~ The Bitterbynde Trilogy ~

Romantasy at its finest.

"'Not since Tolkien's *The Fellowship of the Ring* fell into my hands have I been so impressed by a beautifully spun fantasy."
~ ANDRE NORTON, GRAND MASTER OF SCIENCE FICTION

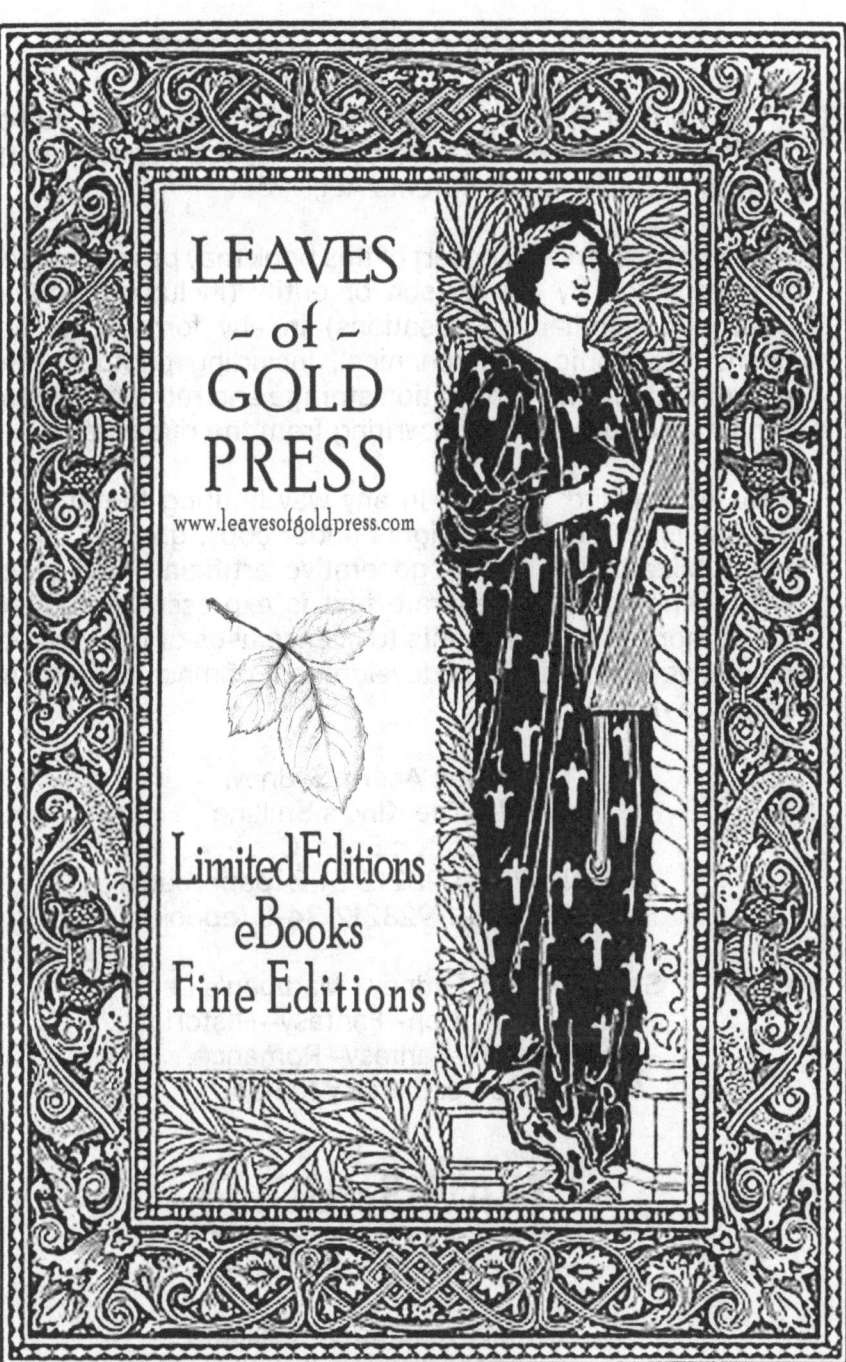

LEAVES
~ of ~
GOLD
PRESS

www.leavesofgoldpress.com

Limited Editions
eBooks
Fine Editions

Author: Acorn, Sydney,
Title: The King's Shilling
Editor: Egan, C.
ISBN: 978-1-923212-31-2 (paperback)
ISBN: 978-1-923212-34-3 (ebook)

Series: Acorn, Sydney ; Madigan's Leap ; 1
Subjects: Fiction--Fantasy--Historical.
Fiction--Fantasy--Romance.
Genre: Fantasy fiction.

www.leavesofgoldpress.com
ABN 67 099 575 078

The King's Shilling

The King's Shilling

Madigan's Leap Book 1

Sydney Acorn

Books in this series:

PROLOGUE

On her wedding night Rose lay alone in the bedchamber, silently awaiting the arrival of her bridegroom. Beyond the tall windows the night sky was a vault of glittering obsidian, sprinkled with stars.

Starlight slanting in through the panes laved the face of the young bride with silver, and made snowfields of the lace pillows. It pooled in her blue eyes; her wide, unblinking eyes that gazed out of the windows like the eyes of a statue. A swift draught stirred the open curtains; it carried the tang of the ocean, and the faint susurrus of waves.

Somewhere on a cliff-top overlooking the sea, someone was playing a plaintive air on a tin whistle. The tune came sliding down the wind as if on a thin wire, its beginnings lost in the evening. Rose shuttered her lids against the sight of the great, silk-canopied marriage bed. A tear glistened on her cheek and she began to sing under her breath, but her song could not keep out the sounds of distant merriment penetrating the chamber's oak-panelled walls. They were the shouts of drunken stags in their ribald revelry, plying Rose's bridegroom with liquor in chased silver cups, anointing his head with it, waggishly stripping off his fine jacket and cambric shirt. Intending to tease him in his eagerness for the first encounter with his bride, they had hoisted him high on their brawny shoulders and now paraded him round and round as though they would keep him forever from the marriage bed, and he laughing and protesting and hiccuping all the while.

"Last night he came to me." Rose sang the ancient song in a sorrowful whisper.

"My dead love came in,

So softly he came that his feet made no din,

As he laid his hand on me and this he did say:

'It will not be long, love, 'til our wedding day.'"

In the stillness of the bedchamber, the bride ceased her crooning and her eyelids snapped open. A faint noise had startled her. Next instant she sat bolt upright, speechless. She could not fully comprehend what she saw before her; thought it a dream, or some effigy rigged as a prank.

There at the foot of the bed stood a man, regarding her intently.

Her incredulous stare took him in from head to toe. The intruder was not her bridegroom. Nor was he any of the wedding guests, eight hours early for the shivaree. Too startled even to think of danger, she returned his measuring gaze.

2

He looked like some weather-beaten sea-captain . . . or a ghost from a shipwreck . . .

CHAPTER 1

Where the Mermaids are Seen
and the Fierce Tempest Gathers

"The Acre by the Sea" 1862 by James Clarke Hook (1819-1907)

*Will you come to the bower o'er the free, boundless
ocean
Where stupendous waves roll in thundering motion
Where the mermaids are seen and the fierce tempest
gathers,
To loved Erin the green, the dear land of our fathers?
Will you come, will you come, will you come to the
bower?*

*"Will you come to the bower?" by Irish poet Thomas Moore (1779-
1852), thought to be based on an earlier song by the same title.*

Rose Delacey had been raised in the village of Allanwell, on
the west coast of Ireland, where cottages nestled beneath
the misty shoulders of green hills marching down to the bay.
Her childhood had been spent at Charter Hall, the stately
mansion high on Whitethorn Hill.

The Delaceys were of the gentry. Their lineage could
be traced back to the Pale, the medieval dominions of the
English in Ireland. The strong Catholic faith of those English
settlers had remained unaffected by the Reformation of
the sixteenth century, and they became known as the Old
English. But through the generations, the Delacey men had
occasionally taken well-born Irish women to wife—by the
year 1790, the blood running in the family's veins was more
Irish than English.

During their childhood at Charter Hall, Rose and her three
older sisters had known the privileges of riches, respect and
influence—but that was before the sunny afternoon in June

1791, the day after Midsummer, when Uncle Frank had come bowling into Allanwell in a coach drawn by six matching horses as black as the hellnight.

From the city of Dublin he had travelled, coming in from the north-east, the iron-shod hooves and wheels of his equipage kicking up billows of dust. The coach rattled along the Valley Highway, traversing the long dale between Whitethorn Hill and Madigan's Leap. It clattered through the main street of Allanwell and past the Well itself, scattering dogs and children and chickens.

A winding private road branched off to the east, climbing the hill up to Charter Hall, before passing between the tall iron gates and along the gravel driveway with its borders of whispering hedges.

What a stir Uncle Frank's coming occasioned amongst the villagers! Such a splendid sight had scarcely been seen in the main street within living memory. Even the Delaceys of Charter Hall only used a team of four, and those were not nearly so mettlesome as the six black steeds, nor was the Delacey family barouche so highly polished. Their driver was never so free with the whip, and they kept only one footman riding at the back. He must be very rich, this visitor calling at Charter Hall. What a grand thing it was indeed, to witness the likes of him driving through Allanwell!

A fine gentleman he looked, young Francis Delacey. He was elegant and pleasing to the eye from the top of his powdered wig to the tip of his gold-buckled shoes; quite the dandy with his white silk stockings, his velvet breeches and jacket, and his waistcoat picked out in gold braid. As ever, his wit and manner soon charmed the entire household at Charter Hall. Francis had not seen his elder brother for six years, for he had been abroad, "making money by the barrow-load", as he put it. Now, he asserted, he had returned to Ireland to find himself a wife and settle down. Unfortunately, all his funds were temporarily tied up overseas, in enterprises in France and Spain. He was forced to prevail upon the kindness of his dear brother who clearly took such admirable care of the ancestral home and its outlying farms. And would John extend his generosity to giving his little brother a roof over his head for one night?

"Of course you shall stay with us, Frank!" cried Rose's father, clapping him on the shoulder, "But you must stay for longer than that! We have much news to catch up on, and besides, the children hardly know their own uncle. Look at them staring at you as if you were the Each Uisge[1] himself, risen out of the Well to steal the unwary! And you'll have a hundred stories to tell them of your travels in foreign parts, not to mention your extensive knowledge of the revolutionary struggle in France. It'll broaden their education. Stay and be welcome!"

But privately he took Francis aside. Twelve-year-old Rose, listening at the door, heard her father ask in a low voice, "Frank, have you changed your ways?"

---

1   The Each Uisge is the malignant water-horse of legend, who is able to turn himself into a handsome young man

To which her uncle replied, "No doubt of it, John. I've made a success of myself."

So Uncle was given the guest chamber, and his driver and footmen were housed with the other servants, and his team was fed and stabled. Even the coach was snugged down in its own shed across the courtyard, for Charter Hall was not short of outbuildings, all solidly constructed from massive blocks of sandstone the colour of toasted soda-bread.

For a week he stayed, then another, and before anyone knew it, two months had passed while still Francis freely availed himself of the hospitality of his brother. His appearance in the village set the single women in a flutter, and many of the married ones also, for he was tall and strong, with a sparkling eye, an eloquent tongue and winning ways. He would offer a woman his spotless white handkerchief if she happened to drop her own—which occurred surprisingly often, the most coquettish ones being the clumsiest—and the gallant way he escorted the elderly ladies down the church steps after mass on Sundays almost broke the hearts of their daughters and grand-daughters.

Father Joseph also pronounced him a fine, upstanding gentleman. During his first week at Charter Hall, Francis had called at the cottage of the old priest to "make himself known over a dram o' the cratur". When he departed, he had left behind the bottle of whiskey he had brought—a gesture that affected Father Joseph deeply.

Always the girls were eager to sit by their uncle and listen to his stories or watch him smoke. They would look on in fascination as he filled his clay pipe with tobacco, tamping down the weed with a fingertip stained the colour of tea-leaves. Next he would light the pipe from a twist of straw he'd jabbed into the fire, and draw deeply, until the weed in the pipe's bowl glowed red. The ends of his handsome moustaches, and the tufts of hair sprouting beneath his lower lip, were coloured the same peaty brown as his fingertip— which, to the children's minds, made him appear awfully distinguished. The details of the pipe-smoking ritual were a source of interest, because the children had never viewed at close quarters any gentleman who puffed tobacco, and it was all the more exciting when he blew smoke-rings to make them squeak with delight.

Once or twice, Francis Delacey travelled to Dublin for a few days, "on business", as he explained, "setting his affairs in order", for he intended to purchase a grand estate of his own, soon, somewhere to the east of the county.

"And what will you have me bring back for you from Dublin?" he asked his brother's children, gathering them to his knee before he departed on one such excursion.

They happened to be in the drawing-room, where an impressive portrait of King George III in full regalia stared down from above the grand fireplace. A gilded chandelier depended from the ceiling like a birdcage full of stars. Its candle-holders dripped with crystal pendeloques, casting shimmers across the room and striking glints from the china laid out on the tea table. A huge mirror of Venetian glass adorned the far wall, reflecting the light, while making the room look bigger. It reflected, also, Frank Delacey, his four nieces and their elegant mother, Anne.

The girls resembled a posy of rare, pastel-hued flowers, dressed in their high-waisted gowns of sprigged muslin, poplin, silk and brocade, with their dark hair falling in ringlets down their backs. Over their shoulders they all wore the fichu scarf of white voile, tied in a loose knot at the breast. Each sister's mouth was a startling splash of brilliant cherry-red against the lily-paleness of her skin. Nature had coloured their faces also with a soft dusting of pink upon the cheeks and gifted them with eyes like orbs of glacial ice; clear, fathomless blue. Should an artist have wished to paint a picture of four water-witches emerging from a woodland mere crowned with marsh-marigolds to seduce a wandering shepherd, he could not have asked for better models.

"What fine presents shall I buy for my pretty nieces, when I'm in town?" Uncle Frank persisted, grinning jovially. "Come now, do not be shy," he added, ignoring their mother's pleas not to spoil them. "Speak up and you shall have what you wish for!"

"I wish for a cameo brooch to pin my Sunday shawl," said Margaret. At almost sixteen summers, she was the eldest. "And I wish it might be carved of ivory, like the brooch Maureen Kelly wears to church, only finer."

"Such a thing would be far too costly," reprimanded their mother, her cheeks flushed with embarrassment. "You'll be making yourself sound avaricious, Margaret. Uncle Frank cannot be throwing his hard-earned money away on fripperies to flatter the vanity of little girls!" She interrupted herself with a sudden cough, short and dry.

"Not at all!" protested Uncle. A serene smile graced his face and he waved his pipe stem expansively. "Let the children be honest with me, Annie. Gadzooks, what's the matter with their own uncle giving them a treat now and then when he's no pups of his own to pamper?"

Resignedly, their mother sighed.

"I have always wanted a collar of Belgian lace," said Katherine, seizing her opportunity. "I have been desperate to have one."

"And I have surpassing need of a new bonnet," earnestly said Elizabeth, clasping her hands as though in prayer. "A cabriolet, Uncle Frank, white with red satin ribbons, red as blood."

The three eldest girls fastened their eyes beseechingly, demandingly on Uncle Frank.

"Meg shall have her brooch," he said indulgently, "and Kate her collar, and Lizzie her hat." His nieces clapped their hands in glee. "But what does Rosie want?" The pipe-stem indicated the youngest sister, who was sitting on the floor at her uncle's feet.

"Well, I have been thinking and thinking," said Rose, "and what I would most fondly love to have is a book."

"A book! Come now Rosie," said Uncle Frank teasingly, "Would you not rather have a handful of pretty ribbons, like Lizzie? What use is it for a young lady to be burying her nose in books when she might be making herself attractive and stealing the hearts of all the young men?"

"Good heavens Uncle, I am not yet thirteen years old," said Rose, unabashed, "and besides, it is not just any book I am thinking of. I saw it in Egan's bookshop, last time we went to Dublin. It is called 'Le Morte d'Arthur' and 'tis written by a gentleman called Mallory, who translated it from medieval French." She did not hesitate to use the French words, and her pronunciation was quite accurate. Almost every day since they were small, Rose and her sisters had been tutored in that language and other subjects by their French governess, Mme. Duval.

"The famous tale of knights and chivalry?" Uncle Frank exclaimed with amused astonishment. "It is a story for boys! Come now, Rosie m'dear—you must be jesting."

She shook her head with finality. "That is what I would like."

Uncle Frank patted her avuncularly on the head. "If that's so, then you shall have it."

CHAPTER 2

Here's to the Dashing Gentleman

"Portrait of a Gentleman" c. 1800 by Hugh Douglas Hamilton
(1740-1808)

Here rides the dashing gentleman with coat of blue and yellow,
A silken hat, a lace cravat—an admirable fellow.
The ladies sigh, and swoon and cry, "Let's raise a glass of brandy!
Here's to the dashing gentleman, so fine and bold and dandy."

Great was the excitement of the children when they heard Uncle Frank's coach rattling up the hill on his return from town. It had seemed a century since he had left—they were beginning to believe he would never come back. They ran to meet him as his conveyance pulled up in the courtyard.

The horses stood stamping and snorting and sweating, after being driven hard and long. The coach door was flung open and there was Uncle like the bountiful St. Nicholas, his arms laden with wrapped parcels. But the parcels were all the same size, and when the children brought their presents indoors and unwrapped them, they each discovered a painted musical box, and each box appeared to be identical.

It was a tremendous disappointment. Their faces fell, but dutifully they struggled to smile so that Uncle would think them pleased with his kindness.

"Oh, what delightful musical boxes," they mouthed effortfully—Margaret rather more enthusiastically than her siblings, since privately she thought the new toys nicer than Maureen Kelly's clockwork serinette, which trillingly played the song of the lark but which by now had grown old and shabby.

"The gew-gaws you asked for were nowhere to be had in Dublin," explained Uncle. "I searched high and low, combing every street and market. But see here, these musical contraptions are made in Britain!" he triumphantly added, "So we can be confident they are of the best craftsmanship!"

"Do you like the Sasunachs, Uncle Frank?" asked Lizzie, puzzled.

He lowered his voice to a confidential level. "Hush colleen, don't call them by that insulting name. Britain is a grand and powerful nation, young Eliza—a conqueror on land and sea. A gentleman could do worse than side with the winning team, eh? That's where the greatest benefit lies. I have important connections in the English court—among them Lord Leighton, who owns two fine estates in this country and a house in Dublin, and who is a close friend of none other than the admiral of the Royal Navy! Besides," he added as an afterthought, "you're speaking their language, aren't you? English is the tongue of the Sasunachs!"

"But Father says we should buy things that are made in Ireland," said Margaret. "He told us that in Dublin they sing a ditty—'Ye noblemen in place or out, Ye Volunteers so brave and stout, Ye dames that flaunt at ball or rout, Wear Irish manufacture.'"

"In Dublin," replied her uncle, "others say that the 'Buy Irish' campaign is nothing but a mischievous chimera. Why should we be compelled to prefer expensive or inferior goods made at home when we can purchase better or cheaper imported articles? Not that your presents were cheap of course, my dears."

"What is a ky—kymeera?" demanded Lizzie.

"No more questions now, Eliza. Run and play."

Fortunately, the clockwork machines each performed a different tune, which made the youngsters hope that their uncle had put some thought into the gifts, after all.

After supper that evening the children withdrew to the sitting room. There they could listen to the new instruments or hold conversation without disturbing father and uncle—who were sipping port in the parlour—or their mother, who was reading in the library.

Katherine left her music box sitting untouched on the sideboard. She sat slumped in a brocade arm-chair that had feet carved like bird-claws. Moodily she stared at the printed wallpaper.

"Why is it we hardly ever have taters for dinner when Uncle Frank is dining with us?" she wanted to know. "It seems to me we're eating a lot more bread when he's about."

"That would be because he's not accustomed to potatoes much, I suppose," said Margaret, opening a small enamelled box containing a manicure set. "He's often in foreign parts where the folk don't eat them as much as we do in Ireland."

"Why don't they?"

"I suppose they like bread better."

"Some folk in this country might like bread better. Yet

18

everyone scarfs taters all the time."

"That is because the land yields a greater quantity of potatoes per acre than corn," said Margaret sagely. "Three times the yield I think it is, or maybe five. In any case, 'tis a good deal more, and that's why Ireland grows potatoes."

"Yes but 'tis taters, taters everywhere you go," insisted Katherine. "I am surprised everyone is not sick and tired of them."

Lizzie interjected, "I could never get tired of taters."

Katherine rounded on her. "But it cannot be good to be growing one crop all the time."

"There's cabbages and onions," Lizzie said.

"No, I mean it cannot be a good thing to be depending on one crop chiefly. What if one year all the taters refused to grow? Where would we be then?"

"I suppose we'd have a terrible famine like there was back in 1749, after the Great Frost, when half the country emigrated to America," said Lizzie. "An Gorta Mor, as Mary calls that dark time."

"Speak English!" Katherine snapped.

"And you talk sense, Kitty!" said Margaret. "Why would potatoes refuse to grow?"

"I don't know, but what if they did?"

"Then we would all be in a terrible pickle," Margaret replied. "But it has not happened yet and it never will, so give yourself a rest now, and play with Uncle Frank's present."

Katherine looked at the toy with loathing. "I hate my musical box," she said savagely. "I should like to kick it across the room."

"If you do, I'll tell," warned Margaret. "We ought to be grateful to Uncle for bringing us presents. 'Tis not his fault he could not find what we asked for."

"I'll wager he did not even look," said Katherine with bitterness. "Likely, he was too busy with his own affairs. Now I do not know how I am to go on. I so desperately needed a superior lace collar. They do draw attention to one's neck, and mine is quite graceful and white, don't you think? Like a swan's."

"Of course it is white," said Margaret, smoothing her fingernails with an emery board. "Since you have been smearing Ilvenna McGinty's pastes all over your skin night after night. Mary says she is fed up with washing the stuff out of the pillowslips. She says she's likely to hand in her notice and go to work for the Kingsleys."

"She says that whenever we vex her. She'll never do it," said Lizzie.

"How do you know I have anything from Ilvenna?" asked Katherine suspiciously. "Have you been down to the McGintys' for somewhat, of late? Tell me!"

Margaret tossed her head. "Only a small jar of May-Day morning dew—"

"I knew it!" Katherine exclaimed furiously. "Those two horrid blemishes have vanished from your nose. To think, I had fancied it pure good fortune on your part! Well, don't keep it to yourself. I shall share my lily-cream if you will share the dew."

"As you like," grumbled Margaret. "But 'tis the tiniest bottle you ever saw. You mustn't use more than a drop—"

Katherine interrupted, flinging herself forward, "No Lizzie, do not touch that key! You are all forbidden to wind up my musical box. If I hear 'Greensleeves' one more time, I shall wind it so hard the spring will break."

"Ooh, do they have springs?" asked Lizzie. "I should like to see inside. I think I shall take mine apart and look."

"Please take mine apart first," said Katherine sweetly.

Margaret's and Lizzie's musical boxes were playing simultaneously. The tunes mingled, with a harsh jangling.

Rose, ignoring the discord, was kneeling on the window-seat gazing out towards the west. Beyond the garden walls, beyond the park with its groves of old oaks and sloping lawns, the land dropped gradually away. Down this gradient stepped the thatched rooves of the village. On the other side of the dale the terrain rose again, to meet the sky along a lofty ridge where sea gulls hovered. The top of that ridge was called Madigan's Leap, and few dared venture there, because everyone knew it was haunted. Upon it was a small private cemetery, in which Anne Delacey's sister lay buried. Her grave, outlined by white stones, lay beneath two wind-warped pines, one green and living, the other as black and lifeless as a burned skeleton, having been struck by lightning during a storm.

This cemetery was unusual in that it contained only a single grave. The ground had never been consecrated, and burial in such ground was seen as a mark of disgrace, reserved for suicides and heretics and other outcasts, but Anne Delacey's sister had insisted that it be her final resting place and the family would not deny her last wish.

To the right of the tiny graveyard, and well removed from it, the ridge jutted forth, forming a small headland overlooking the bay. This vantage point commanded a sweeping view of the ocean to the south, north and west, as far as the horizon, and it was the best place to watch for ships passing by, or vessels that might be bound for Allanwell Bay. On this headland stood the remains of an old fort, the ruins gazing out to sea. The hidden path leading up to it twisted amongst rocks and boulders.

Northwards along the coast, the sea had eroded the shore, forming a shallow bight. At the far end of this bight a second promontory thrust forth, smaller than the first. It was known as Sharpnose. From its northern edge projected a curved claw of land that formed a tiny cove where ships could anchor, unseen from the shore. Because people must bestow a name on all useful geography, this was called Sharpnose Hook, and everyone knew—though nobody spoke of it aloud—that it was sometimes useful to smugglers.

Beyond the Hook, the sweep of the rugged coastline dwindled away into the haze of distance.

From the top of the Leap, the granite cliffs dropped two hundred feet to the sea's edge. Here the rocks were piled high with great springy mounds of kelp, torn by the roots from the ocean floor by the tremendous power of the swell. The ridge itself diminished in height as it extended to the south, finally descending in a long, swift slope to the flat levels and the shores of the bay, and the road that ran along the banks of the river Oranowin.

"What are you looking at, Rose?" asked Lizzie, joining her sister at the window embrasure and pushing aside the heavy velvet drapes.

"Aunt Bridget's headstone," replied Rose, squinting into the distance. "I think I can just make it out from here."

"Oh,' said Lizzie absently. She had noticed she could see her reflection dimly in the mullioned panes, and was arranging her features into what she considered a fetching expression.

"'Tis odd she's buried there," continued Rose. "Mary told me they put her there because she had no one else. Her parents cast her forth without a penny and would have nothing to do with her. They would not even speak of her. There was some quarrel or suchlike. But Mama was still fond of her sister and always believed an injustice had been done. I wonder if Aunt Bridget looked like Mama."

"Mmm," said Lizzie, lowering her chin and peering up at herself coyly to view the effect. She batted her eyelashes. Her sister, preoccupied with far-away thoughts, did not notice.

"I wish't he'd brought the book," said Rose wistfully, after a while.

23

"What?" asked Lizzie.

"The book. You know, King Arthur."

"Oh yes." Lizzie pulled forward some strands of her dark hair and started twisting them around her finger to make ringlets. "Why did you want it anyway? Do we not have enough books here in the library?"

"I want to read it, cloth-head! And besides, it had pictures. Coloured plates!"

"Ooh, pictures," said Lizzie, turning sideways to admire her profile and pouting her lips.

"And the Face was in it," said Rose.

Lizzie stopped playing with her hair. She turned her full attention to her sister.

"The Face!" she echoed. "Truly?"

Rose hesitated. "Well, almost the Face," she admitted. "It was close. The hair was right, and the chin, but the eyes were the wrong colour, and rather too large and, well, womanly. And the brow was not masculine enough. But it was close. As close as I shall ever see, in all likelihood."

"Closer than that tinker's lad we saw on Raglan Road that time?"

Rose nodded.

"Was it Sir Lancelot?"

"No. Sir Lancelot's hair was pale and his eyes were blue. It was Sir Gawaine."

Ever since she could remember, Rose had experienced dreams and visions of a certain Face. They were not frequent, nor were they regular, but they were powerful. She was able to describe the Face and its owner in minute detail to Lizzie, her sole confidante on the topic.

"It is as though you had truly met him," Lizzie would say.

"I have. I meet him all the time in my sleep, and even once or twice when I've been waking."

"When was that?"

"At my birthday party when I was ten years old. Papa gave me my harp. When I first set eyes on it, I wanted to sing for joy. When I looked through the strings, he with the Face was looking back at me with those eyes, the colour of slate after rain."

"Ooh!" said Lizzie, enraptured.

"But it is odd," said Rose, "because I used to dream of a little boy, and now I dream of a youth. It is as though he grows older through the years, as I grow older."

"I wish I could make myself dream of a handsome youth," said Lizzie.

"I do not make myself dream, Lizzie, it simply happens. I have no mastery over it. I know who you would dream of, if you could!"

Lizzie blushed. "Fie, Rose! Don't blither on! I am not so fortunate as you. I dream only of Mme. Duval slapping my hands when I get my arithmetic wrong—have you noticed she never does it when Uncle is nearby? Once I had a nightmare about falling off Madigan's Leap into the sea and the rocks below."

"Yes, and you woke the entire household with your noise!" said Rose.

They both giggled like field mice.

"Well, the Boy with the Face is in my nightmares too," Rose continued. "A long time ago I dreamed I saw him and his friends playing beside a mill-race. One lad toppled in and went under the water. His body was churned and broken by the mill wheel. I saw the water run red and the body came up and over the spinning paddles. Round and round it went, while the Boy had to be held back by his comrades, for he was struggling fiercely to plunge in and get his friend off the wheel. To try would have certainly meant his death. I perceived the wild grief in his eyes and I wanted to reach out and comfort him, but as always when I try to touch him the dream fades."

She turned back to gaze again out of the window. "I wish we could see the ocean from here."

CHAPTER 3

'Tis There the Fairy-court is Holden

From "The Fairy Wood" 1903 by Henry Meynell Rheam (1859–1920)

'Tis there the fairy-court is holden,
And there flow beer and ale so olden,
And there are combs of honey golden,
And there lie men in bonds enfolden,
Seóthú leó, seóthú leó

From "A Bhean Úd Thíos" (Fairy Lullaby)
Collected by George Petrie from the singing of Mary Madden. (1855)

One of the children's favourite evening pastimes was sitting with their parents in the library, listening to their mother's fairy-stories. Here, floor-to-ceiling mahogany bookshelves lined the walls, filled with leather-bound volumes, and classical busts perched atop pedestals, as accents around the room.

Ensconced in one of the deep buttoned-leather armchairs arranged by the fireplace, Anne Delacey told the four girls that the fairies were called, in Irish, the "Tuatha de Danaan" or the People of Danu.

"Entrances to the realm of the fairies are all around us," she said to her listening daughters, "in caves, and tombs, on hills and isles, under ancient tree roots and in the hollows of trees, in wells and woodlands. Some, such as the fairy islands, are visible only once every seven years. Some also abide across the Western Sea, or in an unseen realm that exists alongside our own.

"There are two castes of fairies," she expounded. "The noblest are the Cúirt Sídhe, the Fairy Court, sometimes called the Daoine Sidhe, the People of the Fairy Mounds.

28

They mostly dwell underground, in hollow hills and those mounds we call fairy forts, or raths.

"They are human-like in appearance, and their beauty is matchless. A king and a queen reign over them, and their subterranean halls are vast and high, filled with magical light, splendid in every respect. In those enchanted palaces they indulge in parties, feasts, and drinking. But sometimes after sunset, the doors of their halls swing open, and the lords and ladies ride out under the stars on elegant fairy horses, in a cavalcade called a 'rade'. Their clothes and jewels and trappings are magnificent."

While listening, Lizzie was sketching a fairy on a piece of blotting paper she had found.

"Tell us of the other caste of fairies!" said Rose. Despite having heard the tales over and over, she loved listening to her mother speak, and Anne Delacey never recounted the stories the same way twice.

"Some call them 'wights' for want of a better term," said her mother, "or 'síofra'," (which she pronounced, "shee-fra".) "They are not so human-like as the Cúirt Sídhe. Only the banshee—the fairy weeping woman—comes close. They are of a lower order than the Fairy Court and some may appear grotesque and hideous. Many are shape shifters.

"The síofra include creatures such as the phouka and leprechauns, and cluricauns and merrows, and household brownies. They do not dwell in those jewelled halls beneath the raths, but lurk near water, or in deep pools and rivers, or in high places, or around abandoned buildings, or in the vicinity of certain trees, especially thorn trees. And sometimes they even haunt human dwellings. It is said that some human folk who have 'the gift' can see the fairies, and see, too, some of the places they inhabit. The síofra, like all the Danaan, including the lords and ladies of the Fairy Court, may do good, or do harm."

Lizzie put down her paper and pencil. She was sitting on a cushion at her mother's feet, leaning against her chair, her own slippered feet nestling in the pile of the Turkey rug. "Do harm?" she repeated nervously. "But how?"

Anne Delacey laughed affectionately. "Don't be frightened, darling, these are only folk tales. They are not true."

The children knew that their mother did not believe in fairies, but that she loved the stories anyway, and loved to listen to the local people telling them, and sometimes she even wrote them down. In her view, the tales were invented to explain the inexplicable, or to warn children to stay away from dangerous places such as pools and rivers.

"Mama, why does Mary call them the Good People if they can do wicked things?" asked Katherine. Absent-mindedly she placed her hand on the giant terrestrial globe that stood on the floor near the window and set it spinning, so that the countries of the world, and all the oceans between, flashed past in a blur.

"In case they are listening," said her mother. "She doesn't want to offend them or attract their attention by naming them directly, so she refers to them in oblique ways. It's a term of appeasement—you've heard her sometimes speaking of them as 'The Good Neighbors,' or 'the Fair Folk,' or simply 'The Folk'!"

"How can they be listening everywhere, even in our own home, with the doors locked?"

"People believe they have all sorts of strange powers."

"What powers?" Rose wanted to know.

"They can use their glamour to create illusions. They can put on a different shape, or wrap themselves in a 'feth fiadh', a cloak of concealment."

"Good heavens, I'm glad I'm not Mary," said Katherine. "She's forever seeing fairies behind every gatepost, and tree stumps changing themselves into goblins, and brownies changing themselves into footstools."

"But what harm do they do?" persisted Lizzie.

"The old tales," said her mother, "tell that the fairies, invisible, may pinch or kick those whose behaviour displeases them, until the unfortunate creatures are black and blue."

"What kind of behaviour?" asked Lizzie, and it was apparent that she was making a resolution to avoid whatever it was. Her father glanced up from his book, gave her a sympathetic look, and returned to his reading.

"Things like laziness, unkindness, trespassing. Also they are wont to steal people, especially babies—which they replace with changelings—or folk with golden hair, or those who trespass on their haunts. For they are fierce guardians of their favoured places, whether a rath, a mushroom ring, a hawthorn tree, a hilltop or some fathomless lake. People must avoid such places of fairy merrymaking, or approach them with respect and caution. Trespassing there, or eavesdropping on the Danaan provokes them to retaliate.

"According to the lore," Anne Delacey continued, "if you treat them badly they will respond harshly, but if you behave towards them with respect and generosity, they may reward you. It's said that fairies may help the poor, undertake household chores or farm work, leave money for people or endow favoured persons with some marvellous talent."

"I'm a bit scared of them," said Lizzie plaintively, looking up at her mother.

Anne Delacey smiled. Reaching down, she stroked her daughter's hair. "I didn't intend to distress you, darling," she said. "Only, I have heard Mary telling you tales of the Good People, and I'm sure your friends in the village do so too, and I wanted to ease your minds and sate your curiosity. There are no such things as fairies, and if there were—which there are not—there are many protections and wards against them."

"Oh yes," said Margaret. She was sitting at the oak writing table beneath the windows, surrounded by wax candles in pewter candlesticks. Here she had discovered some long-forgotten primroses pressed between two vellum-bound hymn-books, and had set about removing them. "We've all seen those silly charms people hang up around the place," she said, "the iron horseshoes over the doors of barns and cottages, the red ribbons, the rowan trees, the amulets."

Rose chipped in, "Garlands of marigolds and primroses at the front door are supposed to safeguard people, and the wood of ash, rowan, and blackthorn."

Said Lizzie, "Carrying a pouch of clover on a string around your neck will save you, or turning your jacket inside-out."

"And they don't like salt," said Katherine.

"Mary says the Good People cannot stand the touch of cold iron," said Lizzie, "which is why horseshoes are lucky, and why blacksmiths are magical."

"Blacksmiths aren't magical," scoffed Katherine. Drunken Michael O'Sullivan doesn't look magical to me, with his silly gap-teeth."

"The poor man can't help his teeth," Rose said mildly, gazing into the vitreous flames leaping on the hearth, "and he's only drunk after he finishes work."

"Well they are magical," Lizzie disputed in injured tones, "because they magically conjure useful things out of dull bars of metal."

"But that's just—"

"Girls," interrupted their mother, "don't you want to hear more about the protections?"

"Yes Mama," they chorused.

"Then listen quietly. Now, if anyone is invited to a fairy realm—or abducted there—that person must not partake of so much as a crumb of food or a drop of drink if they wish to ever return to our mortal realm."

"I know another caution," said Rose. "Mary says the Good People are abroad on May Eve and Samhain Eve, so it's best to avoid treading on fairy paths on those nights."

"Just so!" said her mother. "And some folk leave out food to propitiate the fairies. The first drops of milk from the household cow are let fall on the floor for them, or set out on the doorstep, and the first drops of whiskey from a still are splashed on the still-room walls."

If their mother was decidedly sceptical about fairies, the servant Mary, by contrast, had an equally firm conviction that they existed.

Mary told stories of the Good People too, but hers were more disturbing. The girls were never entirely sure how much credence to give them. Their views vacillated between Mary's perspective and their mother's, with credulous Lizzie teetering on the brink of full belief in the supernatural and cynical Margaret poised on the edge of complete scepticism.

Mary spoke interestingly of people seeing fairies, engaging with them and even visiting the fairy realm. She said that people and fairies came into contact with other frequently. The key was to coexist peacefully with them and not do anything that might attract their notice.

She didn't have a separate name for the fairies who were not noble. The children had difficulty grasping which descriptive account of the fairies was officially the correct one, or if indeed there was a correct version, for some folk said one thing and others said another, but in the end they settled on their mother's interpretation of the fairy hierarchy, for they knew she was good and true and wise.

Mary also believed in ghosts, but Mama was scornful of this idea too, and said it was superstition. Even more audaciously, Mama asserted that there was no hell—apart from the way people treated each other in the land of the living—and no limbo, no matter what the priests said—she was quite passionate on that subject. She professed that every soul went to heaven, and that included animals, for she knew they had souls too.

"But girls, you must not mention my ideas to Father Joseph or any other priest. They are mostly good men doing what they think is right, but such notions would shock them. I'm entitled to my own notions, and I am sharing them with my family alone."

CHAPTER 4

Money's the Still Sweet-singing Nightingale

*A five pound note issued by the private banking firm of Gibbons &
Williams in Dublin, Ireland (1833).*

When all birds else do of their music fail,
Money's the still sweet-singing nightingale.

Money Makes the Mirth, by Robert Herrick (1591 – 1674)

As time went on, the children became aware their father's hair had become much greyer than aforetimes, and the lines in his face were graven deeper. His head seemed to have sunk between his shoulder blades, as though he carried some heavy burden. Such was his kindliness and sense of paternal obligation that he never so much as hinted at the cause of his worries in front of his daughters, but their ears were sharp and the servants' tongues were able to be loosened by wheedling, and the children found out a few things.

It seemed their uncle had been borrowing heavily from their father, promising to repay him "when his boat came in". But the "boat" was long in coming. Meanwhile, Uncle Frank went about his business as blithely as ever, as though no trouble touched him. The only difference his nieces noticed was that when he returned from one of his trips to Dublin he arrived on the back of a chestnut mare. His coach and team were gone—sold, he explained somewhat airily, to pay off some impatient creditor. With no equipage to provide work, he had also dismissed from service his driver and footmen. Indeed, it was a relief to John Delacey, for there were eight fewer mouths to feed.

But the children were even more anxious about their mother than their father. She had been suffering from a dry, hacking cough, which had become apparent about a fortnight after Uncle Frank arrived. Recently the cough had grown worse. It seemed to wrack her frame night and day, but she refused to send out for the doctor, and when her daughters offered to get her some potions from Ilvenna McGinty, she refused them also.

"Ilvenna McGinty's no more a wise-woman than you or me or poor old Seamus O'Grady," she would say tiredly. "The girl is deluded."

Mary, the middle-aged servant who had been the children's nursemaid when they were small, told them to tread softly about the place, "so as not to disturb the mistress". A sense of dread and doom settled over the household, deepening with every passing day.

It was late on a stormy night in December. Uncle Frank had been away in town for several days and was expected back at any hour. Beneath the scream of the wind and rain, the beating of hooves was heard on the gravel driveway and he galloped in from the darkness. As he leapt from her back his mare fell dead in the courtyard, her hide flecked with blood and foam. Francis did not falter. He ran up the steps and into the house. Soon he and John were ensconced together in the library. With their mother abed and the servants settled for the night in their quarters, the children found it easy to creep up, avoiding the familiar floorboards that squeaked, and listen at the door.

It was the first time they had ever heard their uncle sound shaken.

"It is all over, Johnnie," he said breathlessly. "The French venture has come to naught, all because of the revolution. My partners in Spain were faithless and they've ruined me. It's all gone. There's no money left and the creditors are on my heels. They'll see me in hell before they've finished with me."

Straining their ears, the children heard their father speaking in an undertone but could not make out what he was saying. Presently, Francis replied.

"The devil knows," he said. "Good God man, how d'ye think I feel? To know I've brought this down like an anvil on your shoulders, and you my only brother and as generous a gentleman as ever helped out his relatives! But look at it from my view. You only have to sell up and you'll be able to pay all the damned usurers you borrowed from on my account. Then you'll be a free man. But I? I shall have to pack what few chattels I have left to me and flee the country. Yes, by God, or they'll find me. If they catch me, they'll hang me up and, no doubt, flay me alive. They've been threatening dire consequences this many a day but I have been able to keep them at bay, until now. Promises and excuses will no longer hold them from me, Johnnie, and I must depart with all haste. This very night I must go, or lose my head. There is a ship leaving from the harbour down here, leaving with the tide in the morning..."

There was more—in fact, discussion went on until midnight. By then the storm had rolled away into the west and from the front parlour of Charter Hall came the slow, rhythmic chime of the standing-clock ringing out the hour.

Uncle Frank had difficulty opening the library door because something was impeding its swing. He muttered a curse and bent down to examine the object. "Damn my eyes," he said to John Delacey, who was peering over his shoulder. "It is young Rose asleep on the floor. She must have been eavesdropping, the vixen!"

"Well then," said John, gently raising his slumbering daughter in his arms, "It matters little. There will be no more secrets now."

Before dawn, the children's father and uncle had ridden away down the road to the bay. As the sky brightened over the back hills, Lizzie woke and looked out of her second-storey bedchamber window. Far away on top of Madigan's Leap she saw two horses standing, one straddled by a rider. The rider waited motionless on the ridge-top, looking out across the bay to a horizon which was obscured from Lizzie's view. Invention lent her a vision of a tall ship, its white sails piled up on the masts like giant sea-shells brimming with the wind, her deck canting steeply as the bows sliced through the water like a blade. After some while the rider turned his mount's head and rode down the slope, leading the other horse on a rein.

Later, their father came in to breakfast.

That same afternoon a party of three horsemen galloped into the village asking after Francis Delacey. They wore black coats and three-cornered hats, and they carried pistols in their belts. Most villainous they looked. It was not long before they stood on the threshold of Charter Hall, hammering on the front door with their fists.

"Open up!" they shouted.

When the manservant unclosed the door, the strangers shouldered their way in with no further ado. John Delacey met them in the hallway.

"Is Francis Delacey here?" the intruders demanded belligerently.

"No he is not, gentlemen. And I'd thank you to show more respect for my household."

"Where is he? If ye're hiding him ye'll rue it."

"I am not concealing him," replied John with quiet dignity.

"Where is he, then?"

"I do not know."

"When did ye see him last?"

"That's my business," said John Delacey. "And I'll not be telling my business to the likes of you."

The leader of the trio stepped forward with a curse, raising his fist as if to strike. At the last instant he changed his mind and dropped his arm. John Delacey had not flinched.

"Come awa' man," his companions said to him, "'tis not this Delacey we're after."

They departed, but for two or three days they hung about the village asking questions before they finally disappeared.

It was a bleak Yuletide that year for the Delaceys of Charter Hall.

From that day onwards life was dramatically altered for the Delacey children. Their father sold the house on the hill with its many rooms, its gardens, its stables and hot-house and other outbuildings, and its splendid wooded park. He auctioned their farms, their carriage and horses, their four-posted beds with the velvet canopies, their fine clothes and all their treasures except the four gold lockets, heirlooms given to each child by their mother. Their harpsichord and other musical instruments he sold with the house, and the old standing-clock in the front parlour with its solemn face, inlaid with mother-of-pearl and gold. He disposed of all the livestock save for his two hounds, for they were loyal and would answer only to him. Keeping only one servant, Mary, the Delaceys went to live in a cottage at the edge of the village.

For almost three hundred years the family had enjoyed wealth and power in Ireland. Due to their English connections, they had retained their position despite the imposition of the Catholic Ascendancy in the seventeenth century. They remained Loyalists, and thus when King Charles II came to the throne, he restored to them the lands Cromwell had confiscated. Under William of Genaro, the Penal Laws did not affect the Old English as severely as they affected the Irish Catholic population, and the Delaceys had continued to prosper.

Now they had lost all.

When the family left the Charter Hall estate the sisters missed many things— not least, the privacy of their own bed-chambers. They missed, too, the fields through which they had walked and played during their childhood years, bordered with stone fences or blackthorn hedges, and accessed by wooden stiles. These enclosures had curious old names such as Smoothing Iron Field, The Eight Acre, The Five Rood, Furze Field, The Doon, The Raheen, Hanging Hill, Raspberry Wood, Orchard Meadow, Crabtree Field and Fair Green; familiar names for places they loved.

The only lament Anne Delacey permitted to escape her lips was regret for the loss of the view from the main bedchamber of Charter Hall. The chamber's French doors gave onto an elegant second-story balcony, accessible by way of an external staircase. It overlooked the gardens and afforded stunning views of the surrounding countryside, the river Oranowin and the coast. On fine days Anne Delacey was wont to stand there, looking out to the west, while the wind lifted her hair and blew it back like dark ribbons of seagrasses streaming underwater.

Once, to her husband, Anne Delacey spoke of this loss, in soft tones, and after that she never mentioned it again.

By contrast, their change in fortune was the cause of a great deal of weeping and complaining amongst the sisters, for whereas it is easy to adapt from rags to riches, it is always difficult to do the reverse. Yet, they were not in rags, and if they had lost their possessions, they had not lost their standing in the eyes of most of the villagers, for the people could not forget that the Delaceys were born of an ancient and noble line which (it was said) could be traced back to the Normans. In addition, John and Anne Delacey had always been well liked and respected by the folk of Allanwell. It had ever been their habit to help the poor and weak, and they had never played the high-handed lords with anyone, not even the coarsest farm hand.

Furthermore, they had been left with enough saved capital to avoid being reduced to the wretchedness of most of Ireland's poor. They were in a position to take the best cottage in the village, a four-roomed domicile amidst a community largely composed of single-roomed earth-floored huts. Besides the largest chamber, the kitchen-and-parlour, it boasted two cell-like bed-chambers with wooden doors instead of curtains or hempen sacks, and an added-on room at the back where Margaret and Katherine could sleep. This bedroom, added by the previous owner, had been built of stones fallen from the ruins on Madigan's Leap, for which reason Lizzie feared it might be haunted and refused to enter it. Unlike the houses of the other cottiers, theirs was floored with stone flags—at least in the kitchen, if not the other apartments. Mary's bed was a mattress of dried bracken-fern and grass in a corner of the kitchen, overhung by a couple of smoked hams dangling from the black rafters between strings of onions and herbs.

Theirs was the only cottage in Allanwell with a wooden fence around the garden, to keep stray dogs and escaped goats out of the straggly flowerbeds. For that matter, it was the only domicile with flowerbeds, and Anne planted roses there.

It was dramatic, the contrast between this humble abode and the four-and-twenty rooms of Charter Hall with its spacious grounds, its stables, its glass-house and its quarters for eight or ten servants. Yet it was not long before even the misery the Delaceys felt at their change of circumstance was eclipsed by a deeper concern. Whether due to the upheaval of their situation or due to the season—the winter was a particularly hard and bitter one—Anne Delacey's health deteriorated. She would take very little food; her face grew pinched and her form wasted. When her husband noticed her coughing up blood, the doctor was called at once. He said she must stay in bed with a poultice on her chest, and he left a bottle of medicine to be swallowed by the teaspoonful every two hours. None of his remedies availed her, and she sank rapidly.

Her plight weighed heavily on her daughters. Margaret, who was wont to go about the house singing her favourite hymns, fell silent. Rose left off her pastime of scribbling fairy-stories on scraps of paper, and Lizzie could no longer interest herself in sketching. Katherine took over the running of the household accounts, but her heart was not in it.

That spring, sickness went through the village. It took very few lives. Most of its victims were elderly, like Tom O'Grady, eighty-five years old, the brother of Seamus—most, but not all.

One cold February day Anne Delacey called her children to her bedside.

"I want you, one and all, to make me a promise," she said, uttering the words between great gasps.

"Of course Mama! Anything!" the children said tearfully, clasping her hands and patting ineffectually at the bedclothes.

"I might not be here to see you grow up," said their mother with a sigh. "Just in case, I want to give you now the words of advice I would have said to you when you were older." She coughed weakly, but for a long while, before recovering her breath. "You must promise me this—" she whispered hoarsely, "that in your future lives you will never lie with any man but your own husband, wedded in the sight of God."

"I promise," Margaret said quickly, and the others, anxious to please, also repeated the words. Inwardly they were all shocked; never before had they heard their mother speak of such delicate matters. By this they knew that their precious time with her had almost run out.

"Mama," said Margaret awkwardly, "you need hardly have asked this vow of us. You have raised us as members of the Catholic Church, and we would never think of doing such a sinful thing."

"Good," said the sick woman. Another bout of coughing seized her and the servant Mary fetched a basin for the blood. Afterwards Anne closed her eyes and lay back, exhausted. Her face was the same colour as the bleached fabric of the pillows.

That night she died.

The whole village came to the funeral service and followed thereafter to the graveyard beside St Finbar's Church.

The sun was setting. The mourners stood with bowed heads as Father Joseph performed the last rites. A salt breeze blew, driven up the sheer face of Madigan's Leap from the waves below, and across the valley to Whitethorn Hill. Beyond the ocean the sky was on fire in streamers of crimson and gold. The lonely cries of sea-birds rose and fell on the wind as long strings of gulls winged their way home, and Anne Delacey was laid to rest.

Then her daughters wept until they could weep no more, and their hearts were as hollow as the broken eggs of blackbirds.

CHAPTER 5

And her Ghost will Walk the Shore

"Maternità" c. 1895-1898, by Luigi Rossi (1852-1923)

*To be a mother and unwedded was her crime, and
death was the sentence. . .
And now the stones answer her cry from the wall
where she lies.
And lake wind whispers her song, and her ghost will
walk the shore all night long.*

Lisa Relander (Irish trad. author unknown)

Rose and Lizzie sat on the front stoop of the cottage, busy at their needlework.

It was a bright spring morning. The air was as brittle as crystal, the sky was sapphire, and in the west a few puffy clouds floated like daubs of clotted cream. Out of the back garden came the staccato clucking of hens as they pecked over the fallow patches of turned earth which on Good Friday would be planted with cabbages and potatoes. From the doorstep the girls could look southwards down the slope over the thatched rooves of the village cottages and bothies towards the gleaming ribbon of the river. To the west they could gaze out over the vale to where the Valley Highway followed the course of the Willowburn to the peatlands and and Moycloon Bog. On the other side of the vale, Madigan's Leap rose against the sky. It could always be seen from anywhere on the western flank of Whitethorn Hill, blotting out the view of the ocean, protecting the vale and the village from the wrath of the harsh, screaming winds that came rampaging over the sea.

Through the boughs of the rowan tree by the front door pale, cool sunlight streamed over the faces and hair of the girls. It picked out the colours of the wildflowers they were embroidering on serviettes of fine cambric. On the garden gatepost a thrush perched, singing.

Rose said, "After the burial I walked up Madigan's Leap and looked at Aunt Bridget's headstone."

"Mmm?" Lizzie said. Her small white teeth were clenched upon a cotton thread she was trying to bite off.

"It's odd, her headstone. Have you ever read the inscription on it?"

Lizzie shook her head.

"It says 'Here lies Bridget O'Day', and then it gives her birth and death dates."

Lizzie cast a dubious look at her sister. "Are you cracked? What's so odd in that?"

"Underneath her name, someone has scratched the words 'and son,' with some more dates. He was born and died on the same day Aunt Bridget died. She had a babe. So why did they not write his name there in the first place?"

"She had a babe!" exclaimed Lizzie, "The poor wee thing. Well, that means the epitaph is even more odd. She must have been married. So, why did they not write her married name on the grave?"

"How d'you know she was married?"

"If she had a babe she must have been married."

"Not necessarily."

51

"But Rose, a woman cannot have a babe if she's not been wed!"

"Yes she can, if she lies down with a man. I once overheard Mary saying so."

Lizzie gaped at her sister in dismay. "I thought it was the words Father Joseph says to God at the wedding, and then God makes the babies come. But its not like the farm animals is it Rose, because if it is I shall vow to remain childless."

"No, I think with men and women it's only the lying down."

"That's fine then." Lizzie sounded relieved. Then she said "Oh," and put down her sewing. She was silent for a long moment, assimilating this information. At last, she said, "So that's what Mama was talking about when she asked us to make that vow."

Rose nodded.

"But don't you see, Lizzie," Rose went on, "they didn't change Aunt Bridget's name and they didn't write the baby on, and when someone did scratch it on afterwards, the baby had no name at all!"

"I don't understand."

"I think it means she was definitely not married, and they didn't have time to baptise the child."

The sisters gazed solemnly at one another. The spectre of a winged cherub fluttered across Lizzie's inner vision.

"That means," whispered Rose, "the child's ghost is still out there somewhere, on Madigan's Leap!"

"No it doesn't," said Lizzie uncomfortably. "You're wrong, Rose. That's not what happens." She picked up her needlework. Then she added, "I wish you would not talk about ghosts."

"If you had seen the Youth with the Face you'd be more willing to credit their existence," said Rose dreamily. "He was there, too, at the burial. I saw him."

Lizzie's needle slipped and she pricked her finger. "Ouch! Now look what you've made me do!" she exclaimed, sucking the wound. Yet despite her annoyance she could not contain her curiosity. "I did not see him," she said. 'What was he doing?"

"Well, of course you did not see him. No one saw him but me; that is for certain. It was when we were standing around the grave and Father Joseph was making a grand mess of his words as usual, leaving out lines and forgetting bits—"

"Mary says the drink has addled his wits," interrupted Lizzie. "She says that's why he's allowed to be a registered priest, because the Protestants think he can't do it properly."

"But I was not really listening anyway," said Rose, "because all I could think of was how much I missed Mama, and how awfully sad Papa looked. I thought my heart would burst, Lizzie, there was so much suffering in it. Then I saw him amongst the mourners from the village. His eyes never left my face and he moved with great purpose through the crowd towards me. I could not speak, but I felt a sigh escape me. As he came up to me I think I cried out, but by then he was gone."

Lizzie had been gazing wide-eyed at Rose, drinking in every word. "I would have fainted, I'm sure," she said, between fear and astonishment.

"No, I was not afraid," said Rose. "In fact, after I saw him I felt, to some degree, comforted."

A thought struck Lizzie. "Maybe he is the ghost of that baby!"

"Oh Lizzie, sometimes you say the stupidest things!" exclaimed Rose. "How can a ghost grow up? How could a ghost be playing with his ghost friends, and one falls into a millrace and gets killed? No, Lizzie. Whatever he is, he is not a ghost. I want you to sketch a picture of him for me."

Lizzie possessed quite an artistic talent, a fact she always humbly denied. She began to demur, but her sister would not hear any excuses. "I cannot draw half as well as you," she insisted, "I will describe the Face to you again, and you must do your best!"

Abandoning her needlework, Lizzie went indoors to find her pencils.

CHAPTER 6

You Choose the Road, Love,
and I'll Make the Vow.

"Cliffs and Ruined Castle by the Sea", by Peter de Wint, (1784-1849)

Come over the hills, my handsome young lad
Come over the hills to your darling
You choose the road, love, and I'll make the vow
And I'll be your true love forever.

Red Is the Rose: Traditional. The earliest recording of this song
was in 1934

Two years went by, and the family continued to live in the cottage.

Very little changed. Allanwell sometimes felt like a backwater half-forgotten by the world. News filtered in from outside: in the autumn of 1791, the Irishman Etan Wolfe and others had founded the Society of United Irishmen, whose membership was composed chiefly of middle-class Protestants. Initially the organization limited itself to calling for democratic reforms, including Catholic emancipation. Responding to popular pressure, the British government—which for all practical purposes ruled Ireland—granted some reforms. But many people believed that the Society would soon begin to demand more, and campaign for independence from Britain.

In France in 1793, the National Convention had abolished the monarchy and declared the day of the autumn equinox—September 22—the first day of the Year One for the new French Republic. They also issued a proclamation offering assistance to peoples of all nations who wished to overthrow their governments. The French success further encouraged the revolutionary ideals of many Irishmen.

But in the remote village of Allanwell, country life went on as usual, showing few signs of the undercurrents which would eventually alter it irrevocably. Even the most recent struggles for Irish self-determination had little effect on the community. Nor did Britain's military conflicts, as yet.

The daughters of John Delacey must work for a living, now. Their father seemed to have aged prematurely since the death of their mother and the loss of his estate. Nevertheless, he obtained a position as overseer of his old farm estates, being employed by the new owners of Charter Hall, the Westbournes. To bring in extra income, his daughters laboured over fine needlework, which their friend and neighbour Flynn McGinty would take to the Ballyganna market once a month.

Katherine taught French, History and Geography to the Kingsley children—their erstwhile neighbors—whose father was among the landed Protestant squires around those parts, while Margaret tutored them in singing and music. Each day the sisters had to walk several miles to The Beeches, but they would rather do so than be quartered with the servants of that household. Besides, their route took them across the beloved, curiously-named fields they had roamed as children. Now, all those pastures, windblown and close to the sky, belonged to Sir Robert Westbourne.

None of their work was well-paid and they all missed many comforts to which they had become accustomed, but their temperaments naturally tended to be cheerful, and after the first long months when grief's talons began to release them, the spirits of the young ladies commenced to rise.

Not that they became meek, and suffered in silence. Loud were their complaints and their squabbles as they bemoaned the loss of their property or fretted over their clothes and hair—for all of them except Rose were pre-occupied with their looks. Margaret and Katherine were always trying to out-do each other in their search for rich husbands, for Margaret had by now reached the age of eighteen and Katherine was only a year younger. But there were no rich husbands to be found in such a far-flung fishing village as Allanwell. The sons of the local squires were either too young or married already, and besides, their circumstances were not as comfortable as the Delaceys had once known. Whenever visitors appeared in the village the two older girls were quick to take the measure of any eligible bachelor amongst them. Margaret always found something to criticise, but Katherine was not so choosy.

"Oh, for heaven's sake Maggie!" she would snap impatiently. "Fifty thousand pounds a year can make narrow shoulders and a bulbous nose appear wondrous handsome."

"Only if you could stuff it in their mouths and stop them talking at all," Margaret would retort with a scowl.

During those long months one message came to Allanwell from Uncle Frank. On an afternoon when Papa was out, Katherine found the paper crumpled into a wad among the cold ashes of the tiny grate in the cheerless lean-to at the back of the cottage, now Papa's lonely bedchamber since

Mama had passed away. After retrieving it and smoothing out the creases, she read the hastily-scrawled letter aloud to her sisters. Uncle Frank was now in Venice. His prospects were "looking bright". The rest of the page was filled up with promises. Having perused it, Katherine crushed the paper tightly in her fist. She flung it straight into the kitchen fire where it flared yellow, like a crocus, and swiftly died.

"Papa will notice it's gone!" exclaimed Margaret, inwardly shocked at herself for agreeing to be party to prying into other people's private correspondence.

"I'll wager he will not," answered Katherine bitterly. "The poor dear is too weary to notice anything these days."

"He threw it in the bedroom fireplace himself, in any case," Lizzie pointed out. "He wanted it burned."

"It is all Uncle Frank's fault!" exclaimed Katherine.

"Hush!" said Margaret, even more shocked. "How can you speak so? The blessed gentleman is blameless!"

Rolling her eyes Katherine whispered to Lizzie, "It is most provoking, this determination of Maggie's to believe the best of our uncle, in the face of blinding evidence!"

Lizzie gazed at her sister solemnly and owlishly.

Since the death of their mother, the three elder sisters were regularly to be found visiting at the home of the McGintys. Ilvenna McGinty, the same age as Margaret, was a self-proclaimed "wise-woman". Some called her a witch, others called her a fanciful young colleen who was "away with the fairies", and who invested more faith in her own abilities than was justified. Many villagers quietly named her—and her mother—bean leighis "woman of healing"', and bean feasa, "woman of knowing". The remedies provided by the McGinty women smacked suspiciously of magical charms, and Father Joseph, for one, did not entirely approve of them.

Despite the wide range of opinions amongst the village folk, there was no doubt that many of them—nay, most of them had visited the McGintys at one time or another, either openly in broad daylight or sneaking in the door after sunset so that others would not spy them. They came to Ilvenna airing all kinds of complaints, from bunions, warts, indigestion and dry skin to coughs, aching bones and sore eyes. They requested love potions, beauty potions and the divining of their future lives. They wanted to know if their next infant was to be a boy or a girl, and why their butter soured in the churn on Fridays, and whether the next season would be a good one for the crops.

Ilvenna helped a great many of them, and some she could not help—but she never turned anyone away, not even the poorest among them, those who could only afford to pay with a pair of fresh-caught mackerel or a bunch of onions. Ilvenna had even been known to accept a song as fee for her services.

Ma McGinty had borne her two surviving children late in life, and she was now in her sixties. She had largely handed over her role of wise-woman to her daughter, but being of robust health, she continued to tend the chickens, the she-goat, the vegetable patch and the lavender fields, and keep house for her daughter and son. Even in the performance of these mundane duties she demonstrated the stubbornness and unflagging determination that had driven her through life—in particular, through the hard years when she had been forced to scrape a living for herself and two babes-in-arms after their fisherman father was lost at sea. The McGintys were relatively well-off compared to most of the villagers, for they owned a small stable beside their cottage, in which they kept a horse and a cart.

Flynn was the same age as Ilvenna, for they were twins. He had spent four years in Dublin apprenticed to a shoe-maker, and now he was back in Allanwell plying his trade. Not that there was over-much trade for a shoe-maker in such a small and isolated bayside-village off the main trading routes, but enough folk wore holes in the soles of their boots to keep him fairly busy with his last and awl.

Besides, Flynn had no need of more brogues to mend, because he played an active part in one or two other enterprises. Time never hung heavily on his hands. The McGintys had planted two acres of lavender bushes on rented land—where in summer, a confetti of bees hummed among the blossoms' purple pageantry—and it was Flynn's task to distil the oil from the crop every year. For this purpose, he and some comrades kept a still somewhere up in the back hills, far enough away from the village "that it would not trouble the village with the overpowering smell". Not that anyone objected to the fragrance of lavender—on the contrary. Everyone knew the still's main purpose was not to distill lavender oil. All turned a blind eye, however, and no-one breathed a word to the Riding Officers of His Majesty's Customs when they suddenly appeared, like something shot out of a cannon, on their brief, unexpected visits to Allanwell. Father Joseph's disapproval of Ilvenna was countered by his tacit approval of her brother's pursuits, from which the priest was a major beneficiary.

Between the two of them, Ilvenna and Flynn eked out a living for themselves and their mother. Once a month Flynn would hitch the horse to the cart. He and Ilvenna would drive off to Ballyganna market with their wares—tiny bottles of lavender oil for the fine ladies, lavender bags to scent their wardrobes and repel moths, several pairs of new shoes and boots, pots and jars and vials of herbal remedies, willow baskets woven by Ma and Ilvenna, and a pile of neatly folded linen embroidered by the aching hands of their friends, the Delacey daughters. The McGintys would return with a few coins, in addition to numerous empty bottles and jars, muslin for the lavender bags and fresh supplies of linen to be decorated for "the Quality". They brought news from the outside world also; the revolutionaries in France had guillotined their king, Louis XVI, on January 21, 1793. His wife Marie Antoinette was was executed on October 16, that same year, at the age of thirty-seven, at the Place de la Concorde in Paris.

"I despise teaching," announced Katherine vehemently, as she arrived home from The Beeches late one February evening. Stamping into the kitchen she held out her chilled fingers towards the blaze in the grate and proceeded to expound on the shortcomings of her students for the information of her sisters, who were seated around the trestle table finishing their meal.

"If only I could find myself a rich husband I should never have to teach again!" she concluded, thumping herself down on a stool. Mary placed a bowl of hot stew in front of her.

"Surely, and 'tis payin' my wages you do be with your teachin'," said Mary tartly, smoothing down her apron. "You would not have to be botherin' yourself with yer fretful pupils if you let me go. Sure, you could be peelin' praties and sweepin' out fire-grates instead."

Katherine banged down her spoon. "You don't have to be saying 'sure' all the time, Mary," she said loudly. "It sounds bog-Irish. Mme. Duval was always after telling us so."

Margaret spluttered, struggling with a mouthful of so many retorts she did not know which to spit out first. "Hearken to yourself Kitty," she eventually burst out. "You with your afters and your pixy-led participles. 'Tis you that sounds bog-Irish!"

"All right Miss Cleverclogs, how am I supposed to say it?" snapped Katherine.

"You ought to say Mme. Duval always told us so."

"Mme. Duval always told us so," recited Katherine, screwing up her face as though she had just eaten a sour plum, "Mme. Duval always told us so." She picked up her spoon—a greying piece of battered cutlery with a dented bowl—and held it aloft, crooking her little finger. "I do like to have good manners at the table," she twittered, "Mme. Duval always told us so."

Lizzie and Rose giggled.

"Hold your blither, Kitty," said Margaret, trying to suppress a smile.

Katherine banged down the spoon a second time. "Hold your blither, she says! How am I supposed to be finding a good example so that I can continue my proper English education? And if I do not end up refined and educated, how in heaven's name can I find myself a rich husband?

Fiercely, she tore off a piece of potato bread and poked it into her stew. "Where's Papa?" she asked, poised with the spoon hovering at her mouth.

"He was called out to a calving," Rose volunteered.

"He's not well enough to be traipsing out of doors in the middle of the night in winter," said Katherine. Hungrily she began to eat her meal. Mary splashed and rattled the dishes in the washing-up tub.

"The ideal husband would love his wife for her humble ways and piety and charity to the poor," said Margaret primly, "not for the way she speaks."

"Oh, do you think so?" cried Lizzie, sounding somewhat alarmed.

"Of course!"

"Well, that's not my idea of the ideal man," said Lizzie rebelliously.

Margaret looked piqued. "I doubt you can think of a better," she said.

"My ideal man would love his wife even if she sometimes forgot to be pious and humble," said Lizzie. "He would be tall and strong, with laughing eyes and a ready smile. He would fear no man, and he would be generous and kind."

"And have red hair," put in Katherine, through a mouthful.

"Kitty!" Lizzie shrieked, mortified. "Rose, did you tell?"

"She didn't have to tell. It is obvious."

"Who has red hair?" asked Margaret. "Do you mean—"

"Please—" Lizzie said in a strangled croak.

"Let the poor child keep her secrets," said Mary over her shoulder, taking pity on her.

"Kitty's ideal husband would be handsome and rich beyond compare," said Rose to divert the topic, "would he not, Kitty?"

Katherine nodded and swallowed. "He would have one manor-house in Ireland," she said, "one in India and another in America. He would own a fleet of ships so fast they could outrun all others. He would dress in velvet and furs, and wear a different hat for every day of the week, each one stuck through with great feathers. He'd have gold buckles on his belt and shoes and he would be a favourite at the court of every king."

"And he would love and honour you above all others and be faithful forever," said Rose.

"Not necessarily," said Katherine with a shrug. "With all that money, why would I care?"

"Katherine! Sometimes you're the very devil," said Margaret exasperatedly.

Mary flourished a dish-rag and began to dry the crockery.

"Mary, what's your ideal man like?" asked Rose.

"Lord, how should I know?" said Mary. "I never t'ought about it. 'Tis a waste of time. A body would be as like to ever find the ideal man as have the brownies do all her housework for her overnight."

"I have heard of that happening," said Rose. "Anyway, if you don't believe in the brownies why do you leave a crock of milk out for them every evening?"

"That's for the cat," defensively countered Mary.

"We do not have a cat," mumbled Lizzie.

"And what's your ideal man," challenged Katherine, turning decisively towards Rose. "You haven't told us yet."

Lizzie and Rose exchanged glances.

"Well," said Rose calmly, "I'll be telling you now, if you wish it." She looked around at their faces. They were all watching her.

"He is tall and strong," she said, "like Lizzie's man—but his hair is as dark as a crow's wing. It falls down his back, and he ties it out of the way like a horse-tail. So handsome is he that the very stars hurl themselves from the sky, just to be near his beauty for an instant. His face is lean and taut, as though carved out of stone, and the bones are proud. Yet his look is not hard and cold, but youthful and lively. His jaw is shaven, the line of it well-moulded and firm. Dark are his lashes and eyebrows. His eyes are like none I have ever seen before. They are silver-grey, like the sea in a storm, but they can flash suddenly if his passion is aroused, and there is a depth to them that is fathomless. His nose is long and aquiline, like that of the eagle." Rose's eyes appeared to be fixed on some far-away point, and she half-chanted the words, as though quoting some ancient saga. "Broad are his shoulders, tapering to an elegant middle, and his belly is flat. He stands as straight as a spear, but moves with the grace and power of a wild horse. He is fearless, loyal and honourable. To his enemies he would appear to be the devil himself, but as a lover, he would be matchless."

Katherine was forgetting to eat. She sat at the table with her mouth hanging open. Mary stood motionless, the dish-rag in one hand and a dripping platter in the other. A small puddle was forming on the flagstone floor at her feet. Margaret was leaning forward, staring at Rose, wide-eyed, and Lizzie had knotted her hands together so hard the knuckles had turned white.

After Rose finished speaking there was silence, except for the sizzle of the fire and the moan of the wind under the eaves.

"Good Lord," Katherine muttered to herself, "I would sell my soul for one exactly like that."

"It's as if you have met him already, Rose," whispered Margaret, breaking the spell. "Have you?"

"No. Well, yes, in a way."

"What do you mean?"

"I sometimes see him in my dreams."

"Heavens above, I wish I could see him in mine," said Katherine fervently. "I am completely in love with him."

"He does sound fine," murmured Margaret, in an uncharacteristically mellow and pensive tone.

"Indeed he does," agreed Mary with a sigh. She turned back to her duties.

"As fine as can be, with the single flaw that he does not exist," Katherine mourned.

Rose said, with some hesitation, "Lizzie drew a picture."

"Let's see it!" chorused her two eldest sisters.

They leaned together over the scrap of paper that Rose produced from her pocket.

"Saints preserve us," breathed Katherine. "If it isn't a very archangel. I didn't know you could draw like that, Lizzie. Will you draw one for me?"

"Is that really like him?" Margaret asked rather too casually.

"To a certain degree," answered Rose. "Lizzie cannot see him, so I had to describe him to her. It's not an exact likeness but it is close. The hair and the nose are right."

"Closer than Sir Gawaine," murmured Lizzie enigmatically.

"Tell us about when you see the vision of him, Rose," Katherine said in eager tones.

Rose waxed reflective.

"Well, it is not often. Maybe once in six months. One time I saw him, and he was walking on a road. Another youth walked beside him. There was a strong resemblance between the two—it was his brother, I suppose. The evening was on them, and the trees drew in close on both sides of the road, dark and dreary, like a crowd of spectres. Out from the trees sprang a band of thieves. They set upon the pair with knives and cudgels. But he with the Face had a stout blackthorn stick in his hand, and the length of the staff was the height of his shoulder. His companion fought off one man, and by the time that man had upped and fled, having had it knocked into his head that he had met his match, the other four rogues were lying on the ground with the wits knocked out of theirs."

The wind moaned about the Delacey cottage, plucking at the thatch. In the distance a dog barked.

"Sometimes," said Rose, "I dream that I walk in some woodland and I see him coming to me through the trees. He leaps towards me and I run to him but just before we meet, I wake up."

"That's the way of all t'ings grand, so it is," Mary said briskly, over her shoulder. "One moment they're right under your nose, the next they've been whisked away and you're left with nary a t'ing."

She began scrubbing at the crockery with unaccustomed vigour.

Margaret passed her hand over her eyes as though waking up.

"Mary," she said, recollecting her self-imposed matriarchal role, "and Kitty and Lizzie—I'll thank you to describe to no-one else these revelations Rose has told us in confidence, lest you bring shame on our family, for they will think our sister mad or under a spell. Yet they are no more than the inventions of an immature and fanciful mind and nothing more should be made of them. Now I am going to bed. Good night."

They bade her good night as she left the kitchen.

"Rose," said Lizzie abruptly, "you ought to go to Ilvenna. Ask her if a gentleman looking like that does exist, or if he ever did. Ask her if he lives as a true man or if he is a ghost, and if he lives, ask her where, and what is his name."

"Oh yes," urged Katherine, "you really should, Rose. You must. And what is his income," she added.

"Well then," said Rose, inspired afresh "I shall."

CHAPTER 7

When Shall I Meet my Own True Love?

*"Landscape with Rustic Cottage" c. 1760 by Francois Fournier
(1703-1770)*

When shall I meet my own true love
Whose face I spy when dreaming?
I close my eyes, he turns his head,
Dark locks like midnight streaming.

Rose wrapped her shawl close around her and went through the village, down the long, gentle stair of Whitethorn Hill. She was carrying a bundle under one arm. The low stone cottages scattered along the road up and down the hill were widely spaced, each on its few acres. They were thatched with heather and turf, the rooves held in place by a network of cordage and weighed down by large stones hanging from ropes around the eaves. Neatly cut oblongs of dry peat stood stacked beside every house. She went past the Rafferty place, which was known as 'Rafferty's Inn' because its tenant ran a tavern and a wayside stop for travellers. Around at the side, a little girl was throwing out scraps for the chickens. She bobbed a curtsey to Rose, who smiled in acknowledgment.

The sky was overcast and a metallic tang in the air threatened thunder. Rose could hear it dimly rumbling, away in the west, below the horizon, like a cauldron simmering. After she left the outskirts of the village, her feet passed amongst the patches of purple moor grass that the fishermen scythed and gathered to use in the weaving of nets. She skirted the hummocks of tufted hair grass called "bull fronts". Several earthen holes indicated where some of the local men had recently been digging up the largest of these to make church hassocks. To the right, further up the vale, someone was driving a horse and cart along Valley Highway. The cart pulled off the road and began climbing along a sidetrack. Northeast of Allanwell, the country rose to a jumble of wild, cloud-haunted hills, and this track led high amongst them. Rose guessed the driver was probably Flynn McGinty, judging by the direction he was taking and the number of large, lumpy sacks in the back of the cart with the dog sitting on top of them.

Down along the floor of the vale the ground was somewhat boggy, but by then Rose had reached a path. Narrow and meandering, it had been built up with stones, and remained dry. The footpath intersected with Valley Highway, then descended rapidly towards a stone bridge crossing over the stream, before mounting the steep incline on the other side.

Wild-haired children were playing by the stream, among the pollarded willows. One of them had made himself a whistle out of a dead-nettle stalk, and was piping an eerie and tuneless air. Others were hunting for frogs. Some were tossing "tatie-craas" high into the air and dancing about as they watched them come down. They had fashioned these toys from orb-like potatoes into which they stuck the points of three or four feathers from herring gulls or crows. Each time a tatie-craa fell out of the air it twirled around very fast, making a loud whirring noise. Rose called out to the children and waved, and they returned her salute. She left behind the whirrings and the whistlings, the sudden shrieks of laughter, the chatter of water over pebbles and the frog-notes, and, lifting her skirts to avoid stepping on the hems, she climbed towards the McGintys' place where it nestled in its hollow beneath Madigan's Leap.

The interior of the McGintys' cottage was redolent with mingled scents of herbs and tallow and tanned leather. Through the open door at the rear could be glimpsed the narrow chamber that was Flynn's work-room. Hides and thongs and implements of the cobbler's trade depended from hooks hammered into the walls.

In the main room, bunches of dried leaves swung from the exposed roof-beams; among them yarrow, wood sage, dandelion, mallow, lemon balm and hart's tongue fern. Some strings of onions dangled there also, and a small leg of ham the McGintys were saving for special occasions. On top of the rafters sat a row of four hens, and a sheepdog was curled up under a settle. In the corner stood an old spinning wheel, its distaff wound with lint. A single rush-light like a yellow hound's tooth burned in the centre of the table. The dancing flame duplicated itself in Ilvenna McGinty's eyes and caressed the curves of her young face as she listened to Rose telling her story. Glows of soft light ran up and down the auburn filaments of her hair, strands of which were beginning to escape from the rather shapeless bonnet on her head. She was clad in drab woollen skirts, with a knitted shawl draped about her shoulders.

A goat's head poked in at the window and emitted a rude bleat. Ilvenna stood up and flapped her apron at it. The head withdrew hurriedly and there was a scuffling sound of hoofs on stones as the goat moved away.

"Ma! Gallytrot's after gettin' into the garden again!" Ilvenna shouted out the back door. Then she came and seated herself at the table as before, opposite her visitor. "Sure," she said, "ye're axin' a very barrel-full o' questions, Miss Rose. 'Tis more than a simple love-divination ye're after." She scratched her head thoughtfully. "I never did anyt'ing like this before."

"I know it is a lot to ask," said Rose. "But even if you could just find out whether he is real or not, that would be enough."

"Would it?" Ilvenna fixed her eyes on Rose.

"Well, no," Rose admitted, "but it would be better than nothing."

Ilvenna scratched her head once more. "I'll have to t'ink about this."

"Would it help you to find him if I show you a picture which is almost his likeness?" asked Rose, fishing in her pocket for the piece of paper.

"A picture?" Ilvenna craned forward as Rose unrolled the sketch Lizzie had made. She studied it in silence. Presently she said, somewhat indistinctly, "Oh aye. Aye, it helps." Fanning her suddenly flushed cheeks with her apron, she added, "'Tis terrible warm for this time o' year, don't ye t'ink?"

"And I can tell you more about the dreams," said Rose helpfully.

"Go on."

Beyond the window a goat bleated. There was a clang, as if someone had dropped a wooden pail with an iron handle, and an old woman's voice shouted, "Get out of here, yer great baraille ramhar!"

The two girls in the cottage continued conversing, oblivious of these diversions.

"I dreamed that there was a band of tinkers," said Rose, "and they were gathered in a lane deeply bordered with flowering hawthorn and elder. And they had a horse which was so old and worn-out that it had fallen to its knees and could not get up. But the tinkers were cursing the horse and whipping it, because they wanted it to get up and pull their wagon. The horse was incapable of moving, but they dug a hole beneath its ribs and lit a fire."

"Sweet Jesus," said Ilvenna, her face grey as ash.

"And then he was there," said Rose, "and it was the wrath of Solomon coming down on the tinkers. First he stamped out the fire, kicking the flaming sticks in the faces of those who had lit it. Then he was on them like the Furies, knocking them this way and that with his staff, and although he was greatly outnumbered they were caught off guard, and seeing the rage burning in his eyes they must have thought him a madman. They ran off, in fear of their lives, and when they were gone he knelt down beside the poor old horse. He stroked its head and said something in its ear; softly, gently. Then he pulled out his knife and he did something very quick. I am not sure what he did, but from that very moment the horse was free from all suffering. My boy cleaned his knife

76

on the grass and rose to his feet, casting one sad look at the dead beast. Then he glanced up and beheld me. He took one step towards me, but then I saw him and the flowery lane no more."

With a swift movement, Ilvenna wiped her eyes with the back of her hand. "'Tis a dramatic life he's leadin', this young man wit' the Face," she observed drily.

"Not so dramatic, I think," replied Rose. "I have only told you some of the dreams that affected me most. But it is not all danger and fighting. There have been times when I've witnessed him playing a fast and furious game of hurling, and his team winning. And I have glimpsed him in a large and fire-lit room, surrounded by talk and song and laughter, he holding a tankard in his hand brimming with black stout."

"And is it always in the night-time you're seein' him?"

"No—sometimes I have seen him during my waking hours. A daydream, I suppose they call it. But when I lie in my bed at night," Rose went on softly, "I have dreamed I am floating above his bed, looking down and watching him sleep. He opens his eyes and sees me. Then he smiles and reaches out. I reach too, but we can never quite touch each other, and after a while the dream fades."

Ilvenna sniffed. "There's much to be done," she said, somewhat hoarsely, "if we be to find this lad."

Rose began to put away Lizzie's sketch.

"Wait!" Ilvenna said hastily. "Might I have just one more look?" She peered long and hungrily at the picture before returning it to Rose. "D'ye love him?" she asked abruptly.

A look of shock crossed Rose's features. "I never thought about it," she answered. "Honestly, I do not know! I only know he is always at the back of my mind. When I see a face that looks somewhat like his, a pang goes through me as though a dart has been shot into my heart and I feel compelled to stare at that face, scanning it over and over to detect the similarities and differences between it and the one I know so well. I catch myself searching for the Face around every corner, in every crowd. He has been part of my life ever since I can remember. But do I love him? If a fierce longing to touch someone is love, then I do. If a sense of terrible desolation every time the dreams are snatched away is love, then I do. If the certainty that he is part of you, like your own blood, and that he is necessary for life, like breathing—if that is love, then I do love him."

"Right," said Ilvenna, "That's important, because we cannot do anything wit' ye if ye don't love him, whateffer." She pushed her stool back, stood up and paced the floor restlessly. "There's many a way of divinin' love," she said, as if thinking aloud. "There's ways o' gettin' a vision o' your future husband, not that you're needin' any more visions. There's ways o' findin' out the first letter o' his name, ways o' findin' out what is his job o' work—and if you already have a sweet-heart, there's ways o' findin' out whether he is faithful or whether he'll leave ye for another. But there's only one way I know to tell if your true-love lives or not. And for that ye must wait till Midsummer's Day."

"I can wait no longer!" exclaimed Rose with impatience. "Can you not simply give me a way of getting some wishes so that I can wish for him to be here beside me?"

"No!" Ilvenna whirled on her heel. "Now listen to me Miss Rose, you don't go wishin' for things like that, not until we know for sure if he's livin' or not. D'ye want to be haunted by a ghost for the rest o' yer days?"

Rose smiled. "Yes. If it were he, yes."

"Ach! Hold yer nonsense," scoffed Ilvenna. "You do not know what ye're sayin'. Ye must never speak lightly o' such matters. Now Rose, if ye're after bein' foolish, I'll not help you."

"I'm sorry," said Rose meekly, knowing that her friend meant to carry out her threat.

Ilvenna was mollified. "On Midsummer's Eve," she said, "You must pick two flowers o' orpine. Name one of them Rose, and the other one Rose's Sweet-heart. Stick them in two empty cotton reels and leave them beside your bed when you go to sleep. In the mornin', look at them as soon as you waken. If the one that stands for your sweet-heart has shrivelled and died, then you'll know he is no livin' man. If it has wilted and bends away from the other flower, you'll know he lives but loves you not. If the two flowers do be bent towards each other, then he lives and loves ye. But when ye're pickin' the flowers ye must say the words I will teach you, otherwise the whole t'ing will never work."

As Ilvenna was speaking, Ma McGinty appeared outside the door. She kicked off her muddy wooden clogs and left them on the threshold, then came inside, stooping to avoid the low lintel. "Good mornin' to you Miss Rose," she said, putting down a pail of water and wiping her large, ruddy hands on her apron. Her brow was shiny with perspiration and her gown had been mended in many places.

"Good morning Mrs. McGinty. I hope you're well. I wish't Mama had let us send for you or Ilvenna when she was ill abed with the consumption."

Ma McGinty nodded understandingly. "There do be folk that will never come to us. They have their reasons, so they do. We might have helped your ma, wit' dandelion roots and leaves of fairy thimble, and mullein and yarrow—we might indeed. 'Tis a shame and I'm sorry for ye."

Rose indicated the wrapped bundle she had placed on the table. "I have brought the embroideries so that Flynn can take them with him on his next trip to market."

Mrs. McGinty nodded dismissively. She said, "Just now I heard my daughter tellin' ye how to find out if a man is livin'."

"Yes," said Rose.

"That should be worth a bit to ye, eh? More than a sack o' meal. Maybe a haunch o' mutton from one o' the farms, or a flitch o' bacon? For sure your Da will be chancin' on such pickings right easily, he bein' the overseer and all. We're savin' the ham up there for Pentecost." She poked her chin at the rafters overhead. "I cannot tell ye how long it is since I last tasted meat."

"Ma, we have already agreed on the fee..." Ilvenna's voice trailed off.

Ma McGinty had always driven a keen bargain. It was only to be expected. She was accustomed to working hard for every mouthful of food, and she expected value for value. Planting work-roughened hands on her broad hips she stood looking at Rose. Her eyes were sunk between folds of freckled skin and her once-copper hair was white as lightning. Somehow, she seemed a formidable adversary.

"Mrs. McGinty," said Rose, calmly meeting her gaze, "if I can find out by Valentine's Day whether this man lives, I will bring you anything you want."

"It cannot be done! It is impossible!" expostulated Ilvenna. "Anyway, why the haste, Miss Rose? You've waited all your life..."

"Hush now," her mother said firmly. "If that's what Miss Rose wants, we can provide."

She lowered herself onto a three-legged stool.

"But Ma—"

"Sit you down, mo cailin, and you will be learnin' something this mornin'," said Ma McGinty, waving a hand at her daughter. Rolling her eyes towards the ceiling, Ilvenna acquiesced.

"Listen well Miss Rose," said Ma McGinty. "I have not taught this to Ilvenna because there's a mite o' peril in it, but not if you use the brains God gave ye. This is what you must do..."

John Delacey's employers at Charter Hall must have been appreciative of his unstinting toil and dedication. On the same morning Rose was visiting the McGintys, Lady

Westbourne sent down to the Delacey cottage a basketful of new peas which had been force-raised in the glass-house. Later that afternoon Rose was sitting at the kitchen table with Mary, helping her strip the sweet green pearls out of their cradles.

"I do miss the vegetables grown out of season," said Rose regretfully, splitting open a pea-pod with her thumbnail. "I never understood how much we depended upon that hot-house until it was taken away from us."

"Now you must keep a lookout for a cosh," instructed Mary. "'Tis a shell containin' nine peas, remember."

"How did you find out about coshes, Mary?" asked Rose, as she slipped the contents of the pod into her own mouth.

"Sure, me ma told me," said Mary. "It worked well enough for her."

When they found a pod containing nine peas, Rose hung it from the head of a nail projecting from a 'lucky' horse-shoe fastened over the front door. The door opened straight into the kitchen—there was no grand entrance hall with a wall-mirror of Venetian glass, as there had been in the mansion on the hill.

"The first person who comes through that door will have the same initial as your future sweet-heart," advised Mary, "or maybe your future husband, I forget which."

"Heavens above, Mary—isn't it the same thing?"

Mary shook her head sagely. "When you get to my age you'll understand, me darlin', that love and marriage do not always go hand in hand."

The garden gate squeaked on its hinges. Katherine and Lizzie came running up the path and squeezed through the door simultaneously—breathless, giggling and jostling each other in their efforts to be first. Under normal circumstances Rose would have laughed at their antics, but with so much depending on the prophecy of the peas, her brow creased with annoyance.

"Well, 'tis either a K or an E," she said to Mary. "Those feckless girls have made a right mess of our charm. But I think it was Katherine who was a little bit first, don't you?"

"Maybe," said Mary uncertainly.

"What's the matter, Rose?" asked Lizzie.

"Nothing."

"Oh, so it's peas is it?" said Katherine, eying the bowl full of jade beads on the table, "That'll make a grand change from sloke and watercress and buttered nettles. You're not doing the cosh charm are you Rose? Sure, I did that once, and who should be first through the door but Father Joseph." She shuddered.

"I brought you a stalk of rye-grass," said Lizzie proudly. She held out a slim stem, heavy with seeds.

Rose gazed dubiously at the offering.

"Am I supposed to dance the Pride of Erin? What's so great about a bit of grass?"

Lizzie's face fell. "At this season, 'tis hard to find a stem with seeds still on it," she explained, "and you can use it to find out what line of work he follows."

"Oh yes, of course," Rose said with renewed enthusiasm.

83

Eagerly she took the stalk from Lizzie's hand. Together they went outside and sat on the front door-step.

"Tinker, tailor," enunciated Rose, plucking off the seeds in turn as she spoke the words, "Soldier, sailor, rich man, poor man—I hope he's not a soldier—plough-boy, thief. Saints in heaven Lizzie, this thing has a sackful of seeds on it."

"That should be beggar-man, not plough-boy," Katherine called out. Her sisters ignored her.

"Tinker, tailor, soldier, sailor, rich man—"

Katherine peered over their shoulders. "Devil take it," she interrupted, "he's a poor man!"

"I could have told you that," said Rose, rising to her feet and scattering seeds.

"You ought to do the apple-pip trick," advised Katherine, "to find out the direction where he's living. Every time I do it the pip flies towards Britain. I think 'tis a good sign—it probably means some baron or earl."

"Or a beggar on the streets of London," said Mary.

"Sure, wouldn't you rather have an Irish peer?" asked Rose.

Katherine shrugged. "Of course, if one was available. But it seems to me that over in Britain the gentry are a lot more numerous to share around."

"Ooh, imagine Kitty married to a Sasunach!" squealed Lizzie, enjoying the sheer ridiculousness of the idea.

"I don't care if he's Old Nick himself, as long as he's got plenty of money," said Katherine with relish.

"You mind your heathen tongue or the Old Boy'll carry you off one day," Mary scolded. "Go and say your rose-beads," she added automatically, with no confidence at all that her command would be heeded.

On Valentine's Eve, after the rest of the household was asleep in bed, Rose went out of the house and climbed the hill to where the Catholic church stood in its grove of yew trees. It was close to midnight. High overhead the moon was a polished sickle. Ragged clouds blew across its face, but there was enough light to see by as Rose entered the churchyard. She knelt beside the grave of a young man who had died ten years earlier, and her lips began to move in silent prayer. The wind was in the north, blowing from the direction of Charter Hall. It carried with it the faint sound of a clock striking twelve—the old standing-clock that had once belonged to Rose's family and now belonged to the Westbournes. As the chimes rang, Rose plucked nine leaves of yarrow that were growing on the grave, and as she picked, she said,

"Yarrow, yarrow, I seek thee yarrow,
And now thee I have found.
I pray to the good Lord Jesus
As I pluck thee from the ground."

Hastily tucking the leaves inside her shawl, she turned and hurried home.

When she entered the bedchamber she shared with Lizzie, she put seven of the yarrow leaves in her right stocking and tied it to her left leg, but saved two leaves, one of which she put under her pillow. The other, she folded and placed inside the small, curled shell of her left nostril. Then she whispered, without waking her sister,

"Green yarrow, green yarrow, you wear a white flower,
If my love lives, my nose will bleed sure;
If my love don't live, it won't bleed a drop,
If my love do live, 'twill bleed every drop."

And as she laid her head on the pillow she murmured,

"Good night, pretty yarrow,
I pray thee sweet yarrow,
Tell me by the morrow,
If my true love lives."

As Rose began to fall asleep, she found herself reflecting that Ma McGinty's spells and potions did not always work; a fact the wise-woman fiercely contended. The thought presently evaporated and her mind drifted. Beyond the walls the west wind carried on its back the crashing roar of the surf at the foot of Madigan's Leap, and the cry of a bittern winging through the night.

CHAPTER 8

The Spell's Words I Entwine

Valentine's Day Card, from the Early 1900s.

The love charm's whispered at the midnight chime,
On Friday eve when Luna's glow is bright,
With dewy leaves, the spell's words I entwine,
And visions of my true love fill the night.

At the dawning of St Valentine's Day the rising sun peeped through a long rent in the clouds over the back hills, edging them with gilt. Its rays streamed out like long fingers, reaching to caress first the eaves of Charter Hall and the tops of the hedges lining the driveway. They wandered across the buttresses of St. George's, the Protestant church, making the stone belfry glow like honey. Down the steeple of St. Finbar's they bled, limning the black boughs of the ancient yews, lightly brushing the ancient, mossy roof over the village Well. Then they pulled back the shadow of Whitethorn Hill to tinge with gold the thatched cottages and bothies of the village, upon whose rooves grew clumps of stone-crop, reputed to ward off thunder.

From one of the outermost houses arose a scream.

The scream went on and on, punctuated with almost unintelligible outbursts of "Jesus, Mary and Joseph!" and "Lord save us!"

John Delacey leapt from his bed. Rushing into the kitchen he found Lizzie running in circles, sobbing. Margaret, Katherine and Mary discovered her at the same time.

"Oh Jesus," shrieked Lizzie, "she's all a'blood. She's killed herself, by God. She's murdered."

Still dressed in their nightshirts, everyone hastened into Rose's bedchamber. There on the bed she lay, but the pillow and the linen all around her was soaked with crimson ichor. Bearded with a sticky, red viscosity, her face was almost unrecognisable.

"Mother of God!" exclaimed Margaret, clapping her hands to her mouth.

Her father looked stricken. "Where's all the blood coming from?" he cried, kneeling beside her. "Where are you hurt?"

"It's nothing," murmured Rose, opening her eyes to prove she was still alive. "'Tis only a nose-bleed."

Her father flinched. At that moment he had caught a strange look in his daughter's eyes, and the phantom of a smile on her face, a smile almost of beatific joy.

"Pinch your nose," ordered Mary, businesslike. "Pinch it hard together, like this. Lizzie, quit your pulin'. Go and rinse a rag in cold water, then squeeze it out and be bringin' it here at once. Maggie, you go and rouse up the fire under the hob. Kitty, pull the sheets off the bed this minute and throw them in the tub with cold salt water."

"I'll not!" squawked Katherine indignantly. "I'm not the servant!"

Mary said sharply, "For goodness' sake, I only have two hands! You're not the lucky ones with ten domestics any more."

Rose caught her sister's eye, nodded and made the secret sign with her hand. It was a signal the sisters had used since childhood, to indicate that there was a private matter they promised to share when others were not listening.

"Oh, very well," mumbled Katherine sourly.

Mary's prosaic method prevailed, and soon Rose's haemorrhage was staunched.

"I've never seen you with such a nose-bleed," fussed her father. "I'd better have the doctor here to make certain you're all right."

"I'm all right Papa," said Rose, "truly. It looked worse than it was."

"We'll have him here anyway."

"Papa, if you go spending money on doctors I'll have another nose-bleed with the strain of it," said Rose energetically.

Her father sighed. "Well then," he said, "Have your way. But you'd better be resting for a day or two, at least."

His daughter noticed the haunted look in his eyes and by it she knew he remembered another face lying amongst blood-stained sheets. Putting her arms about his neck she kissed him. "I'm sorry Papa."

"Nonsense," he said gruffly, stroking her hair.

Mary gave Rose a suspicious look. "Ye're pale as a ghost," she said. "It wasn't anyt'in' Ilvenna McGinty told you to do, was it?"

"Oh no!" Rose said, cursing Mary's astuteness and praying inwardly that this wasn't a lie, since it had in fact been Ilvenna's mother who had advised her, "No, truly, it was not."

After breakfast Papa and Margaret went to work. Mary was

out hanging freshly laundered sheets on the washing-line, Lizzie was looking for eggs in the hen-house and Rose, wrapped in shawls, was sitting in the rocking chair by the kitchen window.

Katherine hissed in Rose's ear, "What were all these leaves of yarrow doing in your bed? I found some tied up in a stocking, and another mixed up with the linen. And there was an awful soggy one floating in the wash-tub." She grimaced. "I threw them away. It was a love-divination, was it not?"

Rose nodded and said happily, "But he lives, Kitty. He is a living man."

"What?" shrieked Katherine.

"Hush! Mary will hear you. Somewhere in this world, Kitty, he walks, even as we speak—the yarrow told me."

"Does Lizzie know?"

"I am going to tell her later. She has not yet forgiven me for giving her such a turn."

"What will you do now?" buzzed Katherine excitedly.

"Well, I know his name starts with a K—or maybe an E— and I know he lives somewhere in the south-west."

"And he's a poor man," said Katherine, helpfully.

"Yes. So now all I have to do is wish for him to come to me."

"And if he comes to you, and doesn't even look your way, why then you'll need another charm to make him love you!"

"I shall cross that stile when I get to it," said Rose.

"I did not know you could use yarrow for love-divinations," mused Katherine. "Last night being such an auspicious night, I slept with five bay leaves pinned under my pillow so that I would dream of my future husband. Before I lay down I had to say a rhyme seven times, and count to seven, seven times over at each interval. I saw him, you know Rose."

"Did you?"

"Yes but not too clearly. I think some of the bay leaves had been chewed by some sort of insects. I am pretty sure he was comely, though. Now that I have an idea what he looks like, I'm going to wish for my Sasunach lord to come to me, too," Katherine continued, "or my Irish lord, or the King of Spain, whatever. Let's wish for them together. What do we have to do?"

"It was Ilvenna who gave me the wishing-charm. She says we have to go to the churchyard at midnight and walk around the oldest yew tree seven times. And then—"

"Oh Blessed Mother," groaned Katherine, "I can't do that. I'm afraid of ghosts."

"But there are no yew trees anywhere else in Allanwell."

"No, and do you know why? Yew trees are planted in graveyards because they thrive on corpses, and that's why the wood of them makes such excellent bows. All those corpses, and the roots of the yews wriggling into them, sucking out their rotting brains, sucking the ghosts into the timber to be used for killing..." Katherine shivered.

"I thought the yews were planted there to ward off evil spirits."

"I don't care even if they do ward them off. I'm not going into a churchyard at midnight."

"I did last night," said Rose.

Katherine gasped, between admiration, envy and horror. "You never! Heavens, Rose, you are a devil of a one, no doubt of it." Since they had left Charter Hall Katherine had, for some reason best known to herself, taken to using forbidden curse-words such as "devil", but only when removed from her father's hearing. "Shall you wish for him to appear right in front of you, right there in the graveyard?" The young woman hugged herself with delicious horror.

"Of course not, cloth-head. I would have to be giving the wish some time to work, wouldn't I? That way, it is more likely to happen."

"Well, while you're doing the charm, will you make a wish on my account?" Katherine asked, without much hope.

"Not if it reduces the chances of my wish coming true," said Rose.

"Well then," gloomily said Katherine, "I shall have to wait until summer, when the dandelion clocks appear, so that I can catch me a floating 'fairy' and make a wish before I release it. Not that it ever has any effect."

"You could wish on a falling star."

"Don't you think I've tried that, a thousand evenings? If the stars are feeling healthy enough to grant my wishes they are taking a long time about it. And every year on my birthday I use up my three wishes blowing out the candles, to no avail. And never has any penny I have thrown into the Well ever done me any good, except once, when I was six and Papa bought me my pony. I need a stronger wish-charm than those children's games."

"Then don't be such a Craven Kitty. Come with me!"

"Not a chance. When will you be going?"

"Tonight."

"Tonight!"

"It'll be St. Valentine's Night. There must be some power in that."

"But you look like a vapour. Can you not wait?"

"No."

Deep in the folds of night everything lay silent. All Christian folk were—presumably—abed beneath their rooves. Out under the moon and stars roamed the nocturnal birds and beasts, while through the minds of sleeping men, and perhaps elsewhere, wandered the immortal beings of the supernatural, forever associated with the dark. It was then, in that profound stillness, that a rustling as of silk or feathers could be heard and Rose glided outdoors into the night, climbing the hill towards St. Finbar's. After she departed, Lizzie and Katherine stepped out of the back door in their night-dresses and shawls, and stood watching their sister disappear, like a glimmer, into the darkness.

They waited.

They could not hear the twelve chiming notes of the standing-clock coming down the breeze. But had they been able to detect it, they would have reckoned it a long time between midnight and the moment they first espied Rose coming back down the hill. By that time, Lizzie and Katherine had fallen into a doze, slumped against the doorjamb, shivering. Lizzie opened one eye, then shook Katherine urgently by the shoulder. Neither girl uttered a word. They saw Rose, almost at the bottom of the slope, collapse upon the ground, and away they sprang, hastening to her side. Their night-dresses gleamed in the shadows like the reflections of white swans in deep water.

Throwing her arms about their shoulders they supported the limp form, half dragging her back to her bedchamber. There they undressed her and put her to bed, and the noiseless way they did this astonished even themselves. Only once did they disturb the peace—when Lizzie spilled hot tallow on her hand from the rush-light and emitted a small yelp. The sisters held their breath, but no sound came from the other sleeping-chambers. Papa and Margaret and Mary slumbered soundly, exhausted from their day's drudgery.

Katherine stroked Rose's ink-dark hair, smoothing it away from the pale forehead. "She is exhausted, poor lamb."

Lizzie leaned forward and murmured in Rose's ear, "So, when will we be seeing him?"

And Rose roused herself sufficiently to whisper back, "Before Midsummer's."

CHAPTER 9

In the May Morning Dew

"In the merry month of May". Ehrhart, S. D. (Samuel D.),
approximately 1862-1937, artist

Summer is coming, Oh, Summer is near
With the leaves on the trees and the sky blue and
clear
And the small birds are singing their fond notes
so true
And the wild flowers are springing in the May
morning dew

May Morning Dew - Irish traditional

The news arrived in Allanwell, somewhat tardily—in February, the French had declared war on Britain. This announcement was greeted by cheers from the villagers, whose immediate reaction was delight that their ancient enemies should be attacked by the very nation which led the way in achieving freedom for the oppressed classes. On reconsideration, delight soon altered to misgivings when they considered the part the English would expect Ireland to play in their conflict.

In the meantime, daily life had to continue.

St Patrick's Day came and went, then Good Friday, with the Planting of the First Potatoes. At Easter, the housewives coloured the eggs by boiling them to a clear yellow with gorse blossoms, or to soft brown with onion skins. Everyone went to church and kneeled on the bull-front hassocks.

Allanwell boasted two churches, one for each faith. In these last years of the eighteenth century, with the spread of the principles of Enlightenment, the application of the penal code was often half-hearted—although, when it was enforced, it was enforced with ruthless zeal. George III occupied the British throne and in Allanwell, at least, the large Catholic population and the tiny Protestant enclave tolerated each other, coexisting in relative harmony. Both churches were positioned on the upper slopes of Whitethorn Hill at exactly the same height above sea-level. Both were kept in excellent repair.

In St. Finbar's, Father Joseph said the mass out of sequence, but nobody complained because in the end he "got all the words in". Margaret, noticing that Maureen Kelly wore a new bonnet, could not avoid a twinge of bitterness. In St. George's, Sir Robert and Lady Westbourne took up an entire pew and more, with their long row of well-dressed children and their nannies.

After mass the congregation milled around at the front of St. Finbar's, spilling over the porch. The talk centred mainly around the conflict between England and France. News had been gleaned from strangers who appeared in Allanwell before Easter—seamen off the Golden Willow, a merchant ship lying at anchor in the bay while she took on supplies of fresh water. The war had begun badly for the British. Their attempts to intervene on land in the Dutch Republic and on the French coast to aid the Royalists in Brittany had all failed. The British Prime Minister, Pitt the Younger, had said he expected the war to be short, but these early defeats seemed to indicate otherwise.

The seasons, meanwhile, knew nothing of men's wars. Blithe were the early months of springtime under a Flower Moon.

On May-Day there was a great deal of dancing and singing on the village green, and a hurling match was held, and Maureen Kelly was crowned Queen of the May. On Ascension Day the cottiers held the traditional Well-Dressing ceremony, surrounding the village's ancient Well with garlands and posies and pictures of the saints done in flowers. Everywhere in the hills and valleys wild-flowers were unfolding; tansy and butterbur, coltsfoot, goldenrod, yellow iris and ox-eye daisy. Down at the stream, flowering rushes thrust forth their pink stars, and green stems of river-crowfoot offered up white cups centred with gold. Dragonflies hovered, scintillating in metallic hues. The hillsides were purpled with heather and mottled green with bracken uncurling its fiddle-headed fronds. Apple and plum trees put forth their foam of lace, and clouds of mayflies filled the blossom-scented air. In the cottage plots, both weeds and cultivars thrived in a glorious jumble of colour.

This vegetable explosion seemed to engender a corresponding eruption of industry among the population of Allanwell and the surrounding areas.

Flynn McGinty and some of the fishermen's lads went up into the hills looking for clumps of tormentil, which they dug up with shovels and loaded onto carts. On the wharf-side they would boil the roots in large vats, then use the strained liquid to tan both fishing-nets and shoe-leather. Turf-cutters were busy in the bogs which filled the hollows of the back hills, and it was there, also, that Ilvenna McGinty went to gather sphagnum moss and other aids to healing and hope.

From dawn to dusk, John Delacey was out overseeing the ploughing and sowing on the Westbourne estates. In his home there was an epidemic of what Mary called "Spring Fever". Day in, day out, the Delacey daughters were preoccupied with enhancing their natural beauty and divining every detail of romance in their future lives.

The first of June was a Sunday. After mass, everyone was home except Mary who, on her day off, usually went out visiting. Papa was taking the rare opportunity of an idle day to catch up on much-needed rest. He was snoring away in his bedchamber, "sleeping like the dead" as Lizzie said— to the confusion of her sisters, who had always assumed the dead did not snore. Nothing could waken him, not the carelessly loud warbling of Katherine, nor the banging of pots and pans as she and Margaret and Lizzie mixed up various concoctions to put on their skin, with the aim of improving their complexions and hair.

Lizzie had saved a "cosh" of nine peas. It was dried and shrivelled, but she hung it over the front door anyway. She would not leave the door, and kept poking her head out anxiously to see who might be coming towards the garden gate. If anybody approached, she would jump up on a stool and remove the pod. This made Rose's task awkward, since she was trying to put Lizzie's hair in curling papers and it was only half-done.

Margaret sat in the kitchen peeling a wrinkled apple. Like her sisters, she was wearing a blue worsted dress, but unlike them her face was entirely covered with white paste, except for two circles around her eyes. She resembled a snowy owl. Having peeled the apple-skin as thinly as possible Margaret threw the peeling over her shoulder. "Look, Kitty, what letter do you think it makes?" she demanded, turning to pore over the apple-peel where it lay on the floor.

Katherine swivelled her head sideways and squinted critically. Decorated with a different complexion-enhancer, she was a green version of Margaret's owl. "Don't ask me," she said lazily. "Apple skin always looks like an S to me, or an O. Maybe you're going to marry poor old Seamus O'Grady so you can sing to his fiddle-playing. Oh, don't look daggers at me Maggie, sure I'm only jesting!"

"Where those two strips of peel cross over, it looks like an 'A'." Margaret half-heartedly re-arranged the peelings with her foot. "Next St. Valentine's Eve I'm going to do the thing with the bay-leaves under the pillow," she said decisively, "same as you. What did he look like, your Sasunach duke?"

Katherine's expression softened as her thoughts drifted back. "Well it wasn't altogether clear, mind, but I saw a gentleman with a kind of yellow shine around his head, and he bearing a young four-legged creature in his arms. I think it was a crown he was wearing, signifying wealth and nobility, or it might have been a golden hat. And the beast was the symbol of all the flocks and herds on his estates."

"It was the blessed Lord Jesus with a halo, carrying a

lamb," said Margaret as she swept the peelings out the back door for the hens. "You're going to be a nun."

Lizzie rushed past with the pea-pod in her hand.

"What in heaven's name d'you think you're doing, Lizzie?" asked Margaret. "Either leave the cosh hanging over the door or throw it to the hens."

"But I can't leave it there," wailed Lizzie, "in case the wrong person walks in."

Katherine and Rose doubled over with silent laughter.

"Lizzie," said Margaret, "that is not how the divination works. You know that as well as I. Anyway," she went on in a more chatty tone, "who would be the right person?"

Her sister refused to answer.

"It's useful, Lizzie keeping watch on the door," said Katherine in her ivory owl-mask. "I want to know if anyone is calling, so that I can hide."

Rose went out into the garden and picked an ox-eye daisy. On returning to the kitchen she offered it to Lizzie, saying kindly, "Here, me darling, at least you can find out whether he loves you."

Lizzie sat down at the table. She plucked off the petals one by one and tossed them randomly about the kitchen.

"He loves me, he loves me not..."

The hinges of the garden gate squealed. The latch went 'click', and the sound of boots came crunching up the path. No greater disturbance could have been caused if a fox had intruded upon a hen-coop. Squawking girls scattered; a door slammed. Only Rose was left in the kitchen when a shadow fell across the threshold and Flynn McGinty knocked at the open door.

"Good mornin' to ye, Miss Rose," he said, removing his hat and ducking his head, which reached the lintel. Behind his back, his dog Madu waited patiently on the garden path.

"Hello Flynn," Rose replied politely, brushing a few daisy petals off her skirts. "Won't you please come in?"

The young man entered with a scatter of last year's leaves in a skirl of a cold breeze, and placed a pair of boots on the hearthstone.

"I've mended your Pa's brogues," he said. His eyes briefly flickered around the room.

"Thank you. How much do we owe you?"

"Naught. He paid in advance."

"How is your mother faring, and Ilvenna?"

"Fit as fiddles the both o' them, Miss Rose, t'ank ye."

Having completed his errand, Flynn did not seem inclined to take his leave. He merely stood there, continuing to examine his surroundings with an expression that could be construed as mildly enquiring. Sensing that propriety demanded something more of her, Rose cast about for something hospitable to say. Her father held Flynn in high esteem, and the young man could be considered almost as a family friend, despite the class barrier.

"Please sit down. Would you take a sip of elderflower wine?"

Instantly Rose regretted the invitation. It was well-known that Ilvenna made the best elderflower wine in the county.

The Delaceys' home-made concoction would not stand up to comparison. It was too late to retract the offer, however.

"Aye, that I would," Flynn replied easily, pulling a stool back from the table. The stool's legs screeched against the flagstones. After uncorking the bottle Rose poured the wine and set it before him. A shaft of sunlight speared in through the east window, momentarily enclosing the visitor in a cage of light. It poured over a pair of wide, work-hardened shoulders covered by his "Sunday Best" shirt. The shirt-sleeves were rolled up to the elbows, revealing brawny fore-arms covered with freckles and tiny golden hairs. The sun sparkled on the short coppery stubble that dusted his jaw, and made flames of the autumn-hued hair tied up with a black band at the nape of his neck. Flynn glanced up and caught his hostess watching him. He grinned.

"'Tis a fine drop indeed," he complimented. "And where would your family be on this fine mornin', Miss Rose?"

"I shall see if I can find them," said Rose. A moment earlier she had heard some scuffling noises coming from the bedchamber she shared with Lizzie. Tactfully opening the door by no more than a crack, she called inside—

"Lizzie, are you there?"

There was no reply. Rose opened the door wider, then jumped in astonishment as Lizzie landed against the door-frame with a thump, as though she had been shoved from behind. The curling-papers seemed to have disappeared from her hair.

"Won't you come out Lizzie dear?" asked Rose, endeavouring to keep her tone calm, as gentility dictated. "We have a visitor."

Glassy-eyed, Lizzie followed Rose into the kitchen. They both sat down at the table, opposite Flynn.

"Good mornin'," said Flynn cordially, "Miss Elisabet'."

Lizzie started to speak, croaked, cleared her throat and began again. "And to you, sir." She sat as stiffly upright as a spoon in a bowl of thick porridge.

On hearing himself so formally addressed, the young man chuckled. His amiable confidence contrasted sharply with Lizzie's agonised gaucherie.

"Papa is otherwise occupied," said Rose, "and so are our sisters. But that is of no account—you are most welcome. Would you like some more wine?"

"Don't mind if I do," said Flynn, holding out the earthenware goblet.

Rose refilled it. As she did so, a white flash in Lizzie's hair caught her eye and she comprehended that two or three curling-papers remained caught in the lustrous locks. It was too late to rectify the problem now.

"Have ye heard the news from Charter Hall?" asked Flynn conversationally. "Has your Pa told ye?"

The girls exchanged mystified glances.

"Pa has told us no news from up the hill," said Rose, "but that is not unusual. These days we rarely have an opportunity to sit with him at leisure and discuss the local goings-on. He works long hours, and when he returns, he barely takes time to wash and eat before he goes to bed."

"The heir is comin' home, so he is," said Flynn.

"What heir?" Rose asked.

"The Westbourne heir, the eldest son."

A stifled squeak emanated from behind the door of one of the bed-chambers. Steadfastly, Flynn refrained from turning in that direction. He continued as through nothing had occurred, "He's been at London these past two years, they say. He's to arrive on Monday next week."

"I was not aware they had another son," said Rose, kicking Lizzie's ankle under the table to make her talk. "I thought it was only the nine children, and the eldest a boy of fourteen."

Flynn shook his fiery head. "Nay, Miss Rose, 'tis ten of 'em. The eldest, he was born the same summer as me and Ilvenna," he said, "so I'm told."

Rose kicked Lizzie again.

"Oh," said Lizzie.

"What?" Flynn directed his gaze at her. Courteously he rephrased his question, "Pardon me, I was not after catchin' your words Miss Elisabet'."

"Nothing," mumbled Lizzie weakly. She quickly turned her head away, then moved to the open window as if to peer out—but not soon enough to hide her ripe-cherry blush.

"However, we have heard other news from Waterford," said Rose, trying to simultaneously sound knowledgeable and divert attention away from Lizzie's acute embarrassment.

"Aye," Flynn nodded, and a shadow flitted over his tawny features. "So have I," he said heavily. "'Tis fifteen stills the gaugers have seized." He snorted. "If they work their way round to Allanwell we'll be givin' 'em a greetin' they'll remember. Also their breeches will be torn to shreds after chasin' t'rough the whins, and they'll have little else to show for their trouble."

"More wine?" said Rose, praying that Lizzie would master her paralysing diffidence sufficiently to enable her to come away from the window.

"No, t'ank ye. I must be leavin'."

Again, the stool screeched on the flagstones.

"And I almost forgot to ask," said Flynn, "would ye be wantin' anyt'ing from Cleary's Haberdashery in Ballyganna, Miss Rose? I'll be lookin' for some buttons next time I go over there."

"I think we are well-supplied in the haberdashery department for the while," said Rose, knowing there was no money to spare for ribbons and such fripperies. "May I enquire, why would you be buying buttons from a shop when you yourself could whittle a set in a minute?"

The villagers made their own buttons out of wood, horn, bone and leather.

"Old Seamus O'Grady axed me to look for some brass buttons," said Flynn, "Shiny ones. A picture on 'em, he wants."

"Whatever for?"

"His Da had some brass buttons, a family treasure. Engraved with little pictures—flowers and shamrocks and the like. Old Tom, Seamus's brother inherited 'em, and when Tom died Seamus thought he'd get 'em but Tom was after givin' 'em to their sister. Seamus is still broodin' about it. Wants his own shiny buttons, God bless him. 'Tis two pennies he's given me. I don't know what they'll buy, but I've promised to look."

"Alas," said Rose, "I fear such fastenings are not to be had for tuppence. But 'tis very kind of you, helping out the dear old fellow. Please relay my compliments to your mother and sister."

"And my regards to your Pa," said Flynn gravely, lifting his hat to Rose before settling it on his head. A glint in his eye led her to suspect that a dry merriment lurked behind the gravity. "He'll be rattlin' over the bogs and fright'ning all the dogs in them brogues, for I've made 'em as stout as ever they were. Good day to ye Miss Rose, Miss Elisabet'." Flynn McGinty whistled for his dog.

"Good day," said Lizzie, finally turning around. She gazed tragically after Flynn as he strode down the garden path and out the gate into the road. Her fingers were knotted together tightly, like two spiders locked in mortal combat.

"What's the matter with you?" cried Rose as soon as he was out of earshot, "You hardly said a word and you wouldn't even look at him. He's going to think you can't abide him."

Lizzie made inarticulate sounds.

"It seems to me," said Rose, "Every time he comes near, you take pains to avoid him. If we're ever at Ilvenna's and he arrives, you suddenly recall some pressing duty awaiting you at home. No sooner has he wished you good morning than you're bidding him good day."

A door opened and two masks, one green and one white, popped out from behind it.

"Has he gone?" they inquired.

"And to make matters worse," Lizzie burst out, "the cosh was not over the door!" She threw down the pea-pod so hard that it split. Nine peas went rolling across the floor.

Rose, glancing wryly at her sisters, sighed.

CHAPTER 10

All Among the Quality

"The Quality"
The Family of Sir William Young. Date: circa 1767
by Johann Zoffany

"So then I took a stroll, all among the quality..."

*The Rocky Road to Dublin, by D K Gavan, 19th century Irish poet.
Published circa 1862.*

Needless to say, throughout the following days the talk in the house of the Delaceys focussed upon the imminent arrival of Edwin Westbourne at Charter Hall. Since the financial ruin of their family, the four girls found themselves in a curious situation. Most of village boys adored them from afar, the class barriers being too formidable to permit them to do more than tip their caps or flash the girls a grin and ogle them ardently when they were looking the other way. The young men were well aware none of them could hope to keep a Delacey wife in the manner to which she had been accustomed, even if society-at-large would countenance such a match, which was unlikely. On the other hand the "quality", with whom the Delaceys had been used to fraternising, now felt awkward in their society, and invitations had ceased. None of Delacey sisters wanted to spend their lives as spinsters, yet if they wanted to marry, there seemed very little choice open to them A newcomer, however, brought fresh hope.

"It is him," said Katherine adamantly. "It is my future husband. All the auguries point to it. He's young, he's rich and he's been living in London. Oh sweet Jesus, I can hardly wait! His father is the Baronet Robert Westbourne, K.P., a nobleman and a knight of the Most Illustrious Order of St. Patrick, and when I marry I shall go back to live in my rightful home and we shall drive to Dublin to see Sheridan's plays at the theatre, just like we used to. He's everything I want."

"And he's a Protestant," said Lizzie.

"No matter," said Katherine. "They believe in God don't they? Underneath all the blither, they're just like us. Besides, he may be heathen but he's Irish, and I'll wager the Westbournes despise the policies of the British government as much as we do."

"But would you change your religion?" Lizzie asked in astonishment.

"Why not? I wouldn't be the first."

"Katherine!"

"I am only joking! At all events, who's to say he won't change his when he realises how much he loves me? True love crosses every boundary, as Mme. Duval used to say." In a rebellious undertone Katherine subjoined, "Anyway, why should a body change their religion just because they marry?"

"He might be bringing a wife with him from London," Rose pointed out.

"He's not!" said Katherine triumphantly. "I asked Papa. No, Master Edwin is my man."

"But every time you throw an apple peel you get a different initial," argued Lizzie. "Besides, Rose got an E with the cosh trick, and all the Westbournes have black hair. This Edwin will be the dark-haired one with the Face, I'm certain of it. He's Rose's man."

"It might have been a K," said Rose.

"It is not black, the hair of the Westbournes," insisted Katherine. "It is very dark brown. And besides, you're forgetting I did the counting with the plum stones and got a rich man. And Rose got a poor man with the rye grass."

"My dears, don't you think you are putting a little too much faith in these rustic auguries?" Margaret queried, in the mood for injecting a note of rationality. "They are merely games. I, for one, participate only for amusement."

They had to admit there was an element of good sense in her observations, even though they were aware she gave the divination rituals more credence than she admitted. But that did not make it any easier to wait patiently for the moment this young man would first set foot in Allanwell, and the Delacey household was restless and peevish all week.

On the appointed date the son of Sir Robert and Lady Westbourne arrived as expected, but the Delaceys and most of the village saw nothing of him until Sunday. By that time the fine weather had turned. Gone was the sunshine; the skies drew close to the earth, low and threatening, as grey and heavy as a ceiling of pewter. Teased-wool clouds rested on the heads of the hills and the rhythmic rumbling of the sea was borne on the wind. On Sunday morning the clouds released their burden—slowly, at first. A fine misty rain began to fall softly through the air, spangling all things unsheltered.

The crowd walking up the hill to St. Finbar's was not covered by any roof or bough. The fishermen had on their oilskins and John Delacey wore his wet-weather gear over his Sunday clothes. Women covered their heads with thick woollen shawls while men trudged along with their caps pulled well down over their eyes.

All wore their Sunday best. The women were in long dresses of coarse wool, stained with age but neatly mended. Ragged petticoats peeked from below the hems, and worn leather shoes with brass buckles green with age. Atop their neatly braided hair rested their linen bonnets, with frayed brims and faded ribbons.

Beneath woollen vests, the men wore linen shirts, faded and patched. Their breeches tended to be threadbare at the knees and frayed at the cuffs, their stockings much-darned, their shoes scuffed. Some wore old brown frock coats, worn at the elbows. The children had on their everyday shirts and skirts, faded and patched many times over, and the poorest among them were barefoot.

The road levelled out, running along the side of the hill and passing by the Protestant precincts before reaching the Catholic lych-gate. As the throng neared St. George's, heavy rain suddenly came slanting down to drench the earth. The silver spears pricked and prodded at the congregation. Droplets found their way beneath collars and cuffs. Water splashed up from puddles, trickled down boot-tops and slyly crept between the stitchings of shoes. Mud oozed. Children stamped in the puddles or slipped and fell in the mire.

The parson, who was standing on the ample porch of St. George's, called out, beckoning the passers-by to shelter. Some turned away, but many others came running.

It was a bedraggled congregation that eventually reached the porch. They stood there, shaking out their shawls and stamping their wet boots, squinting at the sky as if it were possible to reckon the weight of the water still to fall.

Then the glassy curtains of rain parted. All heads turned to watch as two magnificent black carriages appeared, rolling along the driveway. The vehicles pulled up in front of the church. A footman in spotless livery jumped down from the back of the first, and lowered the step. Out came a richly-dressed young gentleman in a long coat of sky-blue gaberdine. His face was hidden by sheets of rain and by the brim of his hat. He stood beside the carriage step and offered his hand to the portly woman who emerged next— his mother, Lady Westbourne. The footman held an umbrella over her head. A second gentleman, recognisable by his single-braided queue wig as Sir Robert, appeared after his wife and was given similar protection by another servant. Side by side beneath their umbrellas, Sir Robert and Lady Westbourne walked the few remaining steps to the church porch. Their eldest son took his place behind them. As he reached the porch he swept the hat from his head, spraying all those in close proximity with a swathe of water-drops, flung in a glittering arc.

He looked up.

In that moment, half the village scrutinised him. Not least among these scrutineers were the daughters of John Delacey. At their father's side they stood in a row wearing anxious expressions, but everyone who observed them

116

could not help comparing them to the four angels depicted in the stained-glass window of St. George's chancel, with the flawless symmetry of their faces, the peach-blossom perfection of their skin—which needed no embellishment— and the shining masses of their midnight hair. The rain had only made them lovelier. Water, beading their faces and hands, gleamed like pearls on silk. Their tresses seemed netted with diamonds.

If young Edwin Westbourne thought anything of the vision confronting him, he did not show it. The crowd parted to let him pass. He walked through their midst and entered the narthex in the wake of his parents. Outside, the raindrops continued to teem down.

The other members of the Westbourne family were shepherded out of the carriages and into the church. The downpour dwindled and the villagers began to trickle away.

As they walked on, the Delacey girls remained quite silent. They had no need to confer, even in whispers. Their mutual glances said it all.

He has not the Face.

CHAPTER 11

Mirror'd Pools Reflect Enchanted Light

Tattercoats dancing while the gooseherd pipes (1927)
By Arthur Rackham

In marshlands, lov'd by frog and dragonfly,
Azure and emerald glints beguile our sight.
Pale will-o'-wisps mimic the starlit sky,
And mirror'd pools reflect enchanted light.

In the long summer evenings, the village children—and some of their elders too—liked to make their way to see the lights at a small peatland downstream of the Willowburn bridge. This place, called Moycloon Bog, was unique, in that fireflies were known to glow there at the height of summer. Such a rarity was, some said, caused by a subterranean upwelling of warm water from the depths of the world— possibly from hell itself—that gave the bog its own milder climate. For, the waters of Moycloon Bog were never as chilly as other waters, and it never froze over, even when winter snow lay all around. So the fireflies presumably thought, or wanted to think, they had found a temperate home.

The bog was said to be a favoured haunt of the Good People, so it was never desecrated by turf-cutting. Not only fireflies, but also ghost-lights manifested there. Some called them will o' the wisp, friar's lantern or jack-o'-lantern, those silently hovering glows of greenish-blue lambency and cloud-white luminosity.

In a lingering summer dusk, the tiny, bright pinpoints of the fireflies and the standing candles of the ghost lights made a pretty—if eerie—spectacle at Moycloon Bog. Loaded with protective talismans, the villagers, especially the younger ones, were wont to wander down there of an evening, to marvel at it.

On such an evening, Mary shepherded the four Delacey sisters along the willow-canopied footpath beside the stream, until they reached the edge of the peatland. Two or three other folk were already standing there, conversing in subdued whispers, pointing their fingers at the lights.

The ground underfoot felt uneven—soft yet firm, holding the memory of countless years within its peaty layers. Every so often, their feet sank slightly into a more saturated patch, a gentle reminder of the waterlogged nature of the bog.

"Go no further!" warned Mary. "Or the very ground will give way beneat' yer feet, and ye'll be sucked under, all the way down to t'other place."

The sisters promised to obey.

A hushed twilight gathered across the glimmering pools and low vegetation scattered throughout the bog. The sun had already vanished, leaving faded streaks of magenta and violet across the dark sky. Constellations pricked through, and as if in imitation, a sprinkling of tiny amethyst stars twinkled across patches of bog-water; the magical gleams of fireflies.

Drifting veils of vapour coiled slowly, dreamlike, just above the water. Ghostly marsh lights flickered fatuously, reflected in sheets of water like shards of shattered mirrors.

A living tapestry of mosses, rushes, and bog heathers edged those pools. Sphagnum moss carpeted the treacherous ground, while the sturdier tussocks of rushes jutted up like slim spears. Among them swayed the delicate pink blossoms of bog rosemary and cotton grass. Water languidly lapped against the vegetation, and nocturnal insects hummed.

Suddenly there appeared, through the streamers of mist floating above the bog, a young woman, slender as an awl, her skirts the colour of bog-heather, stepping towards them across the mirror-pools, her dainty feet barely rippling their surfaces.

"Saints preserve us!" expostulated Mary, crossing herself fervently. "Sure, there's a body walkin' on water. 'Tis either a miracle or heresy, I'm sure I be not knowin' which."

As the figure came closer, they perceived it was Ilvenna McGinty. She was holding a basket overflowing with foliage, and was followed, further back in the haze, by a ghostly figure.

When Ilvenna saw the sisters and their servant she called out a greeting, approached them and bobbed a shallow curtsy.

"Dear Lord above, Ilvenna McGinty," said Mary, retreating from the girl as if she had the plague. "What are you doin' wit' dem spells of yours? Is it walkin' on water now?"

Ma McGinty stepped out of the mist behind her daughter. "What are ye blitherin' about Mary McGee?" she demanded. "If Ilvenna and I know exactly where to place our feet to stay on the dry ground, 'tis what we've learned ourselves, from visitin' the bog week by week since time began, or whateffer."

Mary looked relieved. "Oh," she said feebly.

"'Tis quite easy to keep yer footin' when ye know what to

look for," said Ilvenna.

"Why do you and Venna visit the bog so often, Mrs McGinty?" Rose asked.

"Why, Miss Rose, we're after collectin' the bog plants," said Ma. "The mosses and the heather can bring luck, healing', and protection. The sundews be for love, while the bog myrtle is the plant of peace, used in brewin' and medicine. It also protects against evil spirits."

"'Tis only that we're out a bit later than usual this evenin'," said Ilvenna.

Lizzie said wonderingly, "Aren't you frightened of the lanterns attempting to lead travelers astray?"

"Most be just harmless gas-lights," said Ilvenna somewhat disparagingly.

"Most?" repeated Lizzie. "But what about the ones—"

"That's enough questions," said Mary firmly. "Come now my girls, 'tis time to be wendin' home."

As they departed, they heard the voice of Ma telling someone, "Ilvenna has a kinship wit' the very air, so she does. She can hear what the wind is singin', and them gas-lights, she can hold them in her very hands." Then, in reply to some inaudible question, "Oh, it be not witchcraft. We're from a long line of druids."

The settling twilight softened the shapes of the hills in the surrounding landscape as the Delacey sisters walked back along the footpath. The croak of a distant frog was followed by the rattle of wind through rushes. From somewhere deep within the bog, a curlew cried out hauntingly.

CHAPTER 12

On this Mysterious Eve

Midsummer Eve, a Fairy Tale of Being Loved.

Drawn by T. Creswick, A.R.A. Engraved by W. T, Green.

*... As our fathers did before us in the good old days
so glorious,
Around the ring good luck to bring, we'll dance and
sing
On this Midsummer Eve.
Dance around the Magic Fire we'll dance around the
Magic Fire!
And passing through the Magic Fire we'll go unscathed
another year.
Let wild fiend rage or witch conspire,
On this mysterious Eve.*

*R.J. Noall (1871-1944) Cornish Patriotic and Dialect Songs. Published
by W & J Jacobs, St. Ives, 1934*

The days lengthened as Midsummer's Eve approached. Father Joseph called it "St John's Eve", but the old name still adhered in the minds of the villagers. Allanwell stirred, busy with preparations for welcoming the solstice, or celebrating the Feast Day of Saint John the Baptist, or both. The village folk made a huge pile of driftwood high on Madigan's Leap, well removed from the little cemetery. It was built on the lee side of a decaying stone wall which had once been an outer rampart of the old fort. They brought up a dozen small, round hay-bales, specially made, and lined them up on the ridge-top. In every cottage, festive dishes were being baked.

"Midsummer's Eve is in fact a pagan festival that was celebrated by the ancient Celts," remarked Margaret, helping Mary in the kitchen. "I read it in a book."

"What nonsense," retorted Mary. "The Church wouldn't be allowin' it if 'twere pagan. Don't forget its proper name is St John's, and 'tis the celebration of a saint, so it must be all right. And Father Joseph always joins in. 'Tis both hallowed and joyful, and that's the end of it."

"The book said great sacrificial bonfires were lit in honour of the sun," pursued Margaret, "and the rolling of the twelve lighted hay-bales is asking the sun to stay with us for twelve months of the year. In midwinter, when the sun shrinks so small and cold, the pagans were afraid it might disappear altogether. That's why they tried to propitiate it in the summertime."

"They tried to what?" asked Mary absentmindedly. She was covered in flour and up to her elbows in a batter-filled pudding-basin.

"You know—to worship it, so that it would feel kindly towards them."

"Ha," said Mary, vigorously mixing the batter. "'Tis a good thing we've come a long way from theme old superstitions. An tÁibhirseoir's work was easy in those days." She crossed herself for mentioning the devil. Drops of batter flew from her hand to decorate her shoulders and mobcap.

Lizzie wandered in, flourishing a bouquet of May-blossoms to adorn the mantel-shelf. Against the green buds of their foliage the flowers dazzled like ivory lace.

Mary's eyes snapped fire. "Lizzie! Take them white-thorn blaths out of this house this instant. How many times have I told you, it's bad luck to be bringin' them indoors! Pass the raisins, will ye, Maggie?"

"Why is it bad luck?" said Lizzie, wandering out the door.

"Even the round plum-cakes are a pagan sun-symbol," Margaret continued to lecture, handing over the bag of raisins.

Mary reached for it, knocking the spoon out of the saltbox. It flipped up, flicking out a spill of white crystals which Mary automatically scooped up with her sticky right hand, tossing them over her left shoulder.

"Get along wit' ye, Maggie! You and your pagan rites! Sure, I don't have time for such blither," said Mary good-naturedly. "Go and find the nutmeg."

On the night before Midsummer's Eve, Rose cried out in her sleep. Lizzie woke in fright, then leaned across the bed to shake her sister and rouse her.

"What did you dream?" demanded Lizzie, as Rose opened her eyes. "You startled me half out of my wits, screaming like that. I'm still shaking and I know I shan't get back to sleep now for hours. You must have dreamed something terrible. You'd better tell me, or I shall imagine worse, and have nightmares."

Rose sat up, a bemused expression clouding her features. "I must go," she said. Throwing back the coverlet she made to get out of bed, but Lizzie pushed her back.

"What are you talking about?"

"I have to go up to Madigan's Leap."

"Wake up, Rose. You're not properly awake yet. Look, 'tis me, Lizzie, your sister."

"But—" Rose struggled. "I have to meet him..."

A bolt of fear struck through Lizzie. Meet whom—a ghost? Was her first thought, which she dismissed as being too dreadful to contemplate. She had no desire to see Rose roaming about in the night again, making herself ill. Already she seemed feverish and strange. Yet, how could she stop her? "All right, if you're so keen, come outside with me," she said bravely.

Stealing out the back door into the warm night they slipped by the hazelnut bushes that screened the small outbuilding housing the privy, then went up some shallow wooden steps and past the water-pump. After skirting the rough stone byre, one end of which Mary used for the laundry and butter-making, they stood looking up towards the Leap.

The night was cloudless. Overhead, huge stars bristled with a myriad glittering needles of light. Against the glory of the sky the high spine of Madigan's Leap was outlined as though sculpted black onyx. The ruined fort jutted like the broken crown of some long-forgotten king.

"See!" softly said Lizzie, pointing, "there is nobody up there. It is all silent and deserted. Your bed is warm and safe, Rose. Go back to it." She held Rose's hand so that she could not escape, although by this time her youngest sister had become mild and unresisting.

"But," said Rose, "I saw him there. He was there for the first time!"

Lizzie jerked as though she had been stung. Her heart skipped to a peculiarly uncomfortable rhythm, and her mouth went dry. She did not know whether she felt excited or terrified. With hope and dread, her eyes searched the black horizon of the Leap. "He's not there now," she said, endeavouring to keep her voice calm. "Nobody is. Come away, Rose. Come away now."

After a quiet interval, Rose allowed herself to be led indoors.

On Midsummer's Eve a merry multitude bearing flaming torches was wending its way up the slopes of Madigan's Leap. Most went bare-footed, as was their custom in summer, to save their boots. Those who had already reached the ridge-top were treated to the spectacle of a brilliant sunset stretching across the firmament from north to south. The western sky was all ruby embers melting into gold and amber smoke. Its splendour reflected in the ocean, transforming it into a red tide.

"Red sky at night is the shepherd's delight!" someone shouted poetically.

More and more people gathered along the ridge above the ocean, laughing and talking loudly. Not more than three hundred and fifty people lived in the area around Allanwell, but by the numbers, it seemed nearly all of them were on Madigan's Leap this night. Bottles were being passed around. Some folk were seated on the wiry sea-grass, picnicking on oysters, bread and butter, boiled eggs, cheese, black pudding and plum cakes with caraway seeds. Old Seamus O'Grady started sawing at his fiddle. The notes of a traditional jig floated out from the cliff-top like a thread on which the bright laughter was strung. In the bay below, out on the deeper waters beyond the moorings of the little fishing-boats, a brig rode at anchor with its sails close-furled—one of the merchant ships that occasionally navigated along the coast.

The Delaceys were late.

The three older girls had spent all day fussing with their hair, their bonnets and the trimmings on their dresses. One problem after another had delayed them. A button had fallen off Katherine's boot. The stitching on Margaret's cuff was unravelling. Lizzie could not arrange her hair the way she desired, no matter how many combs and pins she and her sisters stuck into it.

"What if I stumble, with this loose boot, and Edwin Westbourne sees me?" Katherine shrilled hysterically. "How is he going to have any sort of respect for me after that?"

"Be soothed, Kitty, he's never ever noticed you," replied Margaret, "even when Papa introduced us to him."

"He has indeed! He looked at me longer than at you. He's so handsome, and did you notice the gold braid on his hat? Just as my vision foretold—"

"He probably won't even be there tonight. Why would the likes of him be going to a pagan festival?"

Katherine waxed indignant. "What do you mean the likes of him? We are the likes of him. Our family's every bit as fine and blue-blooded as his! And it is not pagan. Tell her, Mary."

"I wash me hands o' the lot of you!" Mary had expostulated on several occasions—but she remained, helping Rose to tack together the fallen-off bits and the unruly hair, in any way they could.

"Rose, yer hands are shakin'!" she reprimanded. "Stand aside. Sure, ye're no good to anyone in this state. Calm yourself, child. If I didn't know better I'd say ye were the light-headedest of the lot o' them, this evenin'. I'm not knowin' what's come over ye."

"But it is only a couple of hours until midnight!" Rose moaned agitatedly.

"Well, so what?" answered Mary, who knew nothing of Rose's bargain with Ma McGinty.

"Aren't you coming with us, Papa?" Katherine asked anxiously.

"No." Their father's smile was weary and his face haggard. "I shall stay in, tonight. Mary will take you."

John Delacey had spent all day ferrying the Westbournes' thoroughbred riding-horses to the neighbouring village of Castlerigg and back, to be shod. Michael O'Sullivan, the Allanwell blacksmith, was also the local farrier. A fortnight earlier, he had fallen in a drunken stupor down the front steps of Kevin O'Flaherty's house and broken his right arm. He would not be able to wield his hammer for many weeks. Deprived of his livelihood, he was reduced to hoeing his vegetable patch with one hand and relying on the kindness of neighbours for donations of victuals.

At last the Delacey daughters were ready, and they set out. Along their way down the hill to the bridge they met up with the Kelly girls and another crowd of latecomers, with whom they gleefully mingled. By now the sun had drowned in the ocean, leaving the last of its coloured veils hanging in memoriam in the west. The stars were appearing one by one, shimmering in the evening sky like strewn ice-crystals. Against the darkness the hand-held torches flared, dazzling the eyes. Satin-moths flew against them like suicidal fairies. The noisy throng crossed over Valley Highway and then the bridge, wooden over-shoes clattering on the stonework, bare feet making no sound.

As she strode up the slope of the ridge with the procession, Rose observed two falling stars streaking down the skies over Madigan's Leap. She dropped back from the crowd and averted her eyes from the torch-glare. On retreating into the blind shadows she felt someone fall into step beside her. She looked up to see who it was, and came to an abrupt halt. He halted, too. The crowd parted around them, hurrying along without pause. For a full minute, Rose and the newcomer stood and stared at one another. They seemed to drink each other in with their eyes, like thirsty wanderers in a barren land who have found a well of clear water.

A youth of perhaps seventeen summers, he was tall and strong, with hair as black and deep and shining as a crow's wing. It fell down his back, tied in a horse-tail, and he wore no cap. He was handsome, oh yes—strikingly handsome, with a masculine beauty that commanded attention. Lean and taut was his countenance, as though carved out of stone, yet youthful and lively. His jaw was shaven and the line of it was well moulded and firm. Dark were his lashes and eyebrows. His eyes were as grey as the sea in a storm, but she who stood before him knew, as if by instinct, that they could flash hard and bright if his passion were aroused. There was a depth to those eyes that was fathomless. His nose was long and curved, like that of the eagle. A white cravat encircled his neck. Over his linen shirt he wore a waistcoat, subtly patterned with the colours of heather and bracken. Beneath the shirt, his broad shoulders tapered to an elegant middle. He was girded with a belt to which a sheath was attached, with a scian tucked therein. The haft of the knife was decorated with a carved, interlocking pattern. The newcomer's long legs were clad in trousers of soft leather, over which were tied leather bams, the ankle-to-knee protectors commonly worn by men of the country-side. He stood now as straight as a spear, but Rose was well aware he could move with the grace and power of a wild horse. To his enemies he might appear to be the devil himself, but as a lover, she had no doubt, he would be matchless.

The faces of these two as they gazed upon each other were the faces of people in pain. To look at them, anyone might have guessed they experienced the keenest agony or the most intense sorrow. Slowly the young man's hand moved towards Rose, and then with a sudden movement he had seized her by the wrist. In the same instant her other hand found its way up to his face. Her fingers slid into his hair and gripped tightly. When at length they released each other, her wrist bore his fingerprints in the form of bruises, and her hand came away tangled with several livid filaments torn from his scalp. Despite the fact that they had inflicted violence on each other, and as if by these actions they had verified the other's existence, the expression of hurt in their eyes softened. It appeared that whatever anguish pierced them had now diminished to an ache. As though at some signal, they turned and began walking side by side, following the last of the crowd up the slope.

They had spoken not a word.

CHAPTER 13

Dwelt the Wise One, Druid's Daughter

'The Return from Market' (1786) Artist: Francis Wheatley (1747 – 1801)

In the land of ancient magic,
Where the herbs and blossoms flourish,
Dwelt the wise one, Druid's daughter,
Gathered wisdom from the earth's lore.

Spoke she to the stars and moonlight,
Spoke to flames that danced at midnight,
Heard the voice of elementals,
Earth and fire, the wind and waters.

The Bean Feasa

It seemed that in the darkness no-one else had viewed the meeting. All were more intent on reaching the top of Madigan's Leap, and participating in the festivities. Times of celebration were treasured by this community. Their lives were hard. Anything that engendered happiness was precious. By now, several other musicians had spontaneously joined in with Seamus O'Grady's jig, which had quickened its pace and become a reel. To the swift, blood-stirring notes of whistle and fiddle and the heart-thump of the bodhran, there was dancing on the Leap. There was singing, and there was eating, drinking, games and horseplay, and the bonfire blazed. Michael O'Sullivan, the blacksmith-farrier, was to be seen with his arm in a sling, leaping about to the music as though his pants were on fire. A jar of spirits was never far from his lips and with his wild antics he seemed intent on breaking the other arm and both his legs into the bargain.

At midnight the twelve bales were lit, one by one, and youths rolled them off the top of the Leap on the seaward side. Whirling like tops they bounded down through two hundred feet of airy space, scattering sparks, coming to rest like strange phoenixes roosting in the untidy nests of rotting kelp at the base of the cliff. The tide was out. The aim of the youths was to send one missile flying far enough out that it would land in the sea, and with the twelfth bale, Flynn McGinty achieved it. A chorus of vehement cheers went up from the cliff-top.

The sea-breeze, gentle as a well-fed cat, fingered the tresses of Lizzie and Katherine as they stood, observing, half-bathed by the glow of firelight. Playfully it plucked at their skirts.

"Where's Miss Rose?" panted Ilvenna McGinty, hastening towards them. "There's somet'ing I must tell her."

The sisters appeared to be drooping dejectedly on each other's arms. This was decidedly uncharacteristic of them; a festive occasion normally gave rise to their highest spirits and most sprightly conduct.

"We don't know," they answered bleakly. "Mary's been right vexed. We told her Rose was off somewhere with Maggie, and Maggie's been forced to avoid Mary all night. If Rose does not show herself soon we shall never be allowed to come to Midsummer's again. Every year we're surprised we are permitted to come at all, since there's so much uncouth rowdiness for ladies to be amongst."

"Your Pa was a bale-roller himself, as a boy—that's why," replied Ilvenna, "and one o' the best, from what I heard. Now, if I could only find that cailín..."

"The only place we haven't looked is the graveyard and the old fort," said Katherine, "but anyone can see from here there's nobody in the graveyard."

"Why didn't ye look in the fort?"

"'Tis goblins," said Lizzie.

Ilvenna snorted. "'Tis not," she said, swiftly moving away in the fort's direction.

High walls loomed amongst the ruins, bounded by a maze of other ramparts at shoulder height or lower. A roofless tower waited in the centre, its single, empty window gazing out to sea. Due to certain legends that had grown up around the long-ago sinking of the forty-nine ton smack Resolution just outside the harbour, this window was known as 'William's Light'.

Of the stones that had been dislodged by storm and time, there was no sign. In Allanwell, it was held to be unlucky to remove building materials from the standing walls of ancient edifices, but blocks which lay already on the ground could be abducted with impunity. And taken they were, because hewn stone was a useful commodity.

In the chinks of the enduring walls, sea-pinks flourished. High on the tower, birds built their nests. Over it all rambled the slender briars of wild roses, intertwining in a natural version of Celtic knot-work. From April to June they bloomed, decorated with tiny rosettes in pastel shades of cambric and faded damask, but their thorns were like tiny, scratching claws. Women used to gather them sometimes, at the peril of their skirts and hands, They rolled the petals and made rosary beads of them.

Moving amidst starlight and shadow, Ilvenna heard voices murmuring on the wings of the salt wind. They drifted from the seaward side of this necrotic bastion.

"Miss Rose!" she called sharply.

A shiver passed through the grasses and weeds choking the footings of the ruins. In that moment, Rose appeared. To Ilvenna she looked as though she were intoxicated or feverish, or else in the throes of waking from sleep. Her eyes were soft, two pools, remote and filled with dreams. She stared blindly, as though she looked but did not see.

"Saints preserve us—'tis there you're at!" exclaimed Ilvenna. "How much longer I could have gone on wit'out tellin' someone, there is not the knowledge at me. He is here, Miss Rose! I saw him, down the hill just now. 'Tis him, your man wit' the Face, your man in the picture, I'd swear it, so I would."

Rose laughed, looking puzzled. "But no, Ilvenna," she rejoined, "that cannot be, for he is here with me."

A shadow separated itself from other shadows. A tall figure moved to Rose's side.

Unaccountably dizzy and disoriented for an instant, Ilvenna steadied herself against a buttress of crumbling rock.

"'Tis my brother Ryan you likely saw," said the handsome young man with the silver-grey eyes. "They say he resembles me."

His voice was beautiful, like music played on the strings of the evening.

"Oh," said Ilvenna. Her tongue felt numb. She was too stunned to think of introducing herself or enquiring as to the stranger's name, and Rose did not seem capable of it either.

Down on the rocks below, the sea sighed as the tide turned.

"Well, Rose, aren't you about to join your sisters at all?" asked Ilvenna after the space of several heartbeats. "They do be wonderin' where you be, and 'tis frantic they'll be."

"Yes, of course!" cried Rose, instantly alert, as though she had suddenly been doused with a bucket of icy water. "Good heavens Ilvenna, I have no idea where the time goes!" She turned to her companion. "Tomorrow, then" she said softly. He responded with a quick nod. Their eyes locked, and to Ilvenna it seemed the keen and searching look that passed between them was as binding and inflexible as a clamp of iron. Before she realised what she was doing she had automatically crossed herself as if to ward off some ill-fortune. The movement displaced her shawl, which fell across the perfumed briars. The young man stepped forward. He leaned down and expertly detached the woven wool from the bite of the thorns.

Handing the shawl back to Ilvenna he uttered the words, "Seo duit é."

She replied, "Go raibh maith agat."

142

"Codladh sámh agat anocht," he said in words of velvet.

She inclined her head. "Ceart goleor. Come, Rose," she added. "Good night to you, sir."

The two girls linked arms and walked away, not without a backward glance. When they looked the first time they saw him leaning on the ruins, watching them, but the second time they looked he was nowhere to be seen.

Nothing could be said in front of Mary, who was supposed to have been the Delacey daughters' chaperon for the evening and who was quite put out by the disappearance of Margaret and Rose.

"I'll tell your Pa!" she had scolded, all the way home. "How d'ye think it looks for young ladies of your age and position to be off unescorted, having a merry old time and hoofin' it with the countryfolk as though you were not the daughters of a gentleman? And hatless too, I've no doubt. "'Tis fine and grand for the village girls but not for you. You ought to know better."

"Please don't tell Papa," they beseeched her, cajoling her with kind words.

And she didn't, as they had known she wouldn't.

The sisters did not have a moment to themselves until the following afternoon. Mary was busy finishing the weekly laundry. Papa had come home for dinner and gone out again to complete some urgent task on one of the farms.

Daylight would linger for hours. Having informed Mary that they were going across the vale to Ilvenna McGinty's, the Delacey daughters put on their bonnets, overshoes and shawls. Margaret picked up the basket, its contents covered with a cloth of gingham. In a state of barely-suppressed excitement they departed before Mary could think of some reason why they should stay.

"Could you be gatherin' some roots of wake robin for me on the way?" Mary called loudly from the laundry end of the byre as the girls went down the garden path. "It's runnin' out of starch I do be." She often used the roots of the wild arum plant—which she called by its old name of wake robin—to make laundry starch. Her hands were blistered from the process.

"We shall look for some," the girls called back as they latched the gate behind them.

"Do you think I should run back to the shed to get a trowel?" Lizzie asked anxiously.

"Nay, we'll just pull them up by hand," said Katherine with impatience. "I have seen some growing in the soft ground near the stream. Let's go!"

As soon as they were away from the house the questions began flooding from the lips of the three older sisters and Rose was kept busy trying to satisfy their curiosity. But to many of their enquiries she could provide no answer.

"So, it's him is it?" they said, all three speaking at once. "To think we did not see him! He is real, a living man! How could anyone have credited it? And he with a brother!"

"Aye, a brother named Ryan, so he told me."

"Are they staying long in Allanwell?" asked Margaret.

"I do not know."

"And why are they here?"

"I don't know that, either."

"Well, what's his name, then?" the sisters demanded in exasperation. Rose stopped in her tracks, thunderstruck.

"Do you know, I never asked!"

Katherine groaned and shook her head. "You're a wonder, Rose, you're a very wonder and no mistake. My ears cannot believe what they're hearing."

"What do you mean, you didn't ask?" Margaret snapped, with evident irritation. "That would be the first thing in anybody's book. Two people meet and they introduce themselves."

"Only if they are meeting for the first time," said Rose feebly, "but it wasn't like that. It was—I cannot explain."

"So, what did the two of you talk about, all that time up there in the goblin-castle?" asked Lizzie suspiciously. "You didn't kiss, the both of you—did you?"

The sisters' eyes fastened on Rose, hungrily, doubtfully, ready to disapprove and vicariously thrill.

"No," said Rose simply, "If it's anyone else's business, we spoke—when we did speak—about the times we had seen each other in our dreams. For, whenever I saw him, he saw me."

"You're joking!"

"Not at all. In a way I wish I was."

145

"Good heavens, why?"

"Because, of all the strangeness of the meeting, the strangest part was that two people who have never met should dream the same dreams, and when I heard him describe the very same visions that had passed through my own head I felt uncomfortable. It is not a natural thing, not of this world, and the thought came to me that maybe it was the devil's work."

"But how can this be the devil's work?" expostulated Katherine, "when it is love and only love, and the devil is working against that! It's angels who watch over lovers."

Rose looked up at the sky. Beyond the headland of Sharpnose a tower of cumulus cloud was forming itself into a sculpture of a Spanish galleon. The sun, behind, outlined the rim with silver fire. "Of course you are right," she said, "for I am certain I can find nothing sinful in this."

"And what more did he say?" Lizzie persisted.

Rose said, "He told me about the boy who died in the mill race, and the poor tinkers' horse, and the hurling match and all. And he told me it was better to call them travellers, not tinkers. I talked about the birthday harp and the tunes I used to play on it. And because he saw me at Mama's funeral I spoke to him of her, God rest her soul. And when we were not speaking there were silences, and we looked out across the sea, where the moon was rising. The wild roses never smelled so sweet. I recall there were more silences than words, but the conversation never ceased."

"Sweet Lord above!" exclaimed Katherine. Surreptitiously, Lizzie crossed herself; more out of habit than alarm.

"For heaven's sake," said Margaret to her sisters, "it is even more important, now, never to speak of Rose's dreams to anyone. Not even Papa, for it would worry him. If it were to get about that one of the Delaceys was pining after a handsome gypsy lad and casting love spells, our reputations would be ruined entirely. Now that he is real these fancies are no longer merely a nonsense and they cannot be lightly dismissed."

"Oh Maggie!" Rose said reproachfully. "How can you believe he is but a gypsy lad?"

Margaret bit her lip. "I hardly know what to believe," she said presently. "It is all too extraordinary."

"Anyway, we're not supposed to say 'gypsy' or even 'tinker', it's 'traveller'," Lizzie interjected virtuously.

"Come dearest," said Rose, linking Margaret's arm in her own. "I am sure it is all much more ordinary than it seems at first glance." They resumed walking, while Rose finished recounting her story of the previous night.

"How can you do it, Rose?" Katherine exclaimed. " How can you just simply wander along with us down the hill and not be mad for finding him again?"

"I am mad for seeing him," cried Rose. "How can you think I'm not? I am burning. I'm in a fever of fire, but what can I do? Last night he said 'tomorrow'. He said he would find me, and today is tomorrow. All I can do is pray, for I don't know where he's biding."

"And were you not jealous, when he spoke to Ilvenna in the Irish language, right in front of you, and we not knowing it ourselves?"

"Of course not," replied Rose scornfully. "Jealousy is for those who doubt. Besides," she added, "he said those words out of courtesy to her, meaning no disrespect to me at all."

They crossed the bridge and began to climb.

Lizzie's eyes began darting about like frightened tadpoles. She was looking everywhere at once, as though dreading that some unwelcome sight might appear.

"Rest easy Lizzie," Katherine said wickedly into her sister's ear. "I can see from here the cart is beside the house and the horse is grazing in the meadow near the lavender. Flynn must be home."

Lizzie paled like milk, but she blanched in vain, because he was not.

The cottage of the McGintys was situated apart from the village, two-thirds of the way up the slope. The rent was lower in such an isolated position.

They found Ilvenna tending her burgeoning garden-plot, pulling weeds from beds of medicinal herbs. The she-goat stood on the other side of the stone wall, looking longingly over it at the flowers and foliage. She was tethered to a stake. When she saw the newcomers she stuck out her chin and bleated insultingly.

"Mind yer manners Gallytrot, yer great lump o' lard," shouted Ilvenna. She straightened up, smiling at the visitors, bobbing a curtsey. "Well Miss Delacey, Miss Lizzie and Miss Rose. 'Tis a grand wishin'-charm!" she crowed, "and that's a fact!"

"So it is, Ilvenna, and I shall never forget what you have done," Rose said fervently. "You're a powerful wise-woman, and that's a fact." She kissed Ilvenna on the cheek as she would have kissed her sisters. The goat fixed everyone with a baleful yellow eye.

The sun's rays were lengthening. Bars of smoky amber and cinnabar stretched across the valley, and a flock of rooks passed overhead like fragments of shattered jet. The breeze smelled faintly of lavender. Ilvenna spread a thick cloth of drugget over the stone coping of the well in the garden, so as not to ruin the dresses of her guests. They seated themselves there. Lizzie, as restless as water, bent down to pluck yellow-eyed wild-flowers from the grasses, and made herself a daisy chain.

"'Tis a fine evenin'," said Ilvenna, "too fine to be indoors. Besides, Ma is rattlin' pots and pans in the kitchen, and she's needin' the elbow-room."

They spoke first, eagerly, about the black-haired brothers. Regarding their background, Ilvenna was as uninformed as they.

"I t'ought the one named Ryan was himself at first," she said, "judgin' by Lizzie's drawin'."

"Lizzie is clever, but she cannot see inside my head," said Rose. "Still, her picture was exceeding accurate, considering she has not my dreams."

"This brother Ryan has a scar at his left temple," said Ilvenna. "That was not in the drawin'. By that, I might have known 'twas not yer man."

"Myself, I could see no resemblance between the two of them at all," said Rose. "Besides, no other man has eyes that color. Not even his brother."

"You must have got an eye-full of this Ryan, to be noticing scars and such," said Katherine.

"Oh, that I did," Ilvenna assured her.

After examining and re-examining the topic in minute detail, they turned to the subject of the Midsummer's festivities. The sisters wanted to find out everything Ilvenna had seen and heard. At last they remembered their other business with the wise-woman. They asked her for a remedy for Mary's heartburn.

"She has lately been suffering from it, groaning when she lies down in her bed at nights," said Lizzie.

"Besides," said Rose, "it is her birthday next week and we would like to give her some presents."

Ilvenna invited them indoors. Into one of the small glass bottles they had brought in the basket, she measured out a tincture: "Seven drops under the tongue at night, washed down with water to which a teaspoon of bicarbonate of soda has been added," she advised, "No liquor for a month, not even beer. Let her be drinkin' cold water or luke-warm chamomile tea. No more souse or pickled walnuts or other vinegary vittles. No more anchovy sauce with melted butter."

For Mary's chapped and blistered hands, Ilvenna prescribed a jar of soothing lotion. Along with this she provided a small pot of the arthritis remedy Mary was wont to purchase from time to time.

"Now 'tis three presents you have at you," she said. "What will be the fourth?"

Rose decided on a tiny bottle of lavender oil, for its sweet perfume.

"Ma says Mary should be after doin' her washin' no more 'n once a month like most people," said Ilvenna. "She wouldn't be blisterin' her hands."

"She won't have that," said Rose. "She says cleanliness lives next door to sanctitude. She stirs the laundry tub with a great blackthorn stick, but it's the starching and the wringing out that's the ruin of her hands."

"Maybe she could be doin' with some help," suggested Ilvenna.

"Two servants would be a terrible extravagance," said Margaret, unwilling to admit, even to their friend, that they could only afford one.

Ilvenna looked at the hands of the sisters, which lay folded in their laps like white doves.

"I suppose your own fingers must be keepin' smooth and sleek for the embroidery," she murmured without conviction.

"And so that the eligible landowners will know we are ladies," Katherine reminded her. "You're not thinking that we could help Mary, surely?"

"It never crossed me mind," said Ilvenna.

When all transactions were concluded, Lizzie lifted the basket and they took their leave of Ilvenna and Ma and the goat.

CHAPTER 14

An Irish Young Man, He Dreamed a Dream

An Irish young man he dreamed a dream,
The most beautiful girl in the nation.
No counsel he'll take but a journey he'd make,
Into Ireland to seek this fair creature.

The Knight's Dream. Sung as a Cornish version to Cecil Sharp in April 1904. By Frederick Crossman of Somerset, UK.

The noisy song of the stream came to meet them as they neared the bridge. Beneath the mossy stonework of the arch, it rushed over cold, clacking pebbles carrying peat-stained waters down from the back hills. A couple of men on the banks were fishing, using nets on long poles. They wore brown jerkins and red neckerchiefs. One was smoking a clay pipe.

"Good health to yez!" he called good-naturedly, a gap-toothed grin splitting his sun-browned face. The men tipped their caps at the young ladies, who nodded politely, as they had been taught.

"And to you yourself," they returned.

The afternoon clouds had scudded away to the east and the sky was clear. It glowed with a soft incandescent blue, like a robin's egg.

On the village road, children were kicking a pigskin ball, running and shouting. A black dog and a couple of wolfhounds were sniffing about on the grassy verge, studiously ignoring five bossy hens who were pecking at a swarm of tiny beetles. The road veered to avoid Rafferty's Inn, and as they rounded the corner, lifting the hems of their dresses out of the dust, the Delaceys saw three youths walking towards them, each carrying a stout stave of blackthorn. Lizzie dropped the basket in the dirt and retrieved it as quickly. She uttered a soft, despairing moan—there was no time for any of them to pinch colour into their cheeks, or tuck away stray locks of hair, or arrange their features into looks of tranquil femininity meticulously copied from the statue of the Madonna in the church. Katherine and Margaret were helping Lizzie wipe the basket clean when the young men strode up, doffing their caps and wishing them all a good evening.

"And good evening to you, gentlemen," said Rose. Her mouth was curved in a soft smile but her pulse was racing.

"Miss Margaret Delacey, Miss Kat'erine, Miss Elisabet' and Miss Rose," said Flynn McGinty, nodding to each in turn, "would ye do me the honour of allowin' me to introduce these two fellers to yez?"

A charge had built up in the atmosphere. Rose felt her senses stretch as taut as a fiddle-string, well-rosined and ready to play. Her skin tingled, as it always tingled before a thunder-storm.

"Certainly," said Margaret. Her voice sounded husky and she cleared her throat with a prim ahem. Her gaze danced from one newcomer to the other.

"It is the delight at us to be meetin' you, ladies," gravely said the taller of the black-haired brothers, "and of one among you 'tis not the first encounter." He looked at Rose with his ebony-lashed eyes. "Mistress Rose." Those who heard him speak somehow knew intuitively that it was the first time he had pronounced her name, and when he said it, his voice was a caress.

Katherine and Lizzie could not help but gape at the beautiful young man with awe and some timidity, and even practical Margaret appeared uncertain in the presence of the one with The Face, the dream-haunter, the imaginary lover made flesh. Here, it seemed to them, was a personage who had stepped almost from legend, or from the pages of a storybook, or the hollow hills and diamond halls of the Good People. After all Rose's tales and Lizzie's drawing and Ilvenna's charms it seemed impossible that this silver-eyed youth was merely mortal, man born of woman, who lived and breathed under the sun.

Yet there he was.

"I do be called Keane O'Connell,"—he pronounced it Kee-ahn—"and my brother's name is Ryan." The speaker concluded with a graceful bow. It was now apparent that his voice was as remarkable as his looks; mellifluous, charismatic, its timbre lingering in the consciousness of the listeners even after he finished speaking.

Murmuring formal responses, the Delaceys curtsied.

"So ye've been and introduced yourself, O'Connell," said Flynn McGinty, leaning on his blackthorn staff, "and taken away my privilege."

"That I have, McGinty," replied the other, "seeing as you're a neighbour to these ladies and have had the pleasure of introducin' people to them all your life, I reckoned it time another fellow had a turn."

"I reckon ye owe me a favour now," bantered Flynn.

"And I reckon I do not," said Keane O'Connell. "For it is four favours."

Flynn gave a shout of laughter.

The O'Connell brothers appeared similar in looks, but by no means identical. Ryan, dark and dashing, lacked perhaps an inch or two of the height of his elder sibling and the side of his forehead was marked by a pale, slim scar. His eyes were brown. Smiling, he said, "Ladies, it bein' the evenin' hour would you be requirin' an escort home in case o' bogles and skrikers on the road?"

"To my knowledge nobody has ever been assailed by a bogle or a skriker on this village highway," said Margaret. "However that is not to say that all travellers are forever safe from such frightenings. Therefore we would fain suffer you three gentlemen to accompany us."

They walked up the road together, the youths retracing their recent steps. They used their staffs like walking-sticks, and any enquirers would have been informed that that was their only purpose. Lizzie linked her arm through Katherine's and lowered her chin, earnestly studying the road in front of her feet so as to avoid pot-holes and loose stones. Flynn McGinty offered to carry her basket, an offer she declined with a murmur and the briefest glance at him.

"Where do you both hail from, Mr. O'Connell?" Katherine asked the elder brother. She, of all of them, was bursting with questions.

"From Kerry," he replied in his mellifluous tones, matching his step to Rose's. "The work there is not much, so we've been walkin' up the coast lookin' for better."

"And have you found it?"

"Indeed we have."

Katherine stole a glance at this strapping, handsome Irish lad as they walked. She noted that while he was conscious of his comeliness, he was indifferent to it. He was seizing every opportunity to take her sister's elbow and guide her through rough patches in the road. It was clear that it was all he could do not to fling his arms around Rose, who leaned towards him as though she had inexplicably been struck with an inability to keep her balance.

"'Twas this very day I met these Kerry boys for the first time, so I did," explained Flynn, "and I axed them if they had a trade at all, and they were after sayin' they could whack hot iron as well as any smit'. So I says to them, I can find ye a job o' work right here in Allanwell. Off we took ourselves to Mick O'Sullivan's, and Mick says he's right pleased to have a couple o' apprentices working in his smithy until his bones mend, because yer man has not been doin' so well since he made a holy show of himself at Rafferty's, getting' gallopin' mouldy and fallin' down and smashin' his elber like a right eejit."

"In ancient mythology, blacksmiths were credited with supernatural attributes," said Margaret, "partly because they work with iron, the bane of the Good People. What a pity Mr. O'Sullivan's magical powers did not protect him from the demons of drink. Can you shoe horses, gentlemen?" she asked the newcomers.

"My brother can do so indeed, Miss Delacey," said Ryan.

"I am sure Papa will be pleased to hear we've a farrier in the village again!"

"'Tis all arranged," Flynn went on. "The lads here were talkin' of lodgin' at Rafferty's Inn, but they can stay at magical Mick's instead. Just now, ladies, you met us traipsin' across to my place for a decent feed. The boyos would prefer me ma's baked salmon with bread sauce and a jug o' punch instead o' rabbit half raw half burnt, which is how O'Sullivan cooks his supper."

"No doubt," agreed Katherine. "And it is a good deed you've done today, Mr. McGinty."

As the party of seven walked through the village, blurred white ovals of faces appeared at windows and folk hailed them from doorsteps. They drew plenty of attention. Flynn

McGinty was a popular figure who bore the added prestige of John Delacey's favour, two strangers were a source of intense speculation, and the aspect of the Delacey daughters drew the eye like the play of sunlight on water.

Rose's heart was too full to allow her to speak. She was going hot and cold by turns, feeling Keane O'Connell walking so close at her side that his elbow, once, brushed against hers and sent a tingling charge through her arm.

Conversely, Katherine was loquacious, directing her enquiries at Keane.

She asked, "And would you be spelling your name with a K or a C?" and then gave a sudden gasp, for as soon as the words had left her lips, she regretted them. The strangers might think she was trying to discover how educated they were, and whether they could write their own names or had to mark their signatures by a cross. She held her breath.

"That would be with a K," calmly said Keane, reading her expression easily. "And yourself, Miss Kat'erine?"

"Oh yes, with a K also," said Katherine quickly, releasing a faint sigh.

"Good, well that's another weighty matter settled," said Flynn McGinty. "'Tis a wonderful t'ing we didn't forget about that, now." He twirled his staff with one hand.

"These details can be very important," said Katherine sagely.

"In that case it is not settled that easily," said Keane O'Connell, "For if this is important to Miss Kat'erine I must add that 'tis only a 'K' in the English tongue. The letter K is not at the Gaeilge alphabet at all."

"But what about the word Kerry?" asked the erudite Margaret, flanked by two stalwart Irishmen, the dark and the red.

"Rightfully 'tis with a C, like cat," said Keane O'Connell, and he spelled it out: "Ciarrai."

Katherine looked anxious. "Are you saying that in Gaeilge your initial would be C?"

A frown creased her forehead.

"Indeed, Miss Kat'erine," he replied, somewhat amused, "same as yours."

Her brow cleared. "Same as mine!" she repeated. "Of course!" Slyly she nudged Lizzie to remind her about the results of the trick with the nine-pea cosh over the door. Lizzie merely looked bemused.

"You are knowing a great deal about the Gaeilge language Mr. O'Connell," said Margaret.

"And where's the harm in that?"

"No harm to us, but maybe harm to you. Mind, there's none here in Allanwell that would be betraying you, except maybe the Protestants on the hilltop. But there's those elsewhere who might think a body had been attending a hedge-school if he knew as much as you. It seems to me that you live dangerously Mr. O'Connell. And that blade at your side—some might call it a weapon."

Katherine and Lizzie exchanged startled glances. There was dread in their eyes, for they knew as well as anyone the dire penalties that would be exacted from any Catholic apprehended for carrying a weapon or obtaining an education illegally. It was no light matter, breaking the penal laws.

"And others might call it a butter-knife," said Keane. "How's a man supposed to divide his bread and bacon? Do not fear for me, Miss Delacey. My father gave me this scian. He was a Chieftain and it is a Chieftain's knife. I have carried it for ten years, one way or another, and I shall carry it yet, in spite of the Protestant code."

Ryan said, "Is it not a queer circumstance, that we might merely open our mouths and profess we do not love the Pope and instantly, without changin' another t'ing, we could all be armed— bristlin' like hedge-pigs with swords and pistols in the very blink of an eye. And sittin' in parliament, whateffer."

"How I do envy them lords with their wigs and starched cravats bein' entertained by them speakers in parliament while we poor Catholic boys be forced to be walkin' in the company of four o' the fairest colleens in Ireland and not a cloud in the sky," said Flynn McGinty, shaking his head regretfully.

"It is mortal difficult," agreed the O'Connells.

"For shame, gentlemen," said Margaret, attempting to sound severe, "you've kissed the Stone, no doubt of it. We'll not listen to your flattery."

"Good, then you will not be mindin' if we do keep on with it," said Flynn McGinty.

"With your nonsense, for sure you've been drinking, Mr. McGinty," gleefully teased Katherine.

"Only the water," said he innocently.

"Of life," she shot back. They all laughed together, for although the Delaceys understood only those few words of Gaeilge they had learned by osmosis, they had long since picked up the fact that uisce beatha literally meant the water of life, and from this was derived the word whiskey.

"How is 'Rose' pronounced in the Gaeilge?" asked Rose, who had heard the elder brother say her name once, and ardently desired to hear it again.

"Bejasus, one of the silent ones speaks!" said Flynn McGinty, "I thought you must have been after chewin' cloves, Miss Rose."

"If I had any I'd be giving them to you, Mr. McGinty."

"It is pronounced Rós," said Keane O'Connell.

"Such a scant difference," said Rose, "yet, sir, the way you speak with your Kerry accent makes it sound like music. Say it again!"

"Rós, Rós, Rós," said Keane. "Now 'tis your turn."

"Keane, Keane, Keane," she returned, laughing.

"And what of the other silent one?" Flynn McGinty said, directing his words towards Lizzie. "A penny for your t'oughts Miss Elisabet'."

"I have none," Lizzie said quickly.

"That's grand, because I have not a penny." The red-haired youth grinned and twirled his staff again.

Judging that decorum was sadly lacking from the conversation and determined to set matters to rights, Margaret said politely to Ryan, "May we take it that you and your brother will be staying for quite some time in Allanwell,

Mr O'Connell?" She lifted the hem of her gown no more than an inch, and demurely avoided a wheel-rut in her path. "At least until Mr O'Sullivan is fit for work again?"

"At least," rejoined Ryan.

"Maybe for the rest of our days," said Keane. He bestowed upon Rose a long and searching look, as though to brand every detail of her aspect on his memory.

"What in the world is in Allanwell to make a body choose to stay here?" Katherine said archly. Margaret shot her an admonitory glare.

Keane replied, "'Tis I who should be askin' that question of you, Miss Kat'erine."

"Oh well," she replied, "it is the constant excitement of course."

With laughter and banter the journey up the hill passed quickly. Rose was uncertain whether her feet had touched the ground; she had been unaware of the usual dusty pot-holes and small obstacles offered by the road.

Out over Madigan's Leap the sun was going down. Against the furnace of its unmaking a white sea-eagle soared in slow circles, its wings stretched to full span. At the gate of the Delacey cottage the party split in two, bidding each other good night—but not before another meeting had been arranged. As the sisters walked up the garden path they heard Mary's voice shrilling from the kitchen—

"And did you bring me the wake robin?"

CHAPTER 15

I'd Gladly Give my Heart and Hand

Once I knew a pretty girl, I loved her as my life
I'd gladly give my heart and hand
To make her my wife, oh to make her my wife.

Once I knew a pretty girl (Traditional)

There were many more meetings. Rose and her sweetheart spent every spare moment together. He was real, and a mortal man; of that there could be no doubt. At the dwindling of each long summer day and through autumn into winter he would come running like a deer over the hill to meet her at the garden gate, and she would invite him to come into the house. In the company of Rose's sisters, they would drink ale or elderflower cordial at the trestle table. On fine days they would go walking out, always with a pair of sisters bringing up the rear a few paces away. Their favoured destination was Madigan's Leap. Somehow as they climbed the hidden path to the fort, between the tall boulders and rocky folds of the hillside, the following sisters would find the going arduous and drop back, or they would lose the path entirely and wander off in another direction. The girls always carried with them a piece of half-finished embroidery and a skein of coloured threads. Wielding the needle and conversing, they would pass the time ensconced in some sheltered nook where the last rays of the sun lingered, until Rose and Keane found them again.

Many a meal did the O'Connells share at the table of the Delaceys, and every evening was jovial. John Delacey grew to look upon both lads with reluctant approval and a waxing fondness. His peers would perhaps have viewed them as being from a class unworthy of mingling with his family. Life, however, had taught him that true affection was of greater value than social standing, and even a blindfolded man could see how much the elder brother cherished and respected his youngest daughter. He sensed that Keane was a young buck who, if he ever made his fortune, might take his daughter from him. At the same time he knew also that such partings would some day be inevitable.

"Is he still in your dreams, Rose?" asked Lizzie, unlacing Rose's stays for her as they prepared themselves for sleep one night.

"We do not dream of each other when we are together. And, as in the past, it only happens at times when one of us is seized by some strong passion."

Lizzie, standing behind Rose and pulling the cord from the eyelets of the wooden bodice, said, "It seems to me you are forever going about wrapped in some strong passion. You hardly eat or sleep."

"I know," said Rose. "It's a heady feeling indeed, but it's also an ache. I can't help thinking about him all the time, and my heart pounds, and there's a knot in my belly."

"Are you certain it's not just smittenness?" her sister asked. "You remember, we read about that in Papa's book, 'The Passions and Faculties of the Human Mind', by Dr. Gilbert Burke."

"I do remember it," said Rose.

"People can make themselves believe an illusion that they want to believe," Lizzie elaborated, "despite the evidence of reality. They convince themselves that the object of their affection is some flawless angel. It's pure infatuation."

"Hmm," said Rose. "Look who's talking! The pot calling the kettle 'black'!"

Lizzie looked crestfallen, but since Rose had her back turned, she did not notice.

"Finished," said Lizzie.

Rose peeled away her loosened stays, turned about and began to unlace Lizzie's. "Mama once told me," she said, "to be wary of believing that the rapturous rush of smittenness is real love. She compared it to looking through a pair of spectacles, in which the lenses are made from the stained glass of the church windows, particularly the golden glass used for the halos. Everything would look all glowy, and better than it really is."

"Mama was wise," said Lizzie sorrowfully.

"She gave an example of a young woman she did not name, but I know she was talking about her own sister. Aunt Bridget fell for the blandishments and assurances of a young man she was smitten with. He begged her to lie with him and vowed he would marry her afterwards. But it all ended up with pain. Finished!"

Lizzie removed her unlaced stays and placed them in the small camphorwood chest. Both girls commenced to remove their chemises and don their shifts.

Lizzie said dolefully, "How can any of us know whether love is true?"

"I make no claim to scholarship in this regard," said Rose. "Truly, I believe 'tis a matter of spending enough time to know someone well, becoming friends with him, and trusting more to your head than your heart. Listen closely to what your trusted friends and kin say about your sweetheart. Often times, your loved ones know best, for your own heart's like to be a fanciful idiot, dreaming too much and leading you straight into trouble."

"Yes," said Lizzie as she slipped into bed, "I recall Mama saying, 'Always trust your head instead of your heart'. But it doesn't sound very romantic."

"If it's any comfort," said Rose, "I think Flynn McGinty is a grand young gentleman."

"Why would I want to know that?" said Lizzie in a muffled voice from beneath the blankets.

Rose laughed, sliding into the bed beside her sister and laying her head on the pillow.

Lizzie peered out at her. "I see you've taken to wearing your locket again."

Rose touched her finger to the tiny gold case on its fine chain. It lay in the hollow where her collarbones met, and it was warm to the touch. "Thank you for the reminder. I did not intend to keep it at my neck while I sleep." Unfastening the clasp, she placed the locket in a little carved box at the bedside.

"I do not know why you ever stopped wearing it," said Lizzie. "I always wear mine during the day. It's not as if we've anything finer to decorate ourselves with."

"Do not tell anyone," said Rose, "but I gave it to Ma McGinty in payment for the spell."

"To Ma! How ever did you get it back? It'd be like trying to pry a limpet off a rock, getting something valuable out of her."

"About a week after Keane arrived—" Rose was forever finding excuses to say Keane's name and she uttered the syllables as though savouring some confection—"Flynn quietly came up to me and slipped the locket into my hand. He said his Ma had given it to him to be pawned in Ballyganna. But he did not have the heart to do it. He had saved some money of his own which he handed over her instead, letting her think it was from the pawnbroker. And don't you go telling anyone the truth, either. I only told you so's you know what a fine and gallant gentleman Flynn is. I hope to repay him some day."

"I already know he's a fine and gallant gentleman," sullenly said Lizzie, pouting her lower lip. "Good night!"

Down at the foot of Madigan's Leap the sea, rocked by its tides, reflected the evanescent colours of the sky. Sometimes, when Rose and Keane stood atop the precipice, they could spy sailing ships approaching, making for the bay. First, the tips of their masts would appear over the horizon, next the clouds of ivory canvas straining at the rigging; last to appear was the hull; a sequence that proved the world was, in fact, round.

One day, on that windblown height, Rose and her sweet-heart pledged themselves to one another. As a token, he showed her a ring of gold inscribed with the words 'Go deo'. The ring had been cleverly cloven in two along the band, not athwart it, forming two slender circles. Yet the cleaving was slightly irregular, so that the two halves fitted precisely into each other like two pieces of a puzzle.

"This was my mother's ring," said Keane. "Now she lies beneath the turf beside my father, far away in Kerry. Long ago she gave me this for my bride to wear."

"What does it mean?"

"'Go deo' means 'forever'. That's how long our love will be

lastin'. Will you let me place one half upon your finger, my darlin'? The other half I will be keepin' on my own hand, and when we be married the two halves shall be joined, and you shall wear it."

"I shall never take it from my hand until it is time for it to be joined again with your half. I swear it!"

"Ach, do be careful in makin' such pledges," he chided her gently. "The Good People might be listenin', and ye know about their mischief!"

She shook her head, smiling. "They can listen. I'll stand by my vow!"

Rose wore her half of the ring on her thumb, since it would have slipped from her narrow fingers. Keane slipped the other half around his smallest digit. He went to her father and asked for permission to wed Rose when she came of age, saying, "I have no wealth, as ye well know, Mr. Delacey. But I have my healt' and strengt' and I do not be afraid of hard work. Your family is of gentle blood, but you do know me to be of good character. Know also that my father was the son of the O'Connell. He'd have been a Chieftain himself, and I his heir, except for the penal laws takin' all that away from us. I ask for permission to wed your daughter, but if ye do give it, the weddin' will not be soon, even after her comin'-of-age. The betrothal shall last as long as it takes me to raise enough money to keep Rose in as much comfort as may be, and she surrounded by every good t'ing my hands can make or bring to her. She's the moon and the sun to me, sir, and the eart' and the sky. I would give my life, sir, to

171

prevent any harm comin' to her, and these words I do say from my heart."

"Have you already asked her, then?"

Keane dropped his gaze for a moment. "That I have indeed, sir," he admitted. "She gave her consent."

And John Delacey, looking at the young man standing before him, cap in hand, dressed in his white Sunday shirt, radiant with youth and vitality, his bearing princely, his handsome countenance alive with sincerity and earnest hope, could only give his blessing. He did so with joy, that one of his children should find such a life-partner.

An extraordinary gentleman was Delacey, for his time, because he was prepared to eschew class distinctions when the happiness of his child was in question. Or, conceivably—and equally uncommonly—he recognised that Keane O'Connell was of noble blood, because an Irish chieftain, or taoiseach, had the status of royalty.

"Rose knows her own mind," he said, "and she's a good judge of character. We've not been long acquainted with you, but I have made some enquiries. You and your family are well-spoken of in Kerry. Had history long ago taken a different turn, you might have been a prince in this dominion. Moreover I flatter myself that I am a good judge of men and I know you to be personally honourable. It is with a glad heart I accept you into our family, Keane O'Connell."

"I t'ank ye sir!"

"But," continued John Delacey, "you are both very young. I consent to your betrothal but not to your marriage, until Rose is at least eighteen. The longer you wait, the better. Besides, it would not do to have the youngest sister married before the rest. I've no doubt I would hear nothing but endless complaints about their being viewed as old maids."

He added, feigning off-handedness, "Would you be thinking of taking Rose back to Kerry with you after you're married?"

"No, sir. We would be bidin' here, so that Rose can be close to her family."

"God bless you, my boy. God bless both of you."

Buoyed by happiness, the couple went to visit Father Joseph. They pledged themselves in front of him also, to make the betrothal official, and he 'took a dram' with them to celebrate.

"Sláinte, my dear Anne," said the old priest as he raised his glass in a toast. "Er, that is—" he peered at Rose—"Sure, it's the image of your mother ye do be. Sláinte, Miss Margaret."

"Rose, Father," she corrected him gently.

"Ah that's it, Rose." The priest drained his glass before further debate could keep it from his lips.

Later, Rose said to Keane, "Father Joseph gets a little confused sometimes. You'll have to excuse him."

"It takes bravery to be a priest these days," said Keane, "when to be hanged, drawn and quartered is just a whisper away for so many of them. If a man's not born with that kind o' courage he might have to find it in a bottle. To keep on like he does, the good father do be a saint."

It seemed to the Delacey sisters at that time that all the world was a happy place, for Rose had found her love against all rhyme and reason, and she had regained her locket, and the weather was fine and sunny, and even their father seemed more content than he had ever been since their mother had passed away.

To add intrigue to their lives, somebody started a rumour that Keane O'Connell had been conceived on a Midsummer's Eve, when two newlyweds, delirious with love, recklessly lay down within a fairy ring, so that somehow the Good People had put their mark upon him.

It was only when the sisters went to visit Ilvenna McGinty that they sensed a shadow. Ilvenna side-stepped their attempts to wring from her the reason for her despondency, but later, when the attention of three of the sisters was directed toward the spectacle of Ma chasing the goat out of the vegetable patch, she said softly to the second-eldest, "Miss Katherine, 'tis for Keane I do be fearin', for I must tell you, I have seen the signs in the flight of birds, the appearance of clouds."

"What signs?" Katherine asked, alarmed at Ilvenna's grave demeanour.

"I have seen the signs," the young woman replied, "of doom. No lucky star be shinin' upon that one, and for this, for Rose, for us all, I grieve."

"Pray do not tell a soul," said Katherine, surreptitiously crossing herself. "Let us hope the clouds are wrong."

An exuberant betrothal party was held at the Delacey

cottage, with music, dancing and feasting, and for weeks afterwards the village girls went about with long faces, as though they were in mourning.

CHAPTER 16

I'll go to Some Hollow and I'll Set up my Still

"The Whiskey Still at Lochgilphead" 1819 by Sir David Wilkie

I've been a moonshiner for many a year,
And I've spent all me money on whiskey and beer.
I'll go to some hollow and I'll set up my still,
And I'll make you a gallon for a ten shilling bill.

"The Moonshiner" is a folk song with disputed origins.

The rest of the year flew by. It was an eventful period.

Europe in 1793 was a seething ferment of politics, instability and violence. On November 10th, the new French Republic abolished the worship of God. England, the Dutch Republic and Spain joined with the Holy Roman Empire in a military alliance against the French, but at Toulon the British were blown into the sea by the French artillery, under the direction of an enthusiastic young gunner named Bonaparte.

Because of the economic and political strain of war against the French, English Prime Minister William Pitt spurred the Irish government into granting Catholics voting rights. It was an effort to pacify the Irish revolutionary threat and win them from enthusiasm for 'godless France'. Catholics were still excluded from Ireland's parliament of Protestant aristocrats, however, and the parliament's administration remained in the hands of a Lord Lieutenant appointed by the British government.

Despite the granting of the Catholic franchise the penal laws had not been revoked. Wolfe Tone and the non-sectarian Society of United Irishmen continued their endeavours to make Ireland a republic according to French principles, and

178

sever the ties with England. The Irish Volunteers formed an armed body to extort further concessions from the English. Notwithstanding the unrest it was a season of prosperity for the privileged class, and in Dublin many buildings of gracious dimensions and stately architecture arose.

Meanwhile in Allanwell, the marsh-mallow golds of summer were transmuting into the heady wine-crimsons and cinnamons of autumn, and from thence to winter's tarnished silver as Christmas came and went. The last roses had withered on the briars in the hedgerows, and on the ruins atop Madigan's Leap. Their fruit had swelled like scarlet lanterns that were eaten by birds or harvested by human hands, or that even managed to fall into the earth which, scant as it was on that rocky height, provided enough sustenance to nurture living things of amazing beauty. The leaves dried and were blown away, until only the black stems remained, knotted and twining in interlocking patterns like those on the haft of Keane O'Connell's scian.

The O'Connell brothers lived at O'Sullivan's smithy, where Keane worked. Wearing Michael O'Sullivan's full-length leather apron he stood at the anvil, his left side lit up by the glare of the fire. With the precise blows of the hammer he shaped all manner of items necessary for daily life: horse-shoes, buckles, hinges and hasps, harness hardware, ploughshares, axles and wheel-rims, sickles and scythes, axles, shovels and chains, andirons, pothooks, locks, gates, lanterns and an assortment of other articles. Sometimes O'Sullivan worked the bellows with his good arm. He forced gusts of life into the forge-fire until it roared hard, like a gale on the ocean, while beads of sweat rolled like raindrops down Keane's brow. Every village girl could find an excuse to go to the smithy with a broken pan-handle or a bent saucepan to be mended.

Ryan, it seemed, was able to turn his hand to most tasks. He was content to be a jack-of-all-trades, doing a little thatching here, a little peat-cutting there, some fish-cleaning down at the harbour when a big catch was hauled in, or tending O'Sullivan's potato patch. Both youths blended easily into the life of the village, going to church on Sundays and taking part in hurling matches on the village green on Sunday afternoons.

The two strapping O'Connell brothers were much sighed-after, but many a heart was broken— for the elder had eyes only for Rose Delacey, while the younger told the girls he liked them all so much he could never decide to give his heart to one only.

Besides, Ryan was often hard to find.

He had taken to helping their friend Flynn McGinty with the running of his illicit still. This apparatus remained hidden in a cave high in the misty hills behind Allanwell. The cave was strategically positioned, being well-concealed and reached only by a roundabout route that darted in and out between marshy puddles, around the wicked thorns of whin, blackthorn and whitethorn, past slippery rockfaces, along the reedy margin of a mirror-surfaced pool and across treacherous scree. A freshet on the upper slopes fed a small stream that trickled through the cave, and there was a hole in the roof to allow the escape of the thin trail of smoke generated by the enterprise within. The smoke mingled with the mists and was thereby disguised. The still was put into operation only on days when the clouds lowered themselves, like grey wolves, to fasten on the hilltops.

It was the job of old Seamus O'Grady to mind the still. He ate and slept at the back of the cave, only coming to town when Flynn or one of his comrades relieved him of his duty for a while. Seamus' black-and-white sheepdog stayed with him. The dog, ever alert, would be sure to warn the man of the approach of strangers. This arrangement had been in place ever since the distillers had heard tidings concerning another still in the east of the county, which had been discovered by the indefatigable Riding Officers of His Majesty's Customs. The still having been left unattended, the law-enforcers had lain in wait and ambushed its operators, catching them unawares. Five men were arrested and flung into prison, where they languished under conditions of severe deprivation and starvation. One died of a flogging, two succumbed to disease and as far as anyone could gather, the surviving pair was still subject to durance. During their imprisonment, their families had been evicted for falling behind with the rent.

Seamus O'Grady was a childlike man, considered to be somewhat "away with the fairies" as the villagers put it—but he was reliable and honest. In addition to being able to play the fiddle with a speed and dexterity that made him popular throughout the region, he possessed another talent. He could mimic the calls of wild creatures. In particular, he could whistle like a hawk and bark like a fox, with uncanny accuracy. This was a useful ability, for whenever they approached the cave by day, Flynn and his friends would perform the warble of the thrush as a signal, to be answered by Seamus' hawk-whistle if all was well. During the hours of darkness, the signal would be a barn-owl, acknowledged by a fox.

"What if it is a real fox that's barkin'?" Ryan had wanted to know. He and Flynn were lugging heavy sacks of barley mash along a narrow, almost invisible track that wandered along a hillside between granite outcrops and heathery dells.

"We must be takin' that chance," said Flynn. "Seamus has the luck on us, because there do be no barn owls in these hills. Not that there do be too many thrushes either, these days. When hungry folk are not stealin' the eggs they do be makin' lark pies, more's the pity."

"And what if O'Grady heard someone comin' and that one makin' no signal?"

"His dog would give a yip. Then Seamus would be out the back way, through his little bolt hole and into the fern as quick as you could say 'get the wind up'. Again he has the luck of it, since only a scrawny wee leprechaun like him could wriggle through that tunnel."

Christmas, which many folk called "Yule", came and went at Allanwell like a brief flare of ruby and emerald light in a drab world, with bright red holly berries and verdant ivy leaves decorating the tiny cottages. Snow rested like powdered diamonds on the flanks of the back hills in January and February of the year 1794, and the sky was coloured a soft, dark silver, like dusty cobwebs. When the snow-clouds came down a fire would be lit in the hidden cave. The copper pot would be warmed, the 'baor' would bubble and the vapours would rise within the coils. Then the strong, honey-coloured spirit would drip from a spout. At such times 'the worm was full o' fire', as the saying went.

In spring, Michael O'Sullivan proclaimed that his arm was mended—although Dr Conway had set the bone crooked— and aimed a few whacks at the anvil with his hammer, to test the theory. On the fourth blow he grimaced and dropped the hammer, allowing he'd have to be patient a while longer.

"Tomorrow mornin' I'll be off wit' Ryan to see the Flanagans," said Keane to Rose as they lingered by her garden gate on an April evening. It was one of those partings that extends for hours, because every time Rose's sweetheart made to leave he took no more than a few paces before hurrying back for one last word, one final look, one ultimate clasp of the hands.

"Well, it is about time," Rose forced herself to say. "How long will you be away?"

"Only the two days."

"That's a terrible long time," she said, with downcast eyes. "But promises must not be broken."

Months earlier, Keane had told her about the Flanagans.

They lived in Castlerigg, the neighbouring village, which lay a long day's walk away, south of the Oranowin River. The O'Connells had passed through Castlerigg on their way to Allanwell. On that occasion the Flanagan family had been very kind to a couple of poor travellers who each possessed nothing more than a bundle and a blackthorn stick. They gave the boys shelter and a hearty meal, and even some extra bread and cheese to take away with them when they found out there was no work to be had at Castlerigg. And when they got to talking in earnest, it turned out that Martin Flanagan had met their father, several years back—in fact, he had known him quite well. When the O'Connell lads departed, they promised they would return early in the new year to visit the Flanagans and let them know how they were faring. But the months had slipped by and it was now April.

"'Tis t'ree messages we've sent the Flanagans already," said Keane gently, smiling down at Rose. "Whenever any feller travels out Castlerigg way we send a message wit' him, just so that our friends won't be t'inkin' we've been swallowed up by a bog, whatever. But a man must keep his word, in the end. I've been puttin' it off for weeks. Do you t'ink I want to go anywhere and you not beside me?"

Rose shook her head, reaching up to touch her finger lightly to his lips.

"I know," she said.

"Besides, I'm not forgettin' 'twill be your birthday on Monday. I'll not be missin' that, if I have any say in it."

"I am sure you wouldn't lose a chance at Mary's fruit cake,"

Rose teased. She gazed her sweet-heart, absorbing him as the earth soaks in the rain. Strands of his hair had escaped their confining band. They lay, tendrils of sable, against the snow and cream of his cravat and shirtsleeves, the pale bronze of his neck. He was like a jet of flame fashioned from the night. "Hurry back," she said. "Safe return and may angels watch over you."

The door of the cottage slammed open. Mary's voice issued forth like the squawk of an indignant hen. "Rose Delacey, get inside this minute before you catch your death o' cold! Haven't I enough to do wit'out bein' forced to play nurse at your bedside?"

Keane kissed Rose's hands. "Slán go fóill!" he whispered with a grin, and he swung away into the gathering gloom, his white shirt glimmering momentarily in the dusk like some vanishing spectre.

At dawn on Friday the eleventh of April the deep boom of a single cannon-shot rang across the quiet hills. A tall ship dropped anchor in Allanwell Bay. She was not the kind of ocean-going craft the village had been accustomed to seeing from time to time; no trading vessel, no brig or snow or brigantine laden with cargo bound for England, or en route to far-off countries.

She was a big British man-o-war, a frigate with deep square sails on all three masts and countless reef-points on every sail. From her bows projected a long flying jib-boom. A row of many-paned windows overhung her stern, as the second-storey windows of a house might overhang a street. Along each side of the massive hull was arrayed a single row of gun-ports. As majestic as a gigantic albatross at rest, the ship rode at anchor in the middle of the bay. Her sails were furled, but her colourful pennants stood out stiffly in the breeze. On board there was little sign of movement except for a couple of sailors with buckets and brooms, swabbing the decks.

A name was painted on her bows: H.M.S. Conqueror.

Down the side of the hull hung a rope ladder. From the base of this ladder, early in the morning, a wide-bellied boat was rowed to shore. The families of fisherfolk who lived at the bay-side had seen a party of men in regimental uniform disembark to the south of the narrow river-mouth.

These men wore scarlet frock coats, deep-cuffed and high-collared, with white frogging across the chest, and white epaulettes. The knee-length skirts were slit up the back to allow ease of movement, and the edges were fastened back to show the lining. Their close-fitting white trousers were tucked into buttoned leather calf-protectors, which from a distance looked like knee-high boots. On their backs they bore packs. From their waist-belts hung scabbarded daggers and round canteens of boiled leather. Two baldrics of white leather were slung diagonally across from each shoulder, forming the shape of an X upon their the breasts of their waistcoats. Their shoulder-length locks, greased with candle-wax and powdered with white starch, had been harshly combed back into a queue, doubled over and tied with a band at the nape of the neck. Atop this neat coiffure they wore black cocked hats.

Leaving one of their number to row the boat back to the ship the rest marched away in close formation. Their long-barrelled muskets rested on their shoulders, the bayonets all leaning back at the same angle, and they matched their steps to the beat of a drum.

The king's sailors made their way along the riverbank until they drew level with the bridge over the Oranowin. It was at this bridge that the rutted and optimistically-titled Valley Highway, winding down from the north, crossed the river and changed its name to the Cliff Highway. From this point it began to climb steeply to the high precipices that formed the southern wall of the harbour. Further south, the cliffs ran in a long, straight line, a granite bulwark veined with green marble, dashed by wild ocean waves. The road followed along the clifftops until eventually it turned east and dipped towards Castlerigg.

Southwards along this road the Admiralty's finest marched, and the fisherfolk watched them until they disappeared over a rise and all that was left was the insistent rat-a-tat-tat of the drum, fading into the distance.

They had not been sighted since.

CHAPTER 17

Drink the King's Health in the Morning

"Having the lead." A Picturesque Representation of the Naval, Military, and Miscellaneous Costumes of Great Britain, in one hundred coloured plates. London: William Miller & James Walker, 1807. Author: Atkinson, John Augustus

I had a young cousin called Arthur McBride,
He and I took a stroll down by the seaside
A-seeking good fortune and what might betide –
'Twas just as the day was at dawnin'
And after restin' we both took a tramp,
We met Sergeant Harper and Corporal Grant
Besides a wee drummer who beat up the camp
With his rowdy-dow-dow in the mornin'.

He says 'Me young fellers, if you will enlist
A guinea you quickly will have in your fist,
Besides a crown for to kick off the dust
And drink the king's health in the mornin',
For a soldier-boy leads such a very fine life,
He always is blessed with a charming young wife,
He pays all his debts with no sorrow or strife,
And he always lives happy and charming.

Arthur McBride (Traditional)

That night, it was all the talk in Rafferty's Inn.

The frigate remained at anchor—aloof, mysterious and real. She offered no explanation for her presence, no apology for her invasion. With the stars tangled in her spider-web rigging, she loomed like an ominous reminder of the complex, cruel, marvellous, merciless world beyond Allanwell. Some folk were terrified, others boiled with hatred. But all were fascinated.

Not much had been seen of any passengers or crew; some more had come ashore for supplies of fresh water, that was all. After that, the word went out—"A recruiting party is abroad. They are offering six-and-twenty shillings to any young men who will sign up as a sailor with the Sasunach Navy, and a set of new clothes and boots and plenty to eat besides."

The village lads scoffed. "Recruiting party be hanged," they said. "We'd not take their Judas' coins if they begged us on their knees. They must be towering eejits if they t'ink we would lift a finger to help their banjaxed country and their right hoor of a king who belongs in Bedlam. We'd rot in hell first."

A chuckle rumbled in Flynn McGinty's chest. "They'd as like sprout orange-trees out o' their buttocks as persuade an Irishman to sell his soul to them divils."

"Beware," said Rafferty, "I've heard they'll use violence." He spat on the floor.

"That's not'in' new," said the lads patronising his inn. "Recruitin' party is just a fancy name for a press gang."

Rafferty said, "Be as it may, I'd advise all you young fellers to lie low from now until the Sasunachs depart."

"Let them come back!" shouted the boys. "We shall be glad to give these gentlemen a fine Irish welcome!"

"Aye, " agreed Flynn McGinty. "Our shillelaghs will be glad to welcome their heads."

Unaware of these events, in the bitter dawn of the following day Keane and Ryan O'Connell walked along the Cliff Highway on their way back from Castlerigg, bearing their blackthorn quarter-staffs in their hands. The leaden blanket of cloud that covered the length of the coast diffused the first dilute rays of the spring sun. A boom as of distant thunder reached their ears, but there was no sign of rain and they soon dismissed the sound. In the steely-grey pre-dawn glimmer, the breath of the two youths hung upon the air in steamy plumes.

They whistled as they went, for they were in good spirits. They had arrived at Castlerigg the evening before, and the Flanagans had welcomed them as though they were long-lost cousins. Martin Flanagan had insisted on bringing out his greatest treasure, a set of uilleann pipes. Extra rush-lights were kindled. While the O'Connell boys feasted on hot stew and soda bread and beer, Flanagan regaled them with plaintive airs that sent thrills up and down the spine and pierced like swords, or with toe-tapping jigs that fired the children and adults to dance.

"The fare's plain but the music is fit for the palaces of kings!" Martin Flanagan had shouted, red-faced, perspiring with pride and the heat of the room, crammed as it was with the nine members of his family and their two guests.

"'Twas a grand evenin'," said Ryan in the morning, recalling it fondly.

"It was that," agreed Keane, quickening his step.

After the dancing was over and the children had gone to bed, Martin said to his visitors, "Ye've come just in time, boys, for we'll all be gone by next week."

"Why, man?" Ryan asked. "Where are ye goin'?"

"We're off to the New World in search of a better life," Martin replied, his eyes alight with excitement.

The brothers regarded their host with surprise. "Good luck go with ye," said Keane at last, "but how can ye afford the fare for a voyage across the Atlantic, if ye don't mind my askin'?"

"Indentured servitude," said Martin. "Molly and me, we've agreed to work as servants in America, in exchange for free passage for the family. After a term of four years it'll all be paid off and we'll be free!"

The O'Connell boys congratulated him on this wise plan and wished him and his family a safe voyage.

"But 'tis a bittersweet thing," mused Ryan as they continued to walk in the direction of Allanwell. "'Tis akin to a death, in a way. For to be sure, we'll never set eyes on any of that family again."

"'Tis joy to them," said Keane, surveying the green hills that rolled away to a horizon banded with streaks of pink and gold, "but it would fair tear my heartstrings to leave this land."

The Cliff Highway rose and fell, following the undulations of the cliff-tops. On the left, the sea lay under the fading stars of morning like rippling grey satin strewn with countless silver coins. To the right the smooth green shoulders of the land rolled away, embroidered here and there by darker lines of foliage.

Ryan glanced wryly at his brother, fully aware that the reason for his impatience waited for him in Allanwell, dark-haired and blue-eyed. He rejoiced that Keane had found love, although the manner in which it had happened had surprised him and, for a time, caused him to feel uneasy.

Never had Keane told his brother of his lifelong dreams about Rose Delacey. To discuss visions and fancies was not their way. The two of them rarely mentioned affairs of the heart; by unspoken consent, that was a matter too tender; a subject only to be discussed with mothers or sweethearts, and since their mother had died when they were young and Keane had had many a lady friend but never a sweetheart, he had never told anyone. He had kept his dreams to himself, and when all was revealed upon the brothers' arrival in Allanwell and their meeting with the Delaceys, the knowledge of his brother's eerie prescience burst like a thunderclap on Ryan.

For a time he had been on the verge of believing that Keane had been granted magical powers by the Good People, or else that the real Keane had been abducted and was trapped beneath a fairy hill and the one he saw before him was a semblance, a changeling who had taken his brother's place. It was hard to be rid of such conjectures when every county of the green land teemed with blessed stones and fairy forts and magical wells and fairy thorns, and many people thought that the entire landscape had been formed by ancient giants. According to popular belief, fairies were lurking everywhere; a man could become lost on his way home from the inn at night simply by stepping on a mischievous 'stray sod', or he could be lured into a mushroom ring by seductive fairy women and dance until he was bone-weary and fell asleep on the ground. Such convictions had never been adopted by the O'Connells, but it was difficult to shake off their influence. Discovering that Keane, since boyhood, had dreamed of a woman who turned out to be real had shaken Ryan, but noting no change in his brother's demeanour other than the signs of being desperately in love, he soon returned to his usual equanimity.

As the youths walked along the cliff top, a faint sound started up before them and began to grow. Ryan listened. He could feel the hairs rising on the back of his neck.

"What d'ye t'ink that could be?"

Keane cocked his head to one side. "'Tis the sound of a drum," he murmured.

Gripping their staves more tightly, the brothers walked on. There was no cover in this treeless region, and the barren cliff-tops offered no place to hide. They might have turned back, but they did not. They whistled louder and more jubilantly, as if to drown out the sound of the approaching drum.

"Bejasus, we've nothing to fear," said Ryan, half to himself. "We're law-abidin' citizens and we don't believe in ghosts."

Keane made a swift and practised movement of his right hand, and suddenly the scian was nowhere to be seen. He had concealed it inside his shirt.

Five figures became apparent, coming towards them: two men and a small boy, followed by two more men a few paces

195

to the rear. The boy had been banging on the drum that swung at his hip. By their uniforms, the O'Connells knew these five to be marines of the Royal Navy. After they came within view of each other, neither group altered its pace. Both continued to press forward on the same road until they barred each other's path. At this point they halted and the drummer-boy finished his tattoo with a roll, and a smug flourish of his sticks.

"Good morning to you on this fine Saturday, my good fellows," said the Englishman with the most gold braid adorning his coat. Without bowing or taking off his hat to uncover his wig, he introduced himself as Sergeant Carter, and his assistant as Corporal Greene. The two privates and the drummer-boy did not rate a mention.

"Good mornin' to you, Sergeant," said Keane, looking him up and down. "My name is Mick McCrackenbot'am and this here's me brother Paddy."

"And as sturdy-looking a pair of fellows as ever I saw!" cried the sergeant. "Just the ticket, eh Corporal?"

"Yes sir."

"You're out tramping the roads very early, aren't you my lads?"

"It is the truth," said Keane. "And so ye do be."

The sergeant laughed abundantly. "A man of pleasant humour, eh?" he said. "And such a broad set of shoulders! You'd make a good sailor."

"You'd make a better one," Keane returned, with an innocent grin.

"And I wouldn't swap my trade with any man," said the sergeant, beaming unswervingly. "The largest and most powerful navy in the world looks after its own, just like a mother, keeping us seafarers well-paid and well-fed, with clean clothes to wear and besides—" he paused to wink his eye, "the ladies are particularly attracted to men in uniform!"

Ryan opened his mouth, then closed it again. He had thought better of saying, "I can see why you need to wear one, then."

"Oh it sounds a grand life indeed," said Keane. "Now if you'll pardon us, we must be gettin' on."

The sergeant, however, continued to block their path. "Now look here, my hearties," he said, "let's not dally about. I've an offer for you. If you will enlist, Corporal Greene shall give you a shilling in your hand here and now, besides a silver crown, to drink a toast to good King George at the end of your dusty journey."

"I'm only sixteen," said Ryan, "and Mick here is seventeen. Is it boys you're wantin' for your navy instead of men?"

"Come now!" The sergeant clicked his tongue reprovingly. "Judging by your height and the breadth of your shoulders you lads must be eighteen and nineteen at least. You live on the coast so no doubt you are fishermen like all the rest, and handy with boats. There'll be a set of new clothes for you, good stout boots and plenty of food. All you have to do is take the shilling, swear the oath and kiss the Bible, then come along with us and see the world. We're offering you the greatest honour brave fellows like yourselves could ever

197

hope for—to fight for king and empire. Now, is that not a better prospect than you've ever been offered?"

The O'Connell's stared at the officers and the officers stared back at the O'Connells. Stony-faced, the marines who had brought up the rear stood to attention, the long barrels of their muskets spearing the sky. The sun began to peep over the eastern horizon, washing the night away. Light glinted from the hilts of the rapiers sheathed at the officers' sides. Besides the swords, each carried a pistol.

"Not really," said Keane. "You see, we imagine you'd have no scruples about sendin' us to France where we would be killed. So, t'ank ye for the offer, we'd be glad to take the money, but we'll have to refuse the job."

The face of the sergeant darkened. So recently benign, it now wore an ugly look.

He said, "My young fellows, if I hear one more word of your insolence, I instantly will out with my sword and run you both through—so, my merry devils, take warning."

"Four against two," said Ryan to Keane, speaking in Gaeilge, "not counting the shrimp."

"Seems unfair to them," replied Keane in the same language, "but they're asking for it."

"None of your jabbering," said the sergeant impatiently, "Come now. Take a shilling each, and swear on the book."

The corporal reached for his purse.

"Like hell we will," said Keane.

The hands of the soldiers flew to their swords, but already it was too late. Two blackthorn staves whizzed through the air

198

with a rushing sound, like the wind. The O'Connell brothers fought like dancers. Four loud thwacks split the morning as bone met wood, and all four sailors crumpled to the ground. The young drummer-boy lost his priggish expression and gaped at their assailants, dry-mouthed with terror. He began gabbling incoherently, begging for mercy, but Keane said, "Whisht buachaillín, we'll not harm a whelp the likes of ye. Just give us the cursed drum and get on home to yer ma!"

Hastily, the boy proffered the instrument, and Ryan seized it from his hands.

"Hey!" he yelled, kicking the drum to his brother. Keane booted it back, and the drummer watched in horrified amazement as for the space of several heartbeats an impromptu game of football took place on the cliff-top, the players whooping with glee. "That way!" said Ryan, ceasing the game and jerking his thumb in the direction of Castlerigg. The drummer boy took to his heels.

A wild mood had seized the O'Connells. Ryan rifled the coat of the insensible corporal and found the bible. He and Keane disarmed the semi-conscious figures. Leaving the seamen groaning on the road, they bundled up the weapons, the bible, the broken drum and the drumsticks, then carried them to the edge of the cliff. Cheering exuberantly, they flung out the booty as far as they could.

"To the devil we pitch you!" they sang, and the ocean answered them with a boom and a sigh as it swallowed the sacrifices.

Half a mile further down the road to Alanwell the O'Connells slowed to a walk. They had spied a small military encampment at the wayside. Amongst about a dozen tents uniformed men were moving, cleaning their guns and stowing rations in their canvas packs.

"Where do ye t'ink they sprang from?" Ryan said softly.

"I'd wager they've come by this very road," said Keane, "which means they've probably got a vessel in the bay."

A sentry challenged the brothers. "Ho there," he called out. "Where are you going?"

"Sergeant Carter told us to go on to the ship, sir," Keane said, squinting and crossing his eyes, "We're wantin' to get fitted up for our fine red coats."

The sentry eyed them suspiciously. "He would have told you to report here."

Ryan gave him a vacuous smile, dribbling slightly from the corner of his mouth in an attempt to indicate he was all brawn and very little brain.

Keane said, "The good sergeant told us to drink to the king's healt' at the pub down the road, sir, so's we could tell the other boys about our good fortune." He jingled a couple of pennies in his pocket. "I like dem fancy scarlet regimentals, I do, sir." He leaned on his staff, practising an idiotic grin.

"Will they truly let us be shootin' wit' dem big cannons?" asked Ryan.

The sentry gave them a contemptuous look. "On you way," he said with a dismissive wave of his hand. "Go and tell your friends of your joy. Make them wish to go with you." He half turned away, then on an afterthought he whirled to face them again. "You'll have kissed the holy book now," he warned. "After you have your drink you'll have to get on board the Conqueror, or you'll burn in hell."

Ryan clutched at his heart. "Mercy me," he muttered weakly. "Come on Mick, let's make haste before me knees give way."

The sentry briefly watched the two simpletons as they departed.

When they were out of his sight, the brothers broke into a jogging run. They knew that when the four seamen picked themselves up, rubbed their sore heads and reported their skirmish, the red-coats would waste no time in organising a swift pursuit.

"T'ank the Lord they have brought no cavalry wit' them," panted Ryan, "or we'd be in irons by now."

"It must be angels watchin' over us," returned Keane.

Ryan said, "Let's pray they keep watchin' till we get home tonight."

CHAPTER 18

Heart of Oak are our Ships,
Jolly Tars are our Men

British Naval Frigate and a Ship of the Line (1862) by Tomaso de Simone (1805-1888)

Heart of oak are our ships, jolly tars are our men,
We always are ready; Steady, boys, steady!
We'll fight and we'll conquer again and again.

"Heart of Oak" is the official march of the Royal Navy.
Music by Dr William Boyce, words by the 18th Century English actor
David Garrick.

At sunset the Conqueror fired a thunderous evening gun, while her sentries discharged their muskets in a volley to show that their powder was dry and the muskets were in good working order. Three hours later, several fishermen and labourers and tradesmen of the village were seated around the trestle tables at Rafferty's place. A half-grown sow was snoring by the fire. The rush-lights had burned low, matching the levels in the men's tankards. One or two had departed already and the rest were thinking about going home to bed when a crunching and scuffing of many boots was heard outside and the door crashed open. The patrons all jumped, startled by the sudden savagery of the noise. A group of heavily-armed men carrying lanterns pushed through the doorway. They seemed to fill up the dim space of the room. The lantern-light magnified their jostling shadows, throwing them up against the rough stone walls like misshapen giants.

Their captain stepped forward. Instead of the sharp words and bullying commands the inn patrons feared, he presented them with a speech, delivered in mild tones.

"My good fellows," he said, ignoring Mrs. Rafferty, "it is my duty and honour to present to any able-bodied men between the ages of eighteen and thirty-five years, the opportunity to join the Royal Navy, in particular men with maritime experience." And he proceeded to deliver to the gathering the same invitation that had been bestowed upon the O'Connell boys on the cliff top.

Shortly thereafter, having received no response from anyone save for a sullen and wary silence, the officer changed his tune. In a harsher voice he enquired as to the whereabouts of two tall, dark-haired youths who had been seen that very day, taking the road from Castlerigg to Allanwell. "Any person who gives information which leads to their capture will be handsomely rewarded," the captain proclaimed, rattling a purse. "Any person found sheltering them will be arrested and punished accordingly."

Silence again permeated the room, broken only by the crackle of the fire and the thin snivelling of one of Rafferty's children out the back. Then one of the fishermen, made bolder by Flynn McGinty's moonshine, said, "What is their crime?"

"You will address Captain Thorpe as 'sir'," said the sergeant at the officer's shoulder.

"Sir," obligingly added the fisherman. He belched and added, "Beggin' your pardon."

"The ruffians have committed a grievous offence against officers of the Royal Navy in pursuit of the execution of their duty," the captain said.

The fisherman scratched his head. "Sounds like a terrible t'ing indeed sir," he said. "Sure, you must not be lettin' these two boyos run loose if they're a danger to the Royal Navy."

Rafferty said, "I t'ink I saw two like that this very afternoon." As an afterthought he added, "Sir." He rubbed his stubbled chin between forefinger and thumb. "Now where was it I saw them?" he mumbled.

"Speak up, man!" sharply rapped the captain.

"Ah, I have it! They was harin' along the Valley Highway, headin' north. In a terrible hurry they was, sir."

"I seen those boys too," said Michael O'Sullivan abruptly, "They came through Allanwell around Christmas time. They do be Dublin boys indeed. They was on their way sout' at that time. Must've turned around and come back."

"Dublin, eh? Are you certain?"

"That I do be, sir."

"And their names?"

"That I never axed."

"Indeed." The officer's lip curled. "What is your name?"

"O'Sullivan, sir."

"Here's something for your pains."

A small silver disc winked, bright and dark, in an arc from the captain's hand. The palm of O'Sullivan's left hand stopped it.

"Why thank you sir," he said, a gap-toothed grin stretching across his countenance. "Glad to be of service."

"There will be more for you, O'Sullivan, if we catch them."

Without another word the musketry departed, ducking their heads as they passed beneath the low lintel. Rafferty and O'Sullivan followed them out. They stood watching them troop along the road, stopping at every house as they went. Some hammered on the doors while others slipped around to the back to check the rear exits. When they had passed out of earshot, Rafferty and O'Sullivan stepped back inside. A roar of cheers greeted them, accompanied by much shoulder-slapping.

"Threepence for tellin' lies!" guffawed O'Sullivan, spinning the coin high. "'Tis easy money!"

"Spread the news," said Rafferty as the patrons made their way out. They nodded significantly. Word for word, the story of what had elapsed would be relayed around the village. It would reach the ears of everyone except the Westbournes.

The O'Connells had reached Allanwell before the pursuit. Already, each of them was secure in a house with a priest-hide, while outside, a couple of boys kept watch. Many of the Allanwell houses had priest-hides—places of concealment under the floor accessed by a trapdoor. They were used if ever an unregistered gentleman of the cloth, a hedge-priest, was staying in the village and needed to be concealed from investigators.

But it was not necessary for the quarry to stay hidden for long. By the following morning, HMS Conqueror had raised her anchor and sailed away with her naval infantry aboard. Once again the bay lay open and untroubled, with only the moored fishing boats bobbing on the waves, or made fast along the jetty. All that remained of the solders' presence were some patches of burned earth where their camp-fires had been, and a broken belt-buckle, and a few gnawed bones.

As soon as they received the signal that all was clear, the O'Connells burst their bounds. Leaving their havens, they reunited at the house of the Delaceys, where the smell of hot griddle-cakes pervaded the kitchen like a blessing. There was much rejoicing at their safety after such peril, after which the two guests sat down around the table—very cramped—with John Delacey and his daughters, while Mary served breakfast.

They were not half as cramped as they became after the meal, when it seemed as though almost the entire village arrived to hear the O'Connells' story told over again.

The room became so crowded that some folk were standing outside with their heads poking in the windows, while others, relegated to the garden, could only hear the tale by way of relay from their relations indoors. But when Father Joseph arrived, a place was somehow found for him at the board.

The gathering had a subdued air.

"Times is evil," pronounced Ma McGinty, "when our sons cannot walk the highways wit'out bein' hunted by the red-coats."

"Ach, you worrit too much Ma," said Michael O'Sullivan with his usual jovial optimism, "The heretics do be gone now, curse 'em. Tell us the tale, boys."

On the previous day when, late in the afternoon the O'Connells had sprinted into the village they had only gasped out one fact—that an English press-gang was at their heels. That single statement was enough; none who heard to stopped to ask why or how—their only concern was to help the brothers elude capture by concealing them as swiftly and completely as possible.

This morning there was no need for haste. It was Sunday. The officers and the naval vessel had gone, and word of the adventure had spread like the Plague through the village. Everyone was avid for the details. These, the O'Connells were happy to supply. Story-telling being a time-honoured Irish pastime the brothers indulged in it to the fullest, beginning with an account of their evening under the roof of the Flanagans and progressing to their early morning jaunt along the cliff-tops. Keane did most of the narration for he was the more eloquent of the pair, there was no doubt, and his voice was quite captivating, a perfect blend of richness and clarity, like a polished gem reflecting light.

By the time he was describing the moment the officers vowed to kill the boys if they refused to enlist, he held his audience spellbound. Such a profound silence ruled all about him, that if anyone had closed their eyes they would scarcely have guessed there were even two people in the Delacey house, let alone a multitude.

"But Ryan and meself, we took in the odds," Keane said cheerfully, "We gave them no chance to launch out their swords before our shillelaghs came whacking over their heads and paid them right smart, I assure ye."

"Ag magadh atá tú!²" roared O'Sullivan, momentarily forgetting he was in the company of the Quality. "You two young buachaillí floored the four o' them swaggerin' eejits wit' your sticks, and they the armed sojers o' the Sasunach navy mallaithe?"

"Aye, and they rollin' on the dusty road, more's the pity for their fine red coats," said Keane regretfully. "But bein' concerned that they might try to enlist other boys as unsuspectin' as ourselves, we proceeded to relieve them o' their weaponry and feed it into the fishes."

"That was after we made a football of their rowdy drum," Ryan added, assuming a disarming air of nonchalance.

The laughter had been rising around them like bubbles. At this point it erupted into howls.

"Yez two boyos saw off His Majesty's Navy single-handed!" said Flynn McGinty, laughing heartily and slapping Ryan on the back. "Ye magnificent, crazy bastards!"

Mirth, in conjunction with fellowship, stories, song, music, dancing and liquor were the great ameliorators of the burden of poverty and oppression. The people of Allanwell easily found cause for laughter. In this case it was triggered not only by the absurd picture of two young Irishmen getting the better of the official representatives of their country's subjugation. Nor was it caused only by the ingenuous manner the tale had been told—without a hint of boasting or arrogance. In part it was due to the release of tension. The strain engendered by

---

2   You're joking!

thralldom stretched through every aspect of their lives, like a garrotte, and the momentary easing of it—as in this case, by the humiliation of those who pulled on both ends of the strangling-cord—gave rise to a sense of euphoria as intense as it must be short-lived.

Holding his sides, O'Sullivan sank to his knees. Tears came streaming from Rafferty's eyes. Flynn McGinty had to lean against the wall for support, while Katherine hid her face in her hands and shook like a leaf in the wind. General hilarity took hold, probably encouraged by the contagiousness of Rafferty's unbridled guffaws.

But John Delacey looked stricken, and Rose had turned as pale as porcelain.

It was quite some time before the uproar subsided enough for the O'Connells to resume and finish their tale.

"I do not like it," said Delacey. "There's something odd. After what has happened, I cannot believe we are rid of them just like that." He snapped his fingers.

"Oh, we're rid of 'em all right sir," laughed O'Sullivan. "We've outfoxed 'em all, taught 'em a lesson! They've run off like whipped curs, wit' their tails atwixt their legs, and they won't be back in a hurry. Ha ha! Dublin's a mighty big place! They'll go searchin' there until the nine circles of hell turn to ice."

"Have ye both quite recovered from your ordeal, Mr. O'Connell?" Ilvenna McGinty enquired of Ryan.

He blinked, turning an acute gaze upon her, and a smile that she forthrightly returned. "Oh, you mean the ordeal of only bein' provided wit' a paltry four English skulls to knock manners into? We have indeed, t'ank ye, Miss," said Ryan, "and none the worse for 't."

O'Sullivan made a noise like porridge boiling over.

"From now until the heat dies down," said Rafferty, "if any strangers come pokin' their noses around the village axin' questions, these boys must be hidden immejatly."

He was answered with general accord.

"Not just the O'Connells," put in John Delacey. "All young men must be wary. In Dublin they are saying that the Royal Navy is in great need of crewmen for its ships of the line doing battle against the French. Conditions aboard men-o-war are harsh, I have heard, and the treatment is cruel. It is no wonder there are few volunteers. I've heard rumours that the Impress Service is going around in Liverpool and other towns along the English coast."

"Well and good! Let the press gangs force their own kind into dem red uniforms," said the men. "'Tis their war, not ours."

"What has me puzzled," said Delacey, "is what a troop of marines was doing camped right on the doorstep of Castlerigg. Why on earth would the British bother to send a war-ship into our little bay, then order a troop of armed men to spend two nights trudging around a pair of country villages, only to withdraw them, lock, stock and barrel. There has to be more behind it, to my way of thinking."

Murmurs of agreement and disagreement rippled through his audience like wind through a barley-field.

"Maybe Captain Thorpe decided to show forbearance in the interest of gettin' some recruits, Mr. Delacey," said Rafferty. "Thought he'd show a gentler side, like, so's our boys would t'ink them nice polite Englishmen to get killed for."

Delacey smiled wryly. He was accustomed to Rafferty's sarcastic barbs against the British.

"'Tis my opinion 'twas all just a monumental b—" Flynn McGinty checked himself, "mix-up," he continued. "On their part, I mean. They probably sailed into the wrong bay, and when the officers understood their mistake they were afraid of admittin' it to the enlisted men, so they told them to get out and wander about the countryside a bit, as if it had some purpose to 't."

Rafferty chortled appreciatively. "That'd be right, Flynn me boy, that'd be right."

"Whatever the reason,"—a hush fell as all ears strained to catch Father Joseph's soft voice, "whatever the reason, they have gone and our prayers have been answered, so let us give t'anks to the Lord for his goodness and mercy, before the mornin' mass."

They bowed their heads while the priest intoned a prayer. After amen, Rafferty looked out of the open window, past the heads of those who crowded there. "Sun's gettin' high," he observed. "Sure, you'll be wantin' to get to church, Father Joseph. We'll be away now, to make ourselves ready for mass. T'ank ye for your hospitality Mr. Delacey. Good day Father Joseph, good day to ye, ladies."

They bade him farewell and at this reminder of the passage of time, the gathering broke up.

The last to depart was Keane O'Connell. As was their wont, he and Rose tarried by the garden gate.

"'Tis your birthday tomorrow, and all," he said. "Sixteen years old, imagine that. And I have been makin' a present for you, at the forge."

"You are a present enough for me," she answered. "You should have hidden yourself here with us. Think how many kisses we might have stolen when all heads were turned the other way. There's a priest's hide right here, under the floor in a corner of Papa's room."

"I'd never put you or your kin in danger my darlin', you know that," her sweetheart replied, encasing her fingertips in his hands and putting his lips to them. "If I'd been discovered you'd all have been tried for harbouring a wanted man, and there's no justice, no mercy in their system. How could I live, knowin' I was the cause of woe to you?"

"You'd never be that!" She smiled, twisting the slender gold band around his sun-browned finger. "You must be careful, now. My heart froze like ice when I heard what happened to you yesterday. I could not bear it if you were harmed."

"I can take care of myself."

"Call me that name," she whispered, leaning closer, "the one like music."

"Leannán," he murmured, "Rós-álainn, mo muirnín. Tá mo chroí istigh inti Rós, mo grá, a chailín mo chroi, tá mé go maith di Rós."

Rose closed her eyes. Her dark lashes fanned like angel-wings against the pearly smoothness of her skin. "I could die when I hear you call me the love-words in Gaeilge. It makes the shivers dance up and down my back and I feel I am floating in the air."

He kissed her hands again. "I d not want to leave you, leannán, but I must go to the forge and work another day and make some money to buy our life together."

"Go, then. You're always leaving."

"It seems that way," he admitted earnestly. "God, it is not easy for me Rose—you'll never know what it costs. I just want to throw my arms around you and keep you with me always. One day there will be no more partings."

"One day," she confirmed, with fierce tenderness. Reluctantly she released him. "Angels guard you, my darling."

"And you, mo grá," he said. Then, when he had finally forced himself to let go of her and step out towards the forge, the last vestige of his apparent equanimity vanished. The tumult within him, caused by the conflict between the hunger to rejoin Rose immediately and the cold knowledge that reason forbade it, re-kindled the restless energy within him. He ran a couple of paces down the road, then leapt high in the air to discharge the vitality of youth that makes stillness impossible, except in sleep. As he landed he blew Rose a last-minute kiss before springing away. He could not bear to look back, knowing he would be drawn again to her side in an instant. Thus he did not see her catch the invisible salute and hold it to her heart like a cherished treasure, or a wounded bird.

CHAPTER 19

Beside the Fairy Hawthorn

The Hawthorn Tree, by Arthur Rackham (1867-1939)

And linking hand in hand, and singing as they go,
 The maids along the hill-side have ta'en their fearless
way,
Till they come to where the rowan trees in lonely
beauty grow
 Beside the fairy hawthorn grey.

The Fairy Thorn: An Ulster Ballad, by Sir Samuel Ferguson (1810-1886)

Late in the afternoon, voluminous, sagging bags of rainclouds lined up along the western horizon, out across the sea. Ryan O'Connell and Flynn McGinty loaded the cart with empty barrels and drove up into the back hills, where they would stay for about a week. The weather signs forecast a few days of rain, providing cover for another distilling. It would be one of the last for the season. By late April all the year's barley would have been used up and potatoes would be too scarce to use for making poitín. May, June and July were traditionally the months when the still was allowed to go cold and the whiskey-makers would cut peat and cart coal in readiness for the next season.

Before a distilling, old Seamus would remain in the cave with Flynn and Ryan until the evening, to help with the stirring of the mash. Since the mash had to be mixed with warm water, a fire must be lit under the vat. Although Flynn was an expert at lighting fires which were well-nigh smokeless, he could not prevent a few wisps from escaping. Flynn kept a close eye on the weather-signs, because fermentation took about two days. Only when this process was complete could distillation begin—thus, they had to be certain in their minds, when they began fermenting the wort to make the wash, that the secretive clouds would come down onto the hilltops for a few days at least. Fortunately for their venture, the weather often favoured them. A clear day during the whiskey-making season was the exception, rather than the rule.

Leaping from the cart, Ryan and Flynn tethered the horse at a distance from the cave, where the equipage would remain until they were certain all was secure. Flynn's dog Madu trotted behind them, swerving to sniff in the secret places at the roots of the bracken. As the two youths approached the hidden entrance, Flynn warbled like a thrush and was answered by the whistle of a hawk. Seamus O'Grady emerged from behind a seemingly impenetrable curtain of creepers hanging down a rocky wall. The wizened little man seemed agitated.

"Flynn, boyo! Mr. O'Connell!" he burst out as soon as he saw them. "The ants is hurryin' to their nests and the crows is flyin' widdershins."

"Remind me o' the meanin' o' that," said Flynn.

"'Tis the t'under comin', the t'under and the levin-bolts," Seamus said anxiously and somewhat incoherently. "And yer know I won't be out in't, I will not, not fer all the gold in Christendom."

"Seamus uses his own weather-signs," Flynn explained to Ryan, "and he's afeared o' t'understorms. He t'inks if he goes out of doors in one he'll be struck by lightnin'."

"That I will, Mr. O'Connell,' said Seamus feelingly. "Them levin-bolts will make an end o' me. So ye see, I'm after gettin' along afore the storm breaks at all." His rheumy eyes peered shortsightedly at Flynn, like a dog awaiting its master's orders.

"The storm's a long way off, if it is to be a storm," said Flynn. "Rain is on the way, but I see no t'underclouds and in any case the weather's slow at the approach. We've a fire to light and barrels to unload. Stay a while, Seamus—stay until we get the wort cookin' nicely. Have ye collected enough water in the vat?"

"That I have," said Seamus, "but them bolts..."

"Rest easy," Flynn assured him. "You'll be snug under a roof if they come."

Casting doubtful looks at the sky, the old man acquiesced.

Some of the peat blocks were damp, and it was hard to light the fire under the vat. Seamus had not sufficiently filled the vessel with mountain spring water, so they had to fetch more. By the time the barrels were stacked neatly against the cave wall, the vat was filled, the water made warm enough for the barley mash to be tipped in, and they had taken turns at stirring the mixture for three hours, it was long past sunset. The rain held off. Darkness covered the translucent scarf of turf-smoke issuing from the cavern's vent. This suited Flynn well. He estimated that the cloud cover would be arriving on the doorstep of dawn.

As soon as his work was done, Seamus scuttled off into the night along a track he knew so intimately that his feet could have followed it while he slept. The black-and-white sheepdog slunk close at his heels. It would take Seamus more than an hour to reach the village.

He took with him his old, battered dark-lantern, but there was no need to light it. A full moon shone through a clear, starry window in the clouds. The rugged, beautiful landscape was laid out in night-shades of gunmetal grey, and silver and black. In the western sky, a leaden wall of shadow reared up, long and high, like a barrier between this world and some other. The cold front sweeping through the atmosphere sent a light wind ahead of it, and in that wind could be felt the sizzle and the charge that is the premonition of massive electrical forces enveloping the firmament.

After the old man had gone, Flynn said to Ryan, in Gaeilge, "You never told him about you and Keane whacking the redcoats, and all."

"Well, that's a fact," Ryan replied in surprise. "With all this work in hand, I never gave it a thought. Anyway, he'll be sure to hear the story when he gets to Rafferty's."

Seamus always went straight to Rafferty's Inn when he was relieved of his post as still-guard. After so long alone, he craved company. He was not a great talker, but he liked to be amongst people. On this night he was in more than customary haste to reach the shelter of Rafferty's roof because he was so worried about the possibility of being caught outside in a thunderstorm. His thoughts dwelled on the proximity of lightning. Fear distracted him.

"Beggin' your pardon, missus," he gasped, bumping into the overhanging bough of an ancient thorn tree. He usually avoided that bough, despite his myopia. Black, gnarled, lichen-covered and hard as iron, the leaning thorn was one of the few remaining trees in the locality. It had escaped being cut for firewood because it was considered to be a fairy thorn. Bad luck would settle on anyone who harmed a tree that belonged to Themselves.

Picking up his cap, which had been knocked off by his collision with the branch, the old man hurried on. He mumbled to himself as he went; "Some of them children have been pickin' the wood anemones, they have, and the speedwell. That'll bring the t'under for sure, pickin' them flowers. I've told 'em but they won't listen." For protection against lightning he usually carried a dried sprig of biting stonecrop in his pocket, but recently he had mislaid it.

"Mother of God protect me," he muttered. "I'll be sure to step on the Foidin Seachrain." It was widely believed that the Foidin Seachrain, or Stray Sod, was a piece of enchanted turf. A human stepping on it would be unable to find his way out of familiar territory and might wander, disoriented, for hours until the fairy spell was lifted. "Themselves will put it under me foot for sure, this night," he mumbled, "after I've been bangin' into their tree, they'll punish me. I'll lose me way, and me havin' missed goin' to church last Sunday to boot, God forgive me. The Black Rider'll be after me wit' his hounds and them levin-bolts too, flingin' 'em at me till I'm as black and burned as the Old One himself, just like the dead tree on the Leap."

Superstition intensified his apprehension, while haste made him reckless. At a sharp turn in the track he lost his footing, slipped, and fell down. The dog whined, nosing at him anxiously. Mumbling oaths, the man picked himself up, but a sharp pain shot through his left leg when he tried to put his weight on it. Limping, he continued on his way. He reached the village just as the first thunder rumbled in the west, like a growl awakening deep in the chest of a gigantic wolfhound.

The hour was late. Seamus hauled himself inside Rafferty's Inn, carefully closing the door behind him, directed by years of habit, to keep out draughts. Aware of the storm-harbingers, the other patrons were leaving. They greeted Seamus affectionately as they made ready to depart, clapping their caps snugly on their heads and buttoning up their coats. Seamus huddled by the fire, a tankard of mulled ale between his hands and his dog at his feet. He nodded to the men but did not speak. His heart was still palpitating after his slender escape from the thunderstorm and his leg was hurting. He could hear the Inn's half-grown sow snuffling about underneath the tables, hunting for scraps.

Rafferty's wife handed Seamus his usual porringer of stewed fish, potatoes, onions and cabbage, the hot meal he always enjoyed when he came down from the hills, having lived on bread, cheese, seaweed and a few dried plums.

"Good evenin' to ye, Seamus," she said wearily. "Do ye be keepin' well?"

"Very well, t'ank ye, Mrs. Rafferty," he said, shifting his foot out of her way. He winced at the movement, but bore the pain without complaint. "Here's somethin' to mop up the gravy," Mrs. Rafferty said, handing him a hunch of greyish soda bread. The old man accepted it eagerly, giving a polite bob of his head.

"Lord, there's been a how d'ye do around here while ye've been away," she said. Suddenly she yelled, "Lordamercy! Get out o' it will ye!" The pig had knocked over a jug of ale. Brandishing a besom, the woman chased it out of the room. Two of her younger children began to wail and in attending to them she forgot about her customer. It was easy to overlook him; he was a quiet, unassuming fellow who kept himself in the background.

After all, the storm's path did not pass directly over Allanwell. A mile or two to the west it rampaged across the ocean, spending its fury on acres and fathoms of cold salt water. On this night, had anyone been standing on Madigan's Leap, they would have seen blue-white, ghostly flickerings; jagged columns of light dancing like lurid skeletons on the edge of the sky. The watcher would have heard the sporadic grumbling, a deep and hollow sound, like the wheels of an iron carriage rolling across a metal bridge.

When the rain came it was a fine, soft drizzle, like a mist— not pelting but shimmering down in a silver blur as sleek as the summer coats of seals.

The moment he was certain the danger had passed, Seamus O'Grady bade good-night to Mrs. Rafferty and her family and, dark-lantern in hand, ventured out into the night, his dog at his heel. As he limped along, splashing through the mud with his shoulders hunched against the cold downpour, his dog growled and he became aware that someone else occupied the road besides him. Raising his eyes to squint through the rain he saw a stranger gaining on him. He was curious about the stranger's purpose, so he stopped and waited, holding up his light.

As he stood, it came to him that the stranger might be a brigand out to rob him—or worse yet, one of the dreaded excise men who had found out about the still and was about to place him under arrest. He shrank into his jacket and the hand clutching the lantern wavered, but it was too late to run.

Moonlight came and went in fitful snatches. By its silken gleam, and the saffron glow of the lantern, Seamus made out a stocky man dressed in a dark brown coat, woollen breeches, leather leggings and stout brogues. A countryman's cap was on his head. From its brim, water was dripping. Despite this discomfort, the man was smiling amiably. Seamus thought this a good sign. It bolstered his courage.

When the smiling man caught up, he said to Seamus, "Luvverly weather fer ducks, innit, Paddy?"

The old man found himself at a loss. The newcomer's accent was difficult to understand. Had he said it was lovely weather? Then the stranger laughed. It must have been a joke. Seamus liked jokes; he laughed too, and the next thing he knew the stranger had thrust his hand into the light of Seamus' lantern, and in the palm of it glittered a small piece of the sun. Seamus stared. It seemed he was not about to be arrested or robbed, but what was the meaning of this?

The stranger said, "Don' often see a gold sov'rin, do yer Paddy? Well, this 'ere's fer you, if yer can 'elp me. Woss yer name?"

Seamus stammered out his name and the stranger said, "See 'ere Shaymuss, my master's got a big fleet o' fishin' vessels, righ', an' 'e's lookin' fer some strong young sailor-lads to employ. Good wages, mind. Bloody good. A bloke could live like a lord on them wages. Yer know any strong young lads Shaymuss?"

The old man's face brightened. This was an easy question. He nodded. "To be sure!"

"An' would they be lookin' fer well-paid work, eh?"

"That they would, sir. Rafferty's boys, they're livin' right over there," Seamus indicated the Inn, "and they're always after sayin' they want well-paid jobs."

"Wha' a good neighbour you are!" encouragingly said the stranger, "Tell yer wot, why doncha point out all the 'ouses where likely lads are livin', eh? You do that, an' I'll give yer this 'ere sov'rin. You'll be 'elpin' yer neighbours an' all."

Something had been worrying Seamus. He realised what it was—the man's accent was English. The Sasunachs were bad, everyone knew that. All Englishmen and all Protestants were wicked. A flicker of alarm pinched his weathered face. But the stranger was pressing the shiny gold piece into the old man's palm, and closing his fingers over it. Somehow, Seamus had already taken the money.

"I, I, I'll not—" he stammered beginning to panic. Then a series of other glints caught his eye. Down the front of the dark brown jacket marched a row of bright hemispheres, incised with flowing patterns.

Seamus was mesmerised. For a long time he had yearned for objects like these. "Ah!" he said, reaching out to touch one. "Dem's grand buttons."

The stranger produced a small knife. He cut off all seven buttons and poured them into Seamus' hand.

"There now!" he smiled. "I've kept my end o' the bargain, and more. Which 'ouses did yer say?"

During the night the hazy rain blew through the village in swathes and showers. It dripped from thatched eaves and trickled from the slate rooves of the churches. It ran down the shingles of the gabled roof over the well-head, and collected in dimpled puddles on the ground. Out in the misty bogs, the frogs sang amongst the bulrushes. The green hills drank the rain, the lakes and pools drowned in it. When the moon peeped through a wandering rent in the clouds, granite glistened.

A dog barked as the wind began to rise. In the Delacey cottage, Rose stirred in her sleep.

At two-o'clock in the morning, fourteen men burst through the door of O'Sullivan's smithy. Keane O'Connell and Michael O'Sullivan sprang from their beds so swiftly that the remnants

227

of their dreams were still tearing away from them in long, miasmic tatters.

Manfully they fought. O'Sullivan's weak arm was not much use to him: he grabbed the nearest utensil—a poker—and laid about him with his healthy arm, but despite the huge strength he had won from years of toil with a sledge-hammer, he was overpowered. After one glance at his crooked limb, the press-gang dismissed him as worthless. A strapping youth like Keane O'Connell would bring in the bounty, but he was even harder to subdue. Four men had fallen injured to the floor by the time the rest had mastered him. They bound him in chains, kicked O'Sullivan in the ribs in payment for the work he had given them and bore Keane away, not without some extra trouble.

On the other side of the hill Rose Delacey sat up in bed. She screamed. Lizzie awoke, startled. Taking hold of her sister's shoulders, Lizzie tried to soothe her. Rose fell silent but her blind eyes followed invisible movements about the room and she moaned as if tormented.

"Hush," crooned Lizzie, trying to cover her own fright with calm words. "Everything is all right. Lie down, now. You're just dreaming."

But high in the back hills Flynn McGinty's dog Madu lifted her head and howled, and the peat-fire under the vat flared briefly and inexplicably. In Charter Hall, the harp that had once belonged to Rose was standing, covered, in the music-room. It jangled with a sudden discord, disturbing the sleep of Edwin Westbourne. This phenomenon may have been caused by a vibration through the earth, for beneath Madigan's Leap a freak wave borne on the high tide smashed violently against the unstable cliffs. A large section of rock broke off, crashing slowly and hugely into the sea.

Far out in the ocean the water boiled. It began to cascade from a dark mound, and presently a whale sounded. A jet of vapour shot from its back with a hiss like steam, and through the brine a long mournful cry rose and fell, an ancient music that the muscular currents carried far away to submerged and sunless caverns.

But the cry of the whale could never reach the ears of land-dwellers.

Through the village of Allanwell the press gang raided, house to house, choosing only certain dwellings. There was relatively little commotion, and the wailing of the wind and the patter of raindrops submerged most of it. Besides, the cottages were spaced well apart, and their stone walls were thick. The mercenaries knew their business. They understood how to go about it with utmost quietness and speed.

"If yer shout fer 'elp, one of yer lads gets the knife in 'is throat," they whispered in the ear of Mrs. Rafferty, pressing the flat of a blade to her son's neck. On her knees she begged hard for her three boys as though she begged for her life, all the while restraining the level of her tone so as not to invoke the wrath of the intruders, or waken the little ones who slept. Her pleading sounded like the continuous cooing of a dove. To it, the ruffians would not hearken.

"The king must 'ave sailors. To the seas they must go," one muttered, "And if yer man was younger we'd take 'im too, missus. Be grateful."

They had tied up and gagged her husband.

Mrs. Rafferty and the other women watched their sons being herded down the road in chains. Keane O'Connell refused to walk. He would not stay on his feet, so they dragged him. A dirty cloth had been bound across his mouth. As the sharp stones cut and bruised his body he might have groaned, but he uttered no sound at all. The captives were driven down to the harbour, where a press-tender waited by the pier, and the women ran after them, barefoot in the rain and mud, without their shawls.

There in the middle of the bay she loomed with festooned sails, like some bizarre sea-creature just risen from the deeps, still draped with skeins of weed. Her gunports stared out from her sides like rows of eyes and her masts, mighty as the quarter-staffs of giants, thrust skywards. The splendid frigate H.M.S. Conqueror had been hove-to all day behind Sharpnose Hook, where nobody had thought to look.

The new 'recruits' were shoved into the dark, cramped hold of the press-tender, after which the hatchway was slammed shut and locked. Guarded by men with muskets, sailors took up the oars and began to row away from land.

Before dawn the ship had sailed. With her, she took half the young men of Allanwell, the flower of the west coast.

CHAPTER 20

The king must have sailors,
to the seas he must go!

"The Press Gang" by George Goodwin Kilburne (1839-1924)

All things were quite silent, each mortal at rest
And me and my true-love lay snug in one nest,
When a full set of ruffians broke into our cave
And they forced my dear jewel to plough the salt wave.

I begged hard for my true-love as I would for my life,
But they'd not listen to me, although a fond wife,
Saying "The king must have sailors, to the seas he
must go!"
And they left me lamenting in sorrow and woe.

But although I'm forsaken I'll not be cast down,
For who knows but my true-love some day may return
And will make me amends for my trouble and strife,
And me and my true-love might live happy for life.

All things were quite silent (Traditional)
Ralph Vaughan Williams collected this song in 1904 from Ted Baines of
Lower Beeding, Sussex

At first, scarcely able to believe what had happened, the cottiers of Allanwell gathered along the jetty and the beach, staring out across the sea, as if expecting the ship to return with its precious cargo. Many sank to their knees. They were still there when dawn broke, shuddering with cold, their prayers mingling with the rain. The clouds in the eastern sky turned pale, and the wind eased off, but the rain continued to pour. As the morning wore drearily away, shock and disbelief gave way to grief and rage.

John Delacey took charge. He issued instructions, "Send out three riders with the news, one to Castlerigg, one north to Ballyganna. The third must look for Ryan O'Connell." Three men were despatched on the swiftest nags that could be found. Meanwhile, an impromptu meeting was held there on the pebbled strand.

"I shall write letters of protest, one to Dublin and one to London," said John Delacey, his voice quivering with barely-restrained outrage. "The Dublin letter, I promise to deliver personally. The other I shall put into the hands of an honest and speedy messenger. I hope I may count on the support of the landlords in our endeavours to right this grievous wrong, this felony which has been committed against God and man today." Taking in the expressions on the faces of those who surrounded him he blinked back tears. In all the tumult, he had neglected even to put on his hat, an omission which was normally unthinkable for such a civilised gentleman. Droplets of rainwater released themselves from his thinning grey hair and ran in colourless ribbons down the shoulders of his coat. His cravat was askew, half-untied. He was about to say more when he caught a glimpse of Rose's face and choked on his words.

"What I want to know," shouted Rafferty in a voice like sack-cloth being torn, "is how did they know which houses to be breakin' into? Who was the informer?" He proceeded to thoroughly and carefully curse the unknown traitor in Irish. The tendons in his neck stood out like cables and in his temple throbbed a purple worm of a vein. People began to

233

look at one another with new-found suspicion. "Whoever he might be I'll find him out," shouted Rafferty. "Bejasus I'll find him out and when I do may the Lord have mercy on his soul, for I will not." He clenched his fists.

Nobody spoke. Seamus O'Grady was standing beside Father Joseph. His eyes bulged and his throat seemed constricted. It had taken half an hour for the implications of his deeds on the previous evening to become apparent in the confusion of his mind. When they did, he knew only the black abyss of horror. It was in this gulf that he now swam, unable to defend or excuse himself, unable say anything at all, paralysed by a situation utterly foreign to him. He had erred, he had somehow sinned without knowing it. He was confounded.

"Had there been no informer they would simply have raided every house," said John Delacey. "I doubt whether lack of information would have swayed them from their purpose."

"That might have given folk a chance to warn others," growled Rafferty.

John Delacey said, "What's done is done. But this must never be allowed to happen again in this village. We must keep our doors barred at nights and set a watch. All families with boys aged from fifteen to thirty-five ought to have a priest-hide in their houses. Families who have lost sons on this terrible day, be assured, I for one shall do my utmost to discover their destination—"

"France, Mr. Delacey! 'Twill be the French wars, no other," shrieked one of the women in a frenzy of sorrow. "They'll put a red coat on our boys' backs and a musket in their hands and they'll send 'em in front of the French cannon and tell 'em to fight for their lives, our poor boys from the hills and the shores. They're dead already, the poor angels."

Several women cried out. Some began sobbing and keening like banshees, agony written like ugliness across their features.

"Nay, do not give up hope," John Delacey said, though his broken tones belied his words. "Have faith. One day we shall see our Allanwell boys come sailing home."

But his words rang as hollow as an iron bell.

The rain continued to fall in diaphanous drifts, stippling and etching the surface of the sea. Grey and blurred, the distant ocean remained empty of any sail.

On that same day Flynn and Ryan returned in haste from the hills where the messenger—who knew a thing or two—had found them. Leaving the fire to burn itself out, leaving everything just as it was when they heard the tidings, they had come. When he reached the village, Ryan wasted no time. He packed his meagre bundle of belongings and bade farewell to all. "I am going to find my brother," he said grimly. "I will follow him to France, or the ends of the earth, if needs be."

His friends begged him not to leave. He listened, but shook his head. Nothing could dissuade him. When she saw that his mind was made up, Ilvenna came forward. From around her own neck she took a fine plaited strand of leather. On it dangled a small, round object the colour of a ripe pumpkin.

Through its translucent depths tiny immobile bubbles could be seen, surrounding the four spread wings of some trapped insect.

"'Tis a lucky charm," she said, offering the amber amulet to Ryan. "I'd be grateful if you would wear it. 'Twill keep you from harm."

He took it, thanking her, and when their hands touched the contact lasted, perhaps, for a little longer than strictly necessary. For a brief instant, his gloom lifted.

"Miss McGinty—Ilvenna—I'm t'inkin' ye're truly Áine in disguise," he gently chaffed, pronouncing the name "Ah-nya".

With her green eyes, she bestowed a quizzical look upon him.

"Do you know who the Lady Áine is, now?" he asked. "Sure, she's the goddess of summer, who brings wealth and authority across our lands. The great healer herself, who commands the crops and beasts, and who taught people the meaning of love."

"I do know who she is," replied Ilvenna.

"Wit' your hair like the sun at mornin', Ilvenna McGinty," he said, "you look as she would look."

She did not simper or blush at the compliment; that was not her way. Instinctively, she knew it was his way of saying, I place you above me.

"Then 'tis Lugh you must be," she said, steadily looking him in the eye, "god of all skills and crafts." And he knew it was her way of saying no, we are equals, and he smiled.

Father Joseph blessed Ryan O'Connell, who then set off, trudging along the Valley Road until he shrank to a small speck in the distance. Ilvenna watched him until he could be seen no more.

News came back from Castlerigg—that village had not been spared, either. A press gang had raided it also, early on the Sunday morning. The raiders were the soldiers who had been camped on the cliffs, under the leadership of Captain Thorpe. They had promised severe retribution if warnings of their business were leaked from Castlerigg within twenty-four hours. Their prisoners, chained together, had been led along the Cliff Road toward the harbour. Out of sight they had been forced to wait, until the H.M.S. Conqueror sailed around Sharpnose under cover of darkness.

"So it was not retribution they were after, for the work of the O'Connells," said the villagers. "It was planned right from the start, even before the hour the vessel entered the harbour."

Rose waited, at first with high hopes of Keane's speedy return. The crippled blacksmith, O'Sullivan, brought her a copper bracelet of intricate Celtic knotwork, which Keane had fashioned as her birthday present. "Keep it for now, Michael," she said, pushing away the blacksmith's outstretched hand. "I'll not take it from any other hand than his own. Keep it, and when he returns he can give it to me."

O' Sullivan eyed her dubiously, placed the bracelet in his pocket and then took it out again. "I'll be givin' it to Ilvenna for safekeepin'," he said at last. "In case I gamble it away by accident."

A week later, Seamus O'Grady was found hanging by his neck from a bough of the fairy thorn. Beneath his dangling feet, a gold sovereign and a handful of brass buttons were strewn, and his dog lay whining. By this, the villagers guessed the truth.

"Seamus!" sobbed Rafferty. "If it had been anyone but you, yer poor old fool."

And his wife blamed herself, for having forgotten to speak to the old man that night. Distraught at the loss of her sons, she took to drinking heavily. Michael O'Sullivan adopted Seamus' dog, and Father Joseph was told the old man had died by accident, so he could be buried on consecrated ground.

As for Rose, she could neither eat nor sleep. She spent every possible moment on Madigan's Leap. "Come back to me," she'd murmur into the wind. "Come back to me."

Until late every evening she kept vigil, scanning the vast plain of the sea. Every approaching ship first brought, then destroyed, hope.

It came to be widely-known that the fairy thorn was haunted by the unquiet shade of the old fiddler. Most people refused to go near it after dark. A shepherd boy who was looking for a strayed sheep in the hills wandered into the vicinity of the tree late one evening. Afterwards, he said he had heard the strains of fiddle music issuing from a fissure in a rock nearby. A wry-necked shadow had arisen from behind the rock, and he had fled in terror.

Happiness deserted Allanwell. Grief ate into the bones of the folk, but they carried on with their lives, as they must.

Another week, then a month went by without news. No letters arrived in reply to John Delacey's missives. No tidings came of the fate of the H.M.S. Conqueror and those aboard. No message was received from Ryan O'Connell. With every passing day, it seemed less likely that any of the boys would ever return.

Rose tried to escape from sorrowful musings by immersing herself in writing her Arthurian fairy-stories, her favourite hobby. Yet she never gave up hope. "From time to time fragments of dreams come, as they always have," she told Lizzie in confidence, "and as long as I dream of him, I know he lives."

"What do you dream?"

"I see a tall ship sailing."

CHAPTER 21

We'll all have tea

A fashionable gentleman taking morning tea with a lady. Etching, late 18th century. Artist unknown.

Polly put the kettle on,
We'll all have tea.

Traditional English nursery rhyme pub. circa 1790–1810

One Saturday evening in May, John Delacey said to his daughters, "Tomorrow morning you must make yourselves as neat as possible, for we have been invited to take tea with the Westbournes after church."

His words had a devastating effect, particularly on Katherine. "But I have nothing decent to wear!" she wailed. "Papa, please ask them to put it off until you can go to Galway and buy a few yards of striped crepe—"

"My dear, what can I buy it with?" he responded affectionately. "There is no money for new morning dresses. You will have to make do with what you have. You look very nice in your usual Sunday clothes."

"You would think so Papa, because you are so kind, and because you spare no thought for fashionable trends," said Katherine desolately, "but we all know we are out of the mode. What will Lady Westbourne and her daughters think of us? What will Mr. Edwin think?"

"They will think you are comely, well-mannered gentlewomen with no airs and graces. How could anyone find you dull, even in the plainest of costume? They might ask you to play for them on your old instruments. Then you could display your musical talents."

"And we not having had a moment to practise our playing

since we left Charter Hall!" Margaret said, scandalised.

Katherine was struck by an idea. "Maybe they will invite us to come regularly to the Hall to practise," she said.

"Don't you dare suggest it!" exclaimed Margaret. "They would think you too forward and presumptuous!"

"Of course I will not suggest it. But I might hint..."

"Why would you do that?" Margaret asked sharply.

"Well isn't it obvious? The better he gets to know me, the quicker he will discover my charms and so arrive at the conclusion he cannot live without me." Katherine tilted her chin smugly.

"I doubt it," said Margaret.

"It will be grand to see our house again," said Lizzie, who had not been paying attention to the conversation. "I wonder whether they have had our old rocking-horse repainted."

"Papa, may I be excused from attending?" quietly asked Rose.

Her father drew breath consideringly before replying. "My dear, if it could be arranged I would do so. I understand your feelings—you have shown no inclination towards social occasions since—since it happened. But my dear, Sir Robert is my employer. Lady Westbourne's invitation specifically asked that all my daughters accompany me. If you do not attend, it will offend."

"Feign illness," Katherine suggested to Rose.

Her father frowned disapproval. "That would be deceptive, Katherine. I will not tolerate lies."

She shrugged. "'Tis not really a lie. She is sick at heart..."

243

Her voice trailed off when she noted her father's thunderous expression. "Come, Lizzie. You must help me redecorate my bonnet. You can make a floral arrangement. Those rosebuds we picked from the garden ought to be dry enough by now."

"They are indeed. The petals are falling off," said Lizzie wanly, drifting after her sister.

Tea with the Westbournes was an elegant affair. It was a sunny day, and the party sat on high-backed chairs out in the garden, on the lawns beneath the wide-spreading foliage of a flowering chestnut tree. The liquid notes of blackbirds and linnets threaded through the leaves. Pale blue butterflies flitted erratically as though jerked on strings. Sir Robert's footmen had strategically positioned the small tea tables to take advantage of the views of the landscape and the shade of the trees. Upon tablecloths of albescent lace, painted porcelain plates laden with enticing cakes and pastries were laid out. The tea service was plated with silver, as were the trays on which the servants carried out more dainties. Two snowy-wigged butlers in immaculate blue and white livery stood at a respectful distance, their gloved hands clasped behind their backs.

Sir Robert presided for the first half hour, his wife at his side. John Delacey sat at Lady Westbourne's right hand. Edwin Westbourne was present, as were his sisters Georgiana, Henrietta and Alexandrina, and his brother Albert. Five younger siblings were cloistered in the nursery, from whose second-storey windows their faces could sometimes be seen peering out like ghostly flowers behind the panes.

The three Westbourne girls—aged about fourteen, fifteen and sixteen—wore immaculately coiffed wigs, and their décolletages dipped fashionably low. They were dripping with fine fabrics, frills, flounces, laces and ribbons. Georgiana was clad in a silk sack gown, pastel aquamarine, with deep lace sleeves. A taffeta scarf wrapped her shoulders, and silk flowers adorned her bonnet. Henrietta had on a dress of pin-striped poplin cut away at the front to display a brocade petticoat. Her straw hat was trimmed with feathers. Alexandrina wore a white muslin frock patterned with sprigs of cherries. Pale, cherry-coloured ribbons trimmed both gown and cabriolet bonnet, while pink shoes and gloves completed the outfit. The Delacey daughters, in their much-mended gowns of blue worsted, privately compared themselves to these damsels like pigeons to peacocks, and it caused them much woe.

After half an hour of polite conversation, Sir Robert, whose fingers had been drumming on his knee the whole time, grew even more restless.

"It is obvious that tea-parties are not Sir Robert's cup of tea, so to speak," Katherine murmured in a reckless aside to Lizzie.

After adjusting his peruke, which had slid lopsidedly over one ear, the landowner rose from his chair and took up his walking stick. "Come with me, Delacey," he said peremptorily. "I want you to look at the bay gelding. He's been off his feed."

John Delacey put down the cake he had been eating, and accompanied Sir Robert to the stables.

"Sir Robert's not one for sitting still too long," Lady Westbourne said worshipfully, watching the two men as they walked across the lawn. "He is a gentleman of action, a sportsman. There's nothing he likes better than riding to the hunt. Master Westbourne likes to hunt too, isn't that right dear?" Directing her last query to her eldest son she absentmindedly patted the fake chignon at the nape of her neck, which was decorated with three ostrich plumes.

"Indeed," said young Mr. Westbourne. "Miss Rose, do you enjoy riding?"

"Oh—I—yes, I find it quite agreeable," said Rose, whose thoughts had been far away.

"I am right fond of it," said Katherine, loudly and ardently.

"We have many fine riding-horses here in the stables," Edwin Westbourne said to Rose. "Perhaps you would like to ride out with Georgiana and Henrietta on occasion?"

Rose was caught unawares. "I couldn't—I mean, I could not possibly presume—"

"I would like to," said Katherine.

"There would be no presumption at all," said Edwin, appearing to be deaf in one ear. "They would be glad of the company, wouldn't you, Georgie and Hen?"

"Absolutement!" cried Georgiana with an impeccable French accent, applauding with quick, light pats of her fingers, "Quelle bonne idée! I do not know why I did not think of it myself. Rose is such a charming girl. I adore her like a sister already."

"And I also," said Henrietta.

Rose noticed with alarm that Katherine's eyes were glistening and her face was flushed. She was struggling to hold back tears of mortification.

"But I could not leave my own dear sisters out of the fun," she said quickly. "Margaret prefers long country rambles, but Katherine and Elizabeth love riding even more than I. If I am to be included, surely you could find steeds for them?"

"Most certainly," Edwin said agreeably.

"Well then, it is all arranged," said Lady Westbourne. "Pending their father's approval, perforce. More tea, Miss Delacey?"

"Thank you, no. I have taken quite sufficient," said Margaret fastidiously. "The almond cakes are delicious."

"Pray, take another." Lady Westbourne blotted the corner of her lip with a linen serviette. Covertly, Margaret examined the violets embroidered on the corners of her own serviette and concluded they had been worked by the hands of her sisters. She felt a stab of embarrassment that they were forced to earn a living.

"Do you sing, Miss Rose?" asked Georgiana.

"Not as well as I would like," said Rose. "I was better at playing the harp."

"But of course!" exclaimed Georgiana. "I had heard you were musical in some fashion. You must play for us."

"She's not had the practise lately," said Katherine stiffly.

Georgiana clapped her hands dramatically to her cheek. "Quelle horreur! The poor child has been deprived of an outlet for her musical talent." She turned to her brother, placing her hand on his sleeve and plaintively begging, "Edwin, you must do something, please."

Edwin's attention flicked to his arm. His sister withdrew her hand.

"I do not require urging from you," he said mildly. "I was about to suggest that the young ladies might wish to rehearse their music at Charter Hall, once or twice a week. Or more often," he added, turning back to address Rose. "Naturally, all are included in the invitation."

"You are too kind, but before any decision is taken we must first consult with Papa," said Rose. Hastily she changed the subject to the first topic which came to mind. "How prettily your milliner has decorated your hat, Miss Alexandrina!"

"Thank you." Alexandrina looked to be about thirteen years old. She also looked bored. At her elbow, her twelve-year-old brother Albert was killing a butterfly on the tablecloth.

Georgiana leaned towards Katherine. "I was just thinking the same thing about your bonnet, Miss Kathy. C'est extraordinaire! How quaint of you, including real rosebuds in the décor. I admire such daring. Alas I am forced to wear silk flowers for if I were to wear real ones, the petals would fall off! Oh look, I have discovered two prodigal petals as I speak! Enchanté!"

Giggling behind her hand, she picked a couple of errant pink flakes from among Katherine's curls.

Katherine's eyes took on a steely gleam. Just then, Lizzie piped up, "Oh my! Miss Westbourne, I do hope you are not afraid of spiders."

"What?" shrieked Georgiana, jumping to her feet and upsetting the tea-service. "Where? Is there one on me? Get it off! Get it off!"

Her two brothers sat back and laughed as she squealed, batting at herself with her hands.

"I can't see one," said Henrietta.

"I can't either, now," said Lizzie, looking as if butter would never dream of melting in her mouth. "It must have fallen down somewhere."

Georgiana tried to peer down behind her decolletage.

"George, you look as though you have two chins when you do that," observed young Albert.

His sister threw down her serviette. "Pray excuse me," she said to the gathering, before flouncing away towards the house.

"Dear me, Georgiana's in a tiff," said Lady Westbourne languidly. "You shouldn't laugh at her, Albert, you know it makes me cross. Edwin dear, might you take a turn around the garden with the young ladies?"

Edwin rose to his feet. He was a strapping youth, tall and athletic-looking, with eyes of a startling golden-brown. Today he was wearing a frock-coat dyed indigo, with gold fastenings, gilt buttons and wide borders of crimson brocade. From beneath it peeped a double-lapelled waistcoat embroidered with a pattern of acanthus leaves. It fitted closely, conforming to the slim, hard lines of his torso. White doe-skin breeches clad his long thighs; they were tucked into knee-boots of brown leather.

Katherine could not help giving him a melting glance. He responded with a smile, offering her his arm. The other, he offered to Lizzie.

"Albert, escort Miss Rose and Miss Delacey," he said. "After one turn, we shall exchange partners." Henrietta and Alexandrina trudged dutifully in the wake of their brothers and guests, while Lady Westbourne sat watching, ventilating herself with a fan of carved ivory.

When it was her own and Margaret's turn on Edwin's arm, Rose considered that they walked around the garden far too many times. Margaret chatted away happily, praising the way the new gardener was looking after the flowers and hedges. Rose could not admire the flowers the way she used to. She kept turning her head this way and that—to the west, towards Madigan's Leap, or to the south-east, in the direction where France lay.

Edwin was telling her something... "...in Dublin, a good friend of Lord Leighton." Rose caught the end of the sentence. Momentarily she wondered where she had heard that name before.

The visit dragged on. At last Sir Robert appeared with John Delacey, and they were all free to depart.

It was a relief.

CHAPTER 22

For Dublin is of high renown

A view of College Green, Dublin (1807) by James Roberts.

*So when in Dublin I arrived, to try for a situation
I always heard them say it was the pride of all the
nation . .
For Dublin is of high renown, or I am much mistaken.*

The Dublin Jack of All Trades (Irish traditional)

"Well, if that visit wasn't a disaster, I'm the King's aunt," said Katherine that evening in the kitchen, when Papa and Mary were out of earshot. "That hussy Georgiana kept trying to turn my darling Edwin against me, while the little brother kicked my shins under the table. As for Henrietta and Alexandrina, they didn't have two words to say between themselves. I found them exceedingly dull."

"I wish you would not gossip behind people's backs," sighed Margaret.

"I thought they were nice," said Lizzie. "Alexandrina gave me a colourful beetle with horns."

"Beetles, is it? At your age," scoffed Katherine. After a minute she added inquisitively, "Have you got it there?"

"Don't let it loose in the garden," warned Margaret. "It is probably a cabbage-eating one."

"I won't," Lizzie assured her. "Roger shall stay in a box and I shall feed him myself. I hope that next time we are invited to Charter Hall we shall be permitted to set foot across the threshold. I want to see what it looks like indoors since they moved in."

"I did think it rather an indignity, to be relegated to the garden," said Margaret. "Roger? Good heavens, Lizzie what a silly name for an insect."

"How can we possibly accept a second invitation?" complained Katherine. "We'd have to wear the same gowns! To think that I once possessed seven outfits and now I have only three, one for Sundays and two for weekdays."

"Count yourself lucky," observed Margaret. "Most women in Allanwell can afford only the one, and that one patched and mended many times over."

"We can scarcely count ourselves among the country-folk!" asserted Katherine. "At any rate, I'm certain the Westbournes have at least fifteen costumes each. I cannot recall ever seeing them twice in the same apparel on the way to church."

"Stop your complaining Kitty!" reprimanded Margaret. "Rose, you hardly heeded Mr. Edwin's conversation. I noted he was forced to pause and await your response while you collected your thoughts. I am afraid he will think you slow-witted or discourteous. You know we must do our best to keep their good favour."

"I am sorry. My intention was not to cause offence," said Rose. "If my mind wandered, it is only that last night I dreamed of him."

"Mother of God!" Katherine exclaimed. "So he is alive, at least?" The room stilled as though the air had frozen solid.

"I believe so."

"Where is he?"

"That I cannot tell. He was lying in a bunk or hammock, in some lightless, sightless place. His shirt was smeared with some dark substance—I thought it was blood. And he was sunburned, his hair cropped short. He caught sight of me, the dream-Rose, and I saw him say my name, even though I could not hear it. I tried to say his, but he had already faded."

"Did you see any of the other boys?"

"No."

Through the window came the sound of Mary returning from the chicken-coop where she had been locking up the hens. She was singing some old folk song in Gaeilge.

"Siúil, siúil, siúil a rún,
Siúil go socair agus siúil go ciúin
Siúil go doras agus éalaigh liom
Is go dté tú mo mhúirnín slán."

The poignant melody and the musical cadences of the Celtic language pierced like slim, silver spears. The song evoked a sense of loss and longing, though she knew not the meaning of the words. To divert her thoughts she said briskly to her sisters, "Anyway, since the tea-party was apparently such a disaster, I don't suppose we shall have to go back again. Thank goodness. I am sure they enjoyed the occasion as little as we did."

"I believe you are mistaken," said Margaret. "At least one of them took delight in it."

Rose quickly left the room.

Notwithstanding, Rose's hopes for no further social interaction with the Westbournes proved vain. They were again invited to tea on the following Sunday. The Saturday after that, Rose, Lizzie and Katherine went riding with Edwin, Georgiana and Henrietta—the Delaceys wearing riding-habits borrowed from the Westbournes. Furthermore, Sir Robert insisted that the four sisters must visit Charter Hall for two hours every Thursday afternoon to improve their instrumental skills in the Music Room, after which their father should join them for dinner.

The Delaceys grew increasingly ill at ease with the number of favours pressed upon them. In their lowly financial circumstances, they could not begin to return this overabundant generosity. They could not even invite the Westbournes on a return visit to their humble cottage, lest their patrons should experience awkwardness and embarrassment. Yet neither could John Delacey refuse the benevolence showered upon them without risking his job— his family's chief source of income. Thus, with every passing week, his obligation to Sir Robert Westbourne deepened and strengthened. He knew himself to be falling into the man's power, both financially and socially. But employment like his, with such comparatively good wages, was rare. He would have to seek long and far to find a similar position, and in the meantime, he would have no means of feeding his family.

The reason for the evolving interest of the Westbournes was apparent, if not stated outright. Edwin would always appear at the French windows of the Music Room when Rose was playing the harp. Whenever they cantered out over the hills he disposed his hunter at the side of Rose's mare. To her he first offered his arm when they all went strolling together, and somehow she invariably found herself seated beside him at table. She was civil to him, for his manner was ever courteous, but she could show no warmth. Pre-occupied with other matters, sometimes she hardly noticed him. She was barely aware of the way his golden-brown gaze would rake her from head to toe, the way his fingers trailed across her palm when he passed her a spoon, the way his knee brushed against her skirts beneath the table. Whenever they went riding he refused to allow her to mount into her side-saddle unaided. This she did notice, because it vexed her.

"I can do it myself. Please sir, unhand me," she would demand, but despite her protestations he would take her by the waist and lift her up.

Even Katherine had to admit, eventually, that it was Rose who was the object of Edwin's attention. She accepted the fact philosophically. "I knew in my heart he gave no thought to me," she sighed, "but I hoped he might change his mind. In any case, if I married him I would have to endure that odious Georgiana as my sister, and a mother-in-law who blithers on forever about nothing, and a father-in-law who thinks he rules at the right hand of God. I do not know how long I could bear such company, even with the wealth and the handsome husband to compensate. Well now, I don't have to worry about such matters. Fate has decided my path leads elsewhere. 'Tis you he wants, Rose."

She uttered the last sentence gravely, like a warning.

"That's impossible," said Rose tightly. "I am betrothed. Besides, he's a Protestant."

"So you are telling me that marriages between Catholics and Protestants are unheard of?"

"No, but—"

"Come, Rose, you know it is the truth. He's after weddin' you and that's a fact. What are you going to do?"

"Well, I cannot wed him, of course."

"Of course! There's no question about that. But how are you going to put him off without leaving Papa in a terrible situation?" Katherine asked.

"Master Westbourne has not declared his intentions to me as yet. He may never do so. His family might find some fault with me, and persuade him to bestow his favour elsewhere. Do not forget, Uncle Frank has lost his reputation in higher circles. The Westbournes might consider that his conduct reflects upon me. I shall make sure two things are clearly understood; that I esteem my uncle and will not break off future communication with him, and that I am officially betrothed."

"What communication? We have not heard from Uncle Frank for years. We do not even know if he still lives. Anyway, what if saying all that does not deter your suitor? What if he should put the question to you?"

"If he should do so, I shall simply refuse and tell him why."

"The likes of Edwin Westbourne do not readily brook denial," said Katherine.

257

"I shall have no other answer for him," said Rose.

Privately, Katherine said to Lizzie, "It is a mortal shame his affections are directed towards the only one among us who will not have him. This family is unlikely to ever again get the opportunity to raise ourselves back to our rightful status. If it were not that I myself love Keane like a brother, and that it is plain he and Rose were made for each other... if it were not against all moral and spiritual principles, I could almost wish she could learn to love Edwin Westbourne just a little..."

The English and the French continued to wage war upon one another. Lord Richard Howe defeated a French fleet off Ushant on the first of June, capturing nine French ships in the Channel and sinking a tenth, but the Battle of Fleurus on the twenty-sixth of June ended in victory for the French. In addition, they forced the Duke of Coburg to withdraw from Belgium.

Young Edwin's esteem of Rose officially became public knowledge in July, when the Westbournes were preparing to go to Dublin. They were to sojourn at their town-house in Giltspur Street for a fortnight. There were matters of business to which Sir Robert had to attend. His wife would take advantage of the opportunity to indulge the children with plays and concerts and some leisurely shopping. John Delacey was presented with a request that Rose might accompany them.

Lady Westbourne took him aside one afternoon while he was at his work in the stables. "You see, we shall only have room for one extra in the carriages," she made a point of saying. "The younger children are to stay home in the nursery—Sir Robert cannot abide their constant noise when we reside in the city. We shall be taking both the carriages, but really, if one is to travel long distances on these dreadful roads, one cannot allow more than four passengers per vehicle. Sir Robert needs to stretch out his legs you know, or his gout bothers him terribly. If Rose joins our party we shall be eight altogether—the perfect number! We would have loved to include your other charming daughters but what can I do?" She spread out her hands, palms upwards, in a gesture of abandonment to destiny. "Georgiana positively refuses to travel without Rose," she continued. "The two dear girls have become virtually inseparable, you know Mr. Delacey. They have so much in common."

John Delacey patted the nose of a horse that had put its head over the half-door to nuzzle his shoulder, its nostrils as warm as two deep velvet pouches. He knew full well how profoundly his youngest daughter grieved for the sweet-heart who had been stolen from her. He perceived she took very little joy in the company of Edwin and his family, and he feared that she might suffer if she were wholly abandoned to their mercy. He searched for inspiration, for a way to evade this invitation on Rose's behalf. It was easily found.

"What about church?" he asked. "Rose will not be able to attend church with you. Yet she must not miss going to mass on Sundays."

Lady Westbourne pursed her lips as though her husband's employee had broached a distasteful subject. "Sir Robert has already anticipated this trifle. The housekeeper and butler at Giltspur Street are followers of your religion," she said, avoiding his eyes and patting at the springy curls of her wig. "Sir Robert suggested that Rose could go with them. She will be in good hands—they have been in our employ for twenty years and are irreproachable." She held a perfumed handkerchief to her nose as though the earthy smell of the stables was too much for one of delicate sensibilities. "You understand, Mr. Delacey, that for the sake of the servants who must rush back to their duties, the mass takes place so very early in the morning. It is well and truly finished by the time our own service begins. Perhaps Rose could be persuaded to attend both services. She would not be forced to participate but she would be most welcome to sit in our pew, and what would it matter?"

"What would it matter?" John Delacey repeated hoarsely, trying to mask his incredulity.

"I am certain dearest Rose will have no objection," Lady Westbourne prattled on. "You know, being the youngest, Rose has not seen as much of the city as her sisters. Sir Robert says this is the opportunity to broaden her knowledge of our capital. Oh, the calibre of the people she will meet! There will be balls and dinner parties, musical evenings, visits to the élite tea-shops and all manner of diversions."

"I am afraid that Rose does not, at present, own a ball-gown—"

"I am sure we can arrange something, Mr. Delacey. Never fear, Georgiana and I shall dress her divinely. Well, that's settled then!"

A stable-hand walked by, leading a horse on a rope halter. He doffed his cap to his employer's wife. Hooves made a comfortable clopping sound against the flagstones and the animal snorted, swishing its plume of a tail.

"I shall put your generous invitation to Rose," John Delacey said stiffly. "Thank you for your kindness, Lady Westbourne."

There seemed no alternative but for Rose to comply.

"But Rosie, they are asking you to enter the doors of a Protestant church," her father said, when he broke the news.

"What would it matter, Papa?" Rose said quietly. "Sir Robert would not be pleased if his Dublin friends discovered that his guest went to church only with the servants. If it will contribute to harmony, I will do it."

John Delacey searched his soul. He thought of his wife, Anne, lying back against the pillows while the wind mourned outside her window. He thought of the look in Rose's eyes as she prayed on the pebbled shore of the harbour, in the rain, after the soldiers had taken away her betrothed. He pictured the infant Rose laughing on her mother's knee in the days when life had seemed full of promise, and then the knowledge broke upon him like a flood; that the true worth of life lay in health and simple kindness and the laughter of children. Nothing else, no ritual invented by man in the name of a higher power, was of any real account to him any more. The world was, after all, round—and it was wide, and high, and filled with more things than he could dream of. Rose might sit in a Protestant church and the universe would not crumble.

Accordingly, two shiny black carriages rolled to a halt outside the Delacey cottage on the appointed day, complete with liveried attendants and drivers wielding long whips across the backs of the teams. A footman leaped down from his perch, opened the door and lowered the step. Edwin descended and handed Rose in, while the footman ported her valise onto the roof and tied it there with the other luggage. As the equipages set off again down the road, Rose leaned from the window, gazing back at her family. They waved to her from the garden gate. She waved back, until she was borne out of sight.

Rose had not been to Dublin for four years, but most of its sights remained as clear-cut as a cameo in her memory. The grand buildings such as the Four Courts and the new Customs House were as stately as she recollected, the Liffey as foul-smelling and crowded with shipping.

Stage-coaches and carriages rumbled up and down the wide, cobbled streets. Horses trotted by, carrying ladies and gentlemen in smart riding-habits. On the lamp-studded footpaths, governesses shepherded clusters of well-dressed children, while groups of gentlemen with canes and top hats strolled along, deep in discussion. On the corners, women with weathered faces were selling food from street stalls. Tall Georgian mansions overlooked the streets, surrounded by iron railings. In the classic facade of Trinity College, four stories of rectangular windows overlooked the intersection.

Rows of dilapidated brick buildings crowded right to the river's edge, their rooves a conglomerate of chimneys and steeply pitched gables. They contrasted strikingly with the new, grand public structures like the Law Court, with its Graeco-Roman columns and grand portico topped by magnificent statuary.

The town-house in Giltspur Street had been built by Sir Robert's father in 1770. It was based on the architectural principles of Sir William Chambers' book "Designs of Chinese Buildings", as Lady Westbourne informed Rose when she and Edwin took her on a tour of the premises. Dutifully Rose exclaimed over the panelled dados, the mahogany staircases and architraves, the floor of the front hall, which was tiled with ceramics from China, and the furniture in black lacquer and gold. The walls of the interior were covered with hand-painted Chinese wall-papers. In the bedchambers, scarlet dragons posed in attitudes of attack on top of all four bed-posts and the canopies resembled the rooves of Oriental temples.

"Of course, Mr. Westbourne prefers the classical styles," Lady Westbourne babbled tediously. "Don't you, dear?"

263

"I prefer any house which is fit for habitation," her son returned. "Free from draughts, filled with light and possessing a roof which does not leak."

"But I thought you said—"

"What style of architecture is your favourite, Miss Rose?" Edwin enquired.

Rose, who was endeavouring to make herself interested in their conversation, happened to hold a definite opinion on this subject. "The neo-gothic, most certainly, sir," she replied. "It is so graceful and romantic. I admire the freedom and invention of medieval decoration—it reminds me of the era of King Arthur."

"I too find the rococo amusing," said Edwin, "infinitely preferable to the classical. I do not know where Mother finds her ideas. You are getting confused, Mother."

"Upon my soul, I am in a muddle," Lady Westbourne cried, opening a gilt-and-lacquer fan with a flick of her wrist and causing it to vibrate while she disappeared behind it in consternation at having inadvertently displeased her son. "I don't know what has come over me. It must be the heat. So warm for July, don't you think?"

Her excuses for blushing conjured for Rose a scene in the cottage of the McGintys, when Ilvenna had set eyes for the first time on a drawing of Keane. Almost everything that was said or done, no matter how inconsequential, drew her thoughts back to him.

Georgiana showed Rose the list of all their forthcoming social engagements. "We shall not have a moment to ourselves!" she said contentedly. "There will never be time for dullness. Our feet shall scarcely touch the ground! But first, Mother and I are going to have the dress-makers in. They are going to alter some of my older gowns, and Henrietta's too, so that they will fit you. After you have gone home we can have the alterations reversed!"

"You are all far too generous," said Rose, helpless against the Westbourne tide.

"But really, Rose dearest, you must try to eat more lavishly," tut-tutted Georgiana, "A tiny waist is trés chic, but think of me! My gowns would not have to be taken in with darts at the sides, if you were a little stouter around the middle. Not that I am stout," she added hastily.

Rose drew a deep breath, biting back the words of indignation that sprang to her tongue. "I shall try to oblige," she said, as calmly as possible.

She endured the dress-fittings as stoically as a children's doll being dressed up by its owners. To seal this impression, when Edwin saw her outfitted in lace and silks with her dark hair hidden beneath a bee-hive wig of ringlets the colour of frost, he commented lazily, "Why Miss Rose, how pretty and dainty you look. You ought to be placed on the mantel-shelf, you are such a china doll!"

Before any of the social engagements commenced, Lady Westbourne took Rose aside. "Now my dear," she said carefully, "there are just one or two items you must keep in your mind. We are going to be rubbing shoulders with some very influential people during our time here in the city. The first item is, when you are amongst them you must never mention your uncle, Francis. He caused his own fall from grace three years ago, as I recall, but it is not forgotten in certain circles and a sensible girl like you would not like to raise the issue, would you? His behaviour is best left undiscussed. Let sleeping dogs lie, as the saying goes. We would not want his conduct to tarnish your excellent family name."

"I understood he was disappointed by some foreign business associates," said Rose coolly. "Why should that be considered shameful?"

"Oh dear!" Lady Westbourne's fan blossomed in her hand and began to quiver like a frightened bird. "Have I said too much? I thought you knew—" she broke off.

"Knew what, ma'am? What is my uncle's fault?"

Lady Westbourne sighed. "Well, I suppose I have let the cat out of the bag now," she said. "If you want to know, dear, his losing all that money was not the result of having untrustworthy partners in enterprise. Oh, no. There never were any enterprises. He gambled it all away."

Rose stiffened like a wax figurine. Her nails bit into the palms of her hands.

"That cannot be true!" After a moment she whispered, "Are you certain?"

"Oh, yes. Sir Robert had it from the most scrupulous of sources."

"What source, pray?"

"Lord Leighton, bless him."

"Lord Leighton? The name sounds familiar. Who is he?"

"Why my dear, he is so very well known in society! He is the Baron of Maughinray and a member of parliament, besides being an old friend of Sir Robert's. He was a friend of your uncle's too, before your uncle made a fool of himself and was forced to flee the country. So you see, it is best not to speak of that relative of yours, for your father's sake, really."

"Very well," Rose said in a despairing monotone, "I will do as you ask. What is the second matter I must remember?"

"Never bring up the subject of your religion."

Rose bowed her head in acquiescence.

CHAPTER 23

___

Since the lad of my heart from me did go

The Cholmondeley Family (1732) by William Hogarth (1697-1764)

His hair was black, his eye was blue
His arm was stout, his word was true
I wish in my heart, I was with you,
Go thee, thou Mavourneen slaun.
Shule, shule, shule agra
Only death can cease my woe,
Since the lad of my heart from me did go
Go thee thou Mavourneen slaun!

~ Shule Agra, a 17th century Irish song.

One afternoon, near the end of their stay, Edwin took Rose to see the Port of Dublin. Mrs. Kerrigan the housekeeper rode with them in the landau as chaperon. A mouse-like woman, she sat knitting in the corner, never speaking unless spoken to.

The equipage rocked and swayed its way down beside the grey waters of the Liffey, where a flag flew from the grand Customs House with its domed clock-tower. Tall ships crowded the quay-side. Their forest of masts let down reflections of an upside-down forest into the water. The opposite shore was lined with small buildings, cranes and sheds. Over the ticket-window of a ferry terminal the words "DUBLIN TO BRISTOL" were painted in the shape of an arch. Beneath the arch, in a straight line, was written "EVERY TUESDAY". Numerous horses drew numerous drays or stood patiently waiting for the drays to be loaded with barrels and bales and building materials.

Rose stared out the window of the landau, her gaze lingering on the ships. There was not a man-o-war amongst them. They were all traders and passenger ferries; large coasting smacks, luggers, small brigs and howkers, bugalets and ocean-going bilanders. An old Dutch flute was moored amongst them like a solitary goose in a flock of assorted ducks.

"A penny for your thoughts," Edwin said silkily in her ear.

She turned towards him. "The ships," she explained. "I was thinking about the great distances they travel, and all the different anchorages that are their destinations."

"Do you like travelling?"

"It was not a journey of my own I was contemplating. My thoughts were with the boys who were stolen away from Allanwell on my birthday."

"Melancholy thoughts. Allow me to cheer and divert you."

"Master Westbourne, I am led to believe that your father has influence among the peerage and certain members of parliament. Is there anything more that might be done to secure the safe return of our boys?"

"Alas, no. We have done all we can."

He must have divined from her look that she did not entirely believe him. "I assure you!" he exclaimed, "All possible avenues have been explored! Miss Rose, you must understand that the English are pressing their own fellows into military service, not only ours. If they treat their own in such a despicable manner, why should they show more humanity to the Irish?"

271

"I see," Rose said deliberately. "Master Westbourne, I have known some of those lads since my childhood. One of them was particularly dear to me. He gave me this ring. I am betrothed—did you know?"

"I knew," said Edwin. After a moment he cast a cursory glance at the ring. "The entire village knows. Why, it is such a sliver of a thing! How easily it would break!"

"It is but half of a ring," she said. "My betrothed wears the other."

Edwin turned his face away. It was now he who stared unspeaking from the carriage window. She watched him for a while, then returned to her viewing of the Port of Dublin. The words of a song kept circling through her head: "Oh the love that I have chosen I'll therewith be content, And the salt seas shall be frozen before that I repent ..."

The cargo-handlers had started a fire in a rubbish-incinerator at the riverside. The smoke was pouring from a squat chimney which stood only about twelve feet high. They would use the fire to consume rubbish, to warm themselves and perhaps for cooking. Skiffs were being rowed from ship to shore; three men at the oars, a coxswain at the rudder and a fifth boatman standing in the bows dipping a long punt-pole into the water. Three wooden rafts or pontoons were moored in the centre of the river. An old woman was bringing a basket of laundry down to the river's edge, where she would wash it in the filthy eddies. A four-arched bridge spanned the river further downstream, and the Westbourne landau clattered across.

Their interchange did not appear to much alter Edwin's attitude towards Rose. If anything, he became more attentive, almost possessive. The visit to Dublin was coming to a close. Rose had weathered it better than she had expected—in many aspects she had found it exciting, even though she had missed her family and continually longed for Keane. Lady Westbourne unceasingly assured her she had made an excellent impression in Dublin society and was considered a charming, accomplished young lady of good taste and decorum. Georgiana also enthused. She seemed to have the idea that Rose's "sudden reappearance as if from nowhere" had put the noses of several haughty young ladies out of joint, which pleased her. Even going to church twice in a row on Sunday mornings had not been as arduous as Rose had prophesied. In the Protestant church she spent the time thinking of Keane and marking the similarities and differences between the services.

CHAPTER 24

Tomorrow shall be my dancing day

Tomorrow shall be my dancing day;
I would my true love did so chance,
To see the legend of my play,
To call my true love to my dance.
(Traditional)

A ball was held at the house of Lord Leighton on the Westbournes' last evening in Dublin. It would be the first time in her life that Rose had attended such an occasion; her debut, so to speak.

On the way to the dance Lady Westbourne leaned forward in her seat and said to Rose, "Now you must not be frightened of Lord Leighton, dear girl. Some people are a little taken aback at first by his famous appearance, but he is quite harmless, I assure you." She patted her guest's hand. "I know I can count on your eminently sensible behaviour."

Rose smiled uncertainly. Georgiana half-hid a knowing smile behind the closed tines of her fan.

The ball was a lavish affair, held in a house of magnificent proportions and sumptuous decoration, brimming with candle-light. Overhead, aerial fantasies of chandeliers sparkled, tier upon tier of prisms rainbow-pierced. Atop marble pedestals, multi-branched candelabra blazed like golden trees budding with flame. Ornate clocks and figurines adorned mantelpieces heavily embellished with arabesques and scrolls. The papered walls were hung with paintings in heavy gilt frames. The price of one of those frames would have fed and housed three Allanwell families for a year. The ceiling was adorned with scenes of smiling cherubs and fleshy women reclining half-heartedly clad in Romanesque togas, apparently made of gauze. In the gallery of the ballroom, a full orchestra was playing.

The numerous guests were gorgeously attired and coiffed. Women wore wide, full skirts with bustles to support and expand the fullness of the gathered material at the back, below the waist. Their waists were pinched in by whale-bone corsets. Long gloves crawled up their arms. Their necks and shoulders were exposed by low necklines which seemed to magically cling in place, as receding foam adheres to a swimmer emerging from the brine. Their skin was creamed and powdered to flawless perfection.

Each lady carried, concealed on her person, a tiny cut-glass bottle of smelling-salts in case she should have to be revived after a fainting-fit due to the excessive restriction of her internal organs. Their faces were dusted with cornflour, their cheeks rouged. From their ears dangled clusters of jewels like grapes; great brilliant wine-drops of amethyst, blood-globules of rubies and ice-crystals of diamond. Around their lily-stem necks, some wore the broad black ribbons fashionable at the time. The necks of others were encircled by ropes of precious stones or pearls which sat tightly about the base of the throat. Fashionably, no jewellery cluttered the broad expanse of snowy flesh which extended from the throat to the pushed-up orbs of the breasts.

Their eyes peeped shyly at the gentlemen from behind fluttering fans of ivory, tortoiseshell, lacquer or flimsy, painted wood, the lathes laced through with satin ribbons. Nets of stars glittered in the complicated curl-structures of their wigs, or absurdly tiny hats wobbled on top, or sprays of long plumes nestled there.

Many of the gentlemen were as powdered, perfumed and pomandered as their feminine counterparts. The fops among them had crayoned their lids with kohl to darken and enhance their eyes, while their lips were reddened with cochineal. Tiny black patches strategically placed on the cheek or beside the nose completed their cosmetic triumph. Their striped silk breeches were gartered the knee with colourful ribbons or gathered lace. Silk stockings clad their calves, and their feet were crammed into small shoes. Their wide-skirted coats were edged with lace or braid and decorated with frogging, tassels and embroidery. Now and then these pretty creatures would produce an intricately-carved snuff-box, from which they subtracted a pinch of brown dust. Placing it on the back of one hand they delicately sniffed the powdered tobacco, first into one nostril, then the other.

Beneath richly embellished waistcoats, the bellies of some of the older gentlemen bulged forth, betraying the intemperance of their dining habits. Their rotund paunches were unattractively accentuated by the close-fitting breeches in vogue, which lent them the appearance of boiled eggs on spindly shanks, with a couple of arms sprouting forth and a painted clown's head stuck on top. Rose secretly thought them exceedingly comical.

Butlers and footmen floated everywhere, bearing highly-polished trays of drinks in crystal glasses, each glass delicately painted with Chinese scenes, or meticulously engraved with grapes and vines. Wine flowed like tears at a funeral. And indeed, it was the funeral of many feathered, scaled and woolly creatures, as was indicated by the number of corpses. On the tables of the dining room a vast array of cold refreshments was laid out. There was a variety of meats, including partridge, pheasant, quail, duck, ptarmigan, grouse, venison, lamb, sausage, ham, veal and salmon. Platters were piled with pyramids of oranges, pears, apples, pomegranates, figs, dates, red grapes and plums. Silver-gilt comfit dishes with latticed sides encompassed raisins, sugar-plums, crystallised apricots, nougat, preserved cherries, marzipan and sugared almonds. There were tall fruit-jellies moulded in the shapes of castles, deep flummeries, date puddings, gooseberry fools and honey-cakes. Rose thought of the

Allanwell women gathering seaweed off the rocks at low tide, and picking nettles from the roadside to feed their children. Inwardly she raged against the blatant injustice of it and ached with the wish to bring the villagers all here, now, to partake of this bounty. How could they imagine such munificence, even in their dreams? Surely, the angels above must be looking down and weeping.

Near Rose and the Westbourne ladies, a peer was giving instructions to a pair of footmen. With arms outstretched, the servants were displaying a huge animal-skin magnificently striped with burning amber, bronze, and black.

"I got the devil in Bengal," the lord was saying. "Shot him meself. Dangerous beasts, tigers. They're lethally armed, you know—look at the teeth in that head, and the claws, like scimitars. They can slash a man's belly open as soon as look at you. We're doing the natives a favour, getting rid of these predators. Most dangerous beasts in the world."

"I beg to differ," said his companion.

"By God, Wilberforce, that's typical of you philosophic types. Well, what is it then? What animal is more dangerous than a bloody man-eating tiger?"

"The animal that has killed far more human beings than tigers ever could."

"Lions? Wolves?"

"Lions and wolves quail before it."

"You've got me baffled. Out with it! What's the answer?"

"Man."

The tiger-slayer laughed. "Ha ha! Jolly good dear fellow,

279

I'll remember that to tell at the club. But you haven't told me what you think of the skin. Not bad, eh?"

Another group within earshot was discussing the banning of the Dublin branch of the United Irishmen and the unrest being demonstrated by the masses in the form of public demonstrations and riots.

"All large assemblies must be prohibited," one gentleman was saying. "It is the only way to keep the rabble from their troublemaking."

Rose was unable to hear more, because Georgiana, simpering behind her fan, whispered in her ear, "I daresay you note a considerable difference between society in Dublin and the types with whom you have been accustomed to associate in the country, Miss Rose." Without bothering to wait for an answer she moved into the crowd, having spied an acquaintance on the other side of the room.

Rose looked around at the faces of the men and women of genteel birth. She observed carefully tended expressions of delicate hauteur, feigned or genuine delight, polite or profound interest, portrayals of wit, grace and refinement and momentary lapses into ennui or weariness,

To Henrietta she said, "Put a cottier's babe in the cradle of a lord and feed him from a spoon of silver, but you will find no difference between him and the blue-blood."

"Do not let Georgiana hear you voice such odd opinions," said Henrietta. "She would scold you for declaring we are all no better than peasants."

"Come Miss Rose, I wish to introduce you to Lord Leighton,"

busily said Lady Westbourne, steering Rose through a knot of butterfly ladies, around a group of grasshopper youths and past a cluster of cockroach lords. The crowd parted. Rose saw Sir Robert standing with a group of gentlemen. He was holding converse with one whose appearance was striking, to say the least. About six feet in height and bull-shouldered, the gentleman was well-padded about the torso. A full wig of marvellous coppery curls fountained from his head to his elbows. From his jaw sprouted a luxuriant beard as red as spice. So profusely did this facial hair grow, that it completely concealed the lower half of his face, and both sides of his cheeks below the ears. It was long enough to obscure his cravat. Gingery eyebrows jutted forth fiercely, like two porches. His piratical air was further enhanced by the black patch covering his left eye. The patch was held in position by a thin silver cord which passed around his forehead and vanished beneath the wig.

Rose could not at first discover the location of the gentleman's mouth, since his moustaches burgeoned well down over his upper lip. She felt the uncovered eye bore her through like an auger as she approached. Perceiving that this formidable gentleman had turned his full attention to her, she dropped into a deep curtsy. A cavern appeared within the beard. A deep voice rumbled, "Who is this?"

"My dear Leighton, I would like you to meet Miss Rose Delacey," said Sir Robert jovially. "She is the daughter of my manager at Allanwell. Miss Rose, Lord Reginald Leighton, M.P., Baron of Maughinray."

"I am honoured to meet you, my Lord," said Rose.

"Delacey, eh?" Lord Leighton gave a short bark of laughter. "Ha, there's a name I've heard before! So, this is one of the nieces, is it? And a pretty little dish, ain't she, Westbourne?"

Sir Robert peered vaguely at Rose. Because she was no goshawk or greyhound or mare, he could not find her very interesting and thus could express no opinion. He grunted in reply and began excavating his teeth with a silver tooth-pick.

Rose's cheeks burned scarlet with indignation and humiliation. How dared this Lord Leighton speak about her so? She had never before been treated with such disrespect, as though she were some culinary item or article of furniture to be measured and judged. After her polite greeting, the gentleman had not deigned to bow or even to address her directly. She had made up her mind to say something that would indicate she was surprised and put out by his discourtesy, hoping thereby to make him feel ashamed, so that he would behave better towards her.

Then she happened to look into that single eye.

What she read therein put a stop to her plan. A look of bored insolence and crass disregard for etiquette burned deep in that socket. Instinctively Rose understood that nothing she or anyone else might say could ever mortify such a personality. On the contrary, Lord Leighton was waiting and indeed hoping for that kind of challenge—he had deliberately provoked it. Arousing strong feelings in others was a game he pursued. He delighted in making people squirm. Even his menacing and eccentric appearance was calculated, designed as a way of biting his thumb at the conventions by which everyone else abided like sheep. It was an implied threat—do you mock my beard? Try!

He had invited her anger, her embarrassment, her politely veiled accusation. All this, her native intelligence understood with one glance. Instantly her strategy altered.

She would be seen not to care.

No matter how he baited her, she would remain indifferent, as though he were nothing more than a fly on her shoulder, to be brushed off. She would not be led on by his devices. As soon as she had decided on this, a sense of tranquility washed through her. She smiled straight at Lord Leighton.

"'Tis most kind of you, sir, to include me among your guests," she purred brightly. "A splendid evening it is, no doubt of that." She heard the country lilt creep defiantly back into her voice.

"I'm glad to hear you are enjoying yourself, m'dear," said the bushy-bearded gentleman, "and I'm sure the young men will be enjoying your company also. Is your dance card full yet?"

"I think so," said Rose, holding up the wrist from which the little booklet dangled. "Master Westbourne has claimed—"

"Write down my name for the quadrille and the minuet," Lord Leighton barked abruptly, grabbing the card and reading it. He pointed to two spaces. "There, you see, and there. Off you go now dearie, and don't forget!"

As she walked away beside the twittering Lady Westbourne, anger seethed in Rose again. He had somehow outfoxed her, the cunning old boar. She would be forced to dance with him, a prospect she could scarcely bear to contemplate. Ruefully she had to admit to herself that the likes of him would always manoeuvre the advantage to himself. She was only sixteen, after all, and he had had twenty more years of experience at these games of brinkmanship which she had only begun to learn, for the sake of survival in aristocratic circles. No doubt he would outwit a novice every time. Then and there she resolved to have as little as possible to do with this repulsive and possibly dangerous being.

Edwin Westbourne appeared in front of her, seeming delightful by comparison, and swept her into a stately dance.

Later the young master of Charter Hall hooked Rose's elbow firmly in the crook of his own and made her stroll with him out to the balcony, where one or two other couples drifted like moths. The balcony overlooked a well-ordered courtyard garden, in which a breeze stirred the foliage of elms, and a fountain tinkled. The cooler air was a welcome relief from the stuffiness of the interior.

Rose surmised that Edwin probably intended the circumstances to lead to a romantic interlude. This she determined to avoid. She began a discussion about Uncle Frank, a topic that had preyed on her mind.

"Mr. Westbourne, why should my uncle be ostracised for gambling when, from what I have seen in the city, the greater part of high society indulges in some form of punting?"

The young gentleman frowned and pursed his lips in a manner that reminded his companion of his mother. Restlessly he tapped his sloughed gloves against his palm, as if he would rather not reply to such a distasteful subject. Ultimately, he sighed as if he had made up his mind, and said, "He gambled and lost. He gambled obsessively and lost heavily, borrowing money to feed his addiction. And if that is not enough culpability for you, it was his own family he ruined in the process. That is why he was cast out of good society. Also because of his indiscreet affairs," he added, speaking rapidly and low.

"Oh." Rose digested these words.

"You come from good stock, Miss Rose, but there is no denying that your uncle has fallen into disrepute and no-one who wishes to retain their own reputation would be seen to associate with him in any way, lest they be considered to be tarred with the same brush. Your father is a pauper. You have no dowry except your beauty. To put the seal upon the charter of your unsuitability, you are a Catholic. Despite this list of drawbacks, I am prepared to cast aside caution." He hesitated, then looked her in the eye and said, "I am willing to give you my hand, my name and my fortune." Rose was lost for words. "My father thinks my attachment pure folly," Edwin continued, "since I could choose from so many Protestant heiresses of irreproachable background and good connections. But it is you, dear Rose, who occupies my thoughts. You can never know how painfully you torment me with every pout of your lips, with every haughty toss of your head and every distant look you bestow in my direction. I ache for you every moment. To be near you, yet not to touch you, is to abide in hell."

"You are eloquent, sir," she said, between dread and compassion—for there could be no doubt he was expending considerable effort on suppressing his own eagerness. He fidgeted, continually adjusting his clothing, and she often found herself edging away from his ever-increasing proximity. She could see it cost him dearly to restrain himself from embracing her and not for the first time, she was grateful to the principles of etiquette that were, she guessed, all that restrained him.

"You are too young to understand your own beauty," Anne Delacey used to say to her daughters when they complained that their eyes ought to be a different colour or their cheeks redder, or their waists more waspish. "When you are older you may yourself as others see you. You are beautiful just as you are."

They never believed her. Rose knew only that sometimes, to greater or lesser degree, some youths seemed afflicted with a kind of madness. A madness with which she was not entirely unfamiliar, though when it touched her it had a quality that was perhaps more magical, perhaps less fierce. Depending on the characteristics of the youth involved, which she could not explain, this rendered either her delighted or uneasy; from the sense of attending an exciting social gathering, to the sense of being hunted prey. The former, she enjoyed. The latter was an alarming feeling from which she shied instinctively.

She said, "If your family believes a match with me would be inappropriate, why do they appear to welcome me with such warmth?"

"Merely because they deny me nothing."

"And so, being rebuffed is a novelty to you, a challenge! You have come to believe that the excitement of the hunt is in fact affection!"

"You are mistaken, Miss Rose—very much mistaken. Granted, I enjoy the thrill of the chase as much as any sportsman. But, were you to run into my arms at this very instant, I should crush you against me, and hold you, and never let you free until I had made you my wife."

"I fear you have taken too much drink, sir. Let us pretend you did not say those words, for you will regret them in the morning."

"Pray do not insult my intelligence, dearest. I'll not regret them. Have you an answer for me?"

"You know the answer. I am already betrothed."

Edwin pulled his arm against his side, and Rose with it. She stood pressed so close against him that she could feel a jolt go through his body like a galvanisation. But he said nothing more, and presently they returned amongst the noise and the congestion and the piquant odours of the party.

After the ball, as the black carriages bowled through the streets towards Giltspur Road, they slowed and then were brought to an unexpected halt by some disturbance ahead. The passengers craned their necks from the windows to see what had caused the hold-up. They were treated to the sight of a group of ragged, rowdy youths swarming across the road. A pool of honey-coloured lamp-light illuminated the stragglers. Drunkenly, they were singing a song more than a century old;

"...Ho by my soul it is a Talbot, Lili Burlero bullen a-la.
And he will cut de Englishman's t'roat, Lili Burlero
bullen a-la.
Though by my soul de English do fret, Lili Burlero
bullen a-la.
Lero lero lero lero Lili Burlero bullen a-la.
Lero lero lero lero Lili Burlero bullen a-la.
De law's on dare side and Christ knows what, Lili
Burlero bullen a-la."

The words became jumbled at this point, as though two or three sections within the group were singing different verses.

"This is a Protestant quarter," Master Edwin snapped, talking partly to himself. "What do those fools think they are doing? They're asking for trouble."

No sooner had he spoken than a second crowd began to spill from the nearby public house in search of the ruckus. They were much better-dressed than the first, and when they heard the song they immediately struck up one of their own ditties, equally antique, sung to exactly the same melody—

"Protestant boys both valiant and stout, fear not the
strength and power of Rome!"

The opposing factions strode towards each other, in and out of the circles of lamp-light. "Turn around!" Sir Robert bawled at the coachmen. "Get us out of here."

The drivers yelled commands to the teams and tried to whip them into a tight turn, but there was not enough room in the street for such a manoeuvre. Spying a gap between buildings the leading driver directed the horses into this thoroughfare, where they plunged with alacrity, having been alarmed by the shouting crowd. Harness jingled, axles squealed and the crack of the whip rebounded off walls, a red weal across the night.

"While with their blood the cause they have sealed," roared the patrons of the public house, "Heaven upon their efforts did frown. . . "

As the carriages gathered speed, the occupants could hear behind them the uproar of a brutal conflict breaking out in the street. Down the side-street the equipages barrelled, the horses cantering at a fair speed and the passengers being jolted around inside their compartments.

"There will be bloodshed tonight," Sir Robert proclaimed over the din, as though it were nothing new.

CHAPTER 25

Could you fancy a poor sailor lad?

*"British Plenty" (c. 1795) by Henry Singleton (1766-1839) showing
British sailor with two girl friends.*

*'Come ye young one, come ye fair one, come now unto me!
Could you fancy a poor sailor lad who's just come
from the sea?'*

*The Saucy Sailor. Collected by Cecil Sharp from Mr Thomas Hendy.
Also collected by George Butterworth in Sussex, England, in 1907.*

They returned to Allanwell on the 26th of July. As soon as she arrived, Rose asked for news of Keane and Ryan and any of the other boys. There was none.

That evening, the Delaceys gathered around the kitchen table to hear Rose's account of her visit. To delight them, she tried to recall every detail—and they were delighted. On one matter only she kept her own counsel—she did not reveal that Edwin had spoken to her of marriage.

To her sisters, now accustomed to the narrow drudgeries of daily life in a struggling community, it seemed that Rose was stepping out of the pages of some fairy tale. They begged her to describe, over an over again, the theatre, the shops, the musical evenings and above all, the fashions and the ball.

"Who did you say hosted the ball?" asked Lizzie.

"Lord Leighton," Rose said. Hoping to dismiss that gentleman from the conversation she went on, "I wish you might have heard the marvellous orchestra—"

"Lord Leighton indeed!" exclaimed Margaret, impressed. "Is he as formidable-looking as they say? Hairy, piratical and huge as an ox?"

"Why, yes," Rose said, resigning herself to the fact that her sisters, starved of social tittle-tattle, intended to dwell on the odious fellow. "Georgiana says he grew his ruffianly beard to hide the terrible pock-marks scarring his face. And he lost his left eye in some kind of accident, which is why he wears a patch over the empty socket."

"You know him, or used to know him, didn't you, Papa?" Margaret asked her father.

"Briefly," replied her father.

"Tell me, Rose," said Katherine, "what does his wife look like?"

"A beaten-down, nervous-looking thing. Quite young and pretty. She is his second bride, Georgiana told me."

"Oh, poor man! Fancy being made a widower!" compassionately said Katherine, thinking of her father.

"Yes. Poor man," repeated Rose. "Anyway, the orchestra was wonderful. They played minuets by Herr Mozart and Herr Haydn..."

When she had exhausted all description, she asked for the news of Allanwell.

"The press-gangs have not been back but the excise men have been nosing around," said Katherine, "Flynn McGinty has not been able to carry on his usual trade. He says if the gaugers get too interested in this locality he'll up and out of here."

"Oh no!" exclaimed Rose. "I hope he does not leave Allanwell. He is needed here, especially now."

"That's exactly what Lizzie said," Katherine returned with a smirk.

The the Riding Officers went away, but they kept returning every few months. In April of the following year[April 1795] they were back, and at the same time reports came in of the Impress Service working its way along the coast again. Some of the remaining Allanwell youths decided to leave the area for a while—among them, Flynn McGinty.

"Now there's two lots o' divils after me hide," he said, laughing. "Allanwell's as hot as hell for me. I'll be away until it cools off a little. I'd not leave at all, except Ma and Ilvenna will kill me if I don't."

"Where will you go?" everyone asked him.

"Maybe I'll follow after Ryan," was all he would divulge. When they asked for more information, he replied with a wink, "The less said, the better me chances." No one asked what he meant—everyone knew that the fairies were listening around every corner, and the mischievous or wicked amongst them liked to spoil people's plans.

Since the outbreak of the Anglo-French war, the period of reform which had begun in Ireland as a response to the demands of the United Irishmen had ceased. Furthermore, after 1794 the class basis of the United Irishmen had undergone a radical alteration. The membership was nearly half composed of clerks, artisans, labourers and apprentices.

When the new Viceroy, Camden, had arrived in March of that year, aristocrats were stoned in the streets of Dublin. Now that all mass assemblies had been forbidden, various strategies were used to allow United Irishmen to meet. Mock funerals were organised, with up to two thousand 'mourners'. Sometimes the coffins would be filled with weapons. In rural areas, mass potato diggings provided the necessary cover.

In June 1795, a group of Irish Protestants gathered on top of Cave Hill, overlooking Belfast. They swore "never to desist in our efforts until we have subverted the authority of England over our country and asserted our independence." Thus the Orange Order was formed, 'to combat Defenderism and popery', and the colour orange became solidly identified as "a Protestant colour". Meanwhile in France, the successful Napoleon Bonaparte was named Commander of the Armée D'Interior.

Nearly seven thousand Catholics were driven out of County Armagh by Orange Order pogroms. Many of the expelled families found shelter in the Protestant households of the Presbyterian United Irishmen. These expulsions spread the fear of the Orange Order all over Ireland, and many young Catholic men felt compelled to join the Defenders so that they could retaliate.

The Defenders were an organisation that had been born as a local faction in Armagh. When they started they were non-sectarian, their first captain being a Presbyterian, and in Dublin there were Protestant Defenders. After the armed attacks of the Orange Order on Catholics, however, people had begun to see the Defenders as purely a Catholic sectarian organisation, a green reflection of the Orange Order. Some of the remaining youths of Allanwell went away to join up with the Defenders. To the cottiers left behind, deprived of half a generation, the countryside seemed emptier than ever.

Intermittent dreams of Keane continued to haunt Rose. They comforted and sickened her simultaneously. She glimpsed a nightmare world of extreme peril and cruelty. Often, what she saw seemed incomprehensible—a shadowy cavern in which every dangling object swayed back and forth in unison; a hellish confusion of smoke and flame; blood and water running across slippery floor-boards, men's faces contorted with screaming; a toy-sized ship pendulating at the lower end of a pole so long that perspective tapered the tip to a matchstick; the world upside-down, with the sky a drowning mass of water about to collapse on everybody's heads, and nothing but clouds and vacancies where solid ground ought to be.

The only part that made sense was the sight of Keane, dirty, grim-faced and tight-lipped, yet miraculously, living still. When Rose was not keeping vigil on the heights of Madigan's Leap, gazing out at the horizon and whispering her true-love's name like a prayer, she spent much time at Ilvenna McGinty's. Having exhausted the usual wishing-charms, Ilvenna and Ma racked their brains for some spell of safe return, but nothing had any efficacy.

"I must have used up the goodness on the wish that brought the O'Connells here in the first place," said Ilvenna. "The goodness of me powers, that is."

"Ye'll just have to keep tryin' until it comes back," said Ma.

The weekly visits of the Delacey daughters to Charter Hall continued. One Thursday afternoon as Rose lingered in the Music Room to slide the dust cover over the harp, she caught a movement from beyond the French windows. Young Edwin rode his hunter right onto the lawn and slid from its back. Leaving it loose-reined, to wander among the flowerbeds, he strode in at the open windows. He was dressed in a smart riding habit; a swallow-tailed coat, waistcoat, buck-skin breeches gartered at the knee and calf-boots with spurs at the heels. Wisps of hair fell untidily across his face. In one hand he carried his hat, in the other, a riding crop. His face glistened and he smelled of horse-hair and leather. He was still breathing heavily from his ride. Sunlight streamed in behind him, like lances of gold. A fragrance of wet grass and damp loam drifted in. Behind his head the sky was a clear bowl hewn of sapphire, enamelled with a row of birds winging their way home.

"Rose," he said.

Her back was turned to him, but she caught a curious edge to his tone. "Mother of God," she whispered to herself. "What demon rides his shoulders?"

"Will you wed me?"

Catching her breath, she turned. "I will not," she said agitatedly, tracing the slim ring on her finger. "My betrothal promise was made in front of Father Joseph. It is a binding thing."

"But your fellow is dead." Impatiently, Edwin tapped the riding crop against the side of his boot.

"You don't know that. Nobody knows that!"

"You've had no word from him in a year, have you?"

"That does not mean—"

"Rose, you know there is no chances of those Allanwell chaps being alive. If they've not been killed yet, they will be by the time this war is over."

"You are harsh!"

"I speak the truth and you know it. Forget the dead. Here is a living gentleman who needs you as he needs breath."

"I am pledged," she said.

Confronted with the young man's vital magnificence, Rose was poignantly aware of her own faded attire. She smoothed her hands down the skirts of her old worsted dress.

He took a step towards her, his gaze now steely. "Very well," he said, "if you will not be altered, you will lose me. I will depart from Allanwell like the rest of the wild geese, and when I return it will be with a wife. Fare thee gently, Rose. I hope you find happiness."

And he kept his word about leaving. On the morrow he departed for the Port of Dublin. Word went around that he was sailing to England to apply for a commission with the Royal Rathskillen Dragoon Guards.

For the Delacey daughter, the invitations to Charter Hall ceased.

Life felt dreary.

In December[December 1795], something happened to change the tenor of the monotonous days. An unusual vessel sailed into Allanwell Bay. At first glance she might have been taken for a war-ship, for she was well-armed and sported plenty of gun-ports. But in the form and build of her hull she differed from a man-o-war. The full underbody, flat floor, sharp turns of the bilges and quick rises stamped her as slower and more capacious. Furthermore, many aspects of her rigging were peculiar to the merchant service: the form of the halyards and some of the stays, the fittings of studding-sail booms and the lead of many ropes. In addition, the arrangement of the decks clearly showed she was a cargo-carrier, a trader.[Information from "The Book of Old Ships" by Henry B. Culver, first published by Doubleday, Page & Co in 1924.] Written on her side was the name Spice Queen.

"'Tis an East Indiaman she is!" said one of the fishermen, who had once seen such a vessel in the Port of Dublin. "A Sasunach vessel that plies the routes to India. They are built to carry expensive cargoes and 'tis well-prepared they are in case of attacks from pirates or the enemies of the Sasunachs."

"By Christ, we're enemies of the Sasunachs," said another old salt. "Are they wantin' to blow us up wit' their guns, or what?"

But the cannon of the East Indiaman remained silent. Her captain had directed her into Allanwell Bay only because several barrels of fresh water had leaked, being of inferior manufacture. He required new barrels and further supplies.

As it happened, the vessel anchored on a Friday night. The next day, the weather changed and the wind began to blow hard. It swung about, making it impossible for the ship to leave the bay. The captain—perhaps injudiciously—gave his crew shore-leave. They rowed ashore in an open tender, and, after making some inquiries, headed for Rafferty's Inn.

There they were met with stony glares from the regular patrons.

"Good afternoon to ye, gentlemen," said the Spice Queen's first mate chirpily, pushing the oilskin hood off his head. "We come 'ere ter drink, not ter fight. We've got brass in our pockets an' we wan'a spend it."

"If ye're after our women ye'll get a fight," said Rafferty. "We know what you sailor-boys is like and we won't be havin' it. This is a good Catholic village."

"We'll not touch your wimmin," said the sailors, jingling the money in their pockets.

Sullenly, the village men made room for the English sailors at the benches, keeping well away from them and muttering profanities into their beer. The sailors, enjoying their freedom, ignored the scowls. They did indeed carry money in their pockets, and they commenced to outlay it. After the first mate had bought a round of drinks "for everyone in the 'ouse", the icy atmosphere began to melt and crack. After the second round, a decided warmth was starting to spread, especially when the sailors began to praise Allanwell Bay for being a fine place to drop anchor, and enquired as to the strange light atop the cliff that had helped to guide their ship through the night.

"For the charts show no light'ouse here," the mate said, "but the watch spied it, shinin' through the darkness like a square eye, 'igh up. But in the mornin' when the sun came up, we saw naught on the cliff-top save for some broken stone walls. So tell us, 'oo is the generous soul what 'angs a ligh'ed lan'ern in the roons every night in case o' poor sailors tryin' to find their way 'ome?"

"Well dere's an old fort on Madigan's Leap," said Kevin O'Flaherty, as an expectant hush fell over the gathering, "and one o' the towers still stands, wit' one lonely window looking out over the sea. Dat window we call 'William's Light'."

The sailors leaned almost imperceptibly towards the speaker and some nodded gravely. Intuition told them there was a ghost story brewing.

"On Madigan's Leap in the ruins," said O'Flaherty, "often at nights, from the sea, sailors will see a light glimmerin' in the winder, which cannot be seen from da land. Even on the stormiest of nights the wind cannot blow out the light. They say the light gleams dere to call the child home."

"The child?" repeated the mate.

"The child indeed," said O'Flaherty, crossing himself. "There was a ship, the Resolution, a smack of forty-nine tons, under the command of a Captain Quested. She'd been chartered by Castlerigg landowner Thomas Goundry to take his entire family to Galway for a holiday, and on the night of the fourt' o' November 1750 she was returning to Allanwell

301

Bay when the disaster happened. In bad weather at evenin' the vessel went onto the rocks and began to list, takin' water. So wild was the sea dat they could not put a boat out and the passengers could not land, but the crew abandoned ship and swam to shore, since they were so close in. The family clung to the sinking hull, and by dawn the Goundry children, from the twelve year old to the two year old, all wit' golden hair, had died of exposure."

Nobody spoke, until Mrs. Rafferty murmured, "Sometimes my boys were after findin' a broken bit o' willow pattern crockery washed up on the beach."

"What 'appened to the parents?" the mate asked.

"The entire village came down to the shore," said O'Flaherty, "and the bravest fishermen rowed out and rescued the poor mother who had been clingin' to a spar all night. They saved the father too, and the captain, but it was too late for da poor wee angels. Five o' their corpses was recovered but the sixth was never found—the second boy, William, eight years old. They've a common grave in Castlerigg Churchyard. William's name is written on't wit' the rest, even though no one ever saw him again."

"Yer man was seen again!" Mrs. Rafferty broke in. "Twenty years after it happened, a boyo came walkin' though Allanwell, on his way to Castlerigg, and he said his name was William Goundry."

"Ah, but dat one was away wit' Themselves, Aileen," said Michael O'Sullivan. That was not yer man, but the real one

302

was seen again, O'Flaherty, did you not have the knowledge of 't?"

O'Flaherty shook his head and the English sailors leaned even closer to the speakers. There was not a sound in the hostelry, save for the moan of the wind sliding over the thatch.

"T'irty years after the wreck," said O'Sullivan, "a housemaid up at the big house, Charter Hall, woke one night to see an angel wit' golden hair standin' at the foot of her bed."

Presently the awe-struck quietude was broken by a sigh.

"Is that all?" enquired a sailor.

"Quite so."

"Well we jack-tars is gra'ful for the light, no ma'er who put it there or why," said the mate briskly. "Let's 'ave another round o' drinks."

The eerie mood dissipated when the sailors started a game of dice, inviting all present to join in. This might have proved the trigger for a brawl, except that they lost as good-naturedly as they won. In the end, the sailors were the poorer. By this time the village men were slapping them on the back and calling for songs. The sailors responded with a rendition of the popular "Oh Dear, What Can the Matter Be." After the first couple of verses they began to substitute their own lyrics, with a naughtier, nautical version. It was received with hoots of laughter by the Irish, who came up with a similar ditty. Soon they were falling upon each others' shoulders, weak with hilarity.

Watching the revelry from a corner of the room, the fisherman said drily to the old salt, "By my soul, there's not'ing like a dram o' the cratur for makin' a man discover his long-lost brudders."

"But only till it wears off," said the other. "In the mornin' they'll be wantin' to kill each other again."

"Or maybe tonight if the drink is puttin' the anger on them."

"And good riddance to them Sasunachs," said another fisherman, spitting on the floor. He had always hated the English with a vengeance, and his nephews had been taken by the press-gang.

At the waning of the windy afternoon, Mary burst through the door of the Delacey cottage. She sat down on a stool and fanned herself with her apron.

"Good Lord, Mary, what's amiss?" Katherine asked anxiously.

"Nothing's amiss. I've just run back from Flanagan's, and the word about the place is that the English sailors are at Rafferty's. They've come all the way from India and one of them has brought a vegetable lamb!" She struggled to regain her breath. "Get your clogs on, you've got to go down there with me to see it!"

"Ooh, a vegetable lamb!" cooed Lizzie, dropping her embroidery. "What a shame Papa is not here to see, or Maggie and Rose either. Let's go, Kitty!"

As they hastened down the road, their skirts flapping as they held them up to avoid the mud, Lizzie said, "Mary, what exactly is a vegetable lamb?"

"Well, how should I know?" exasperatedly said Mary. "They told me it was one, that's all I know."

"It's all the way from India is it?" asked Katherine with shining eyes.

"India or Cathay or some such foreign place," panted Mary. "Will you quit your questions? I'm too old to be runnin' and jabberin at the same time."

Word of the manifestation of a vegetable lamb had spread, and many inquisitive onlookers, both men and women, were accumulating inside Rafferty's, forming a circle around one of the sailors, who apparently was the possessor of the amazing object.

A hush descended. Outside the wind keened around corners, plucking again at the thatch.

The sailor loudly intoned, "Beyond the Land of Tartary there groweth a manner of Fruit, as though it were Gourds. And when they be ripe, Men cut them atwo, and Men find within a little Beast, in Flesh, in Bone and Blood, as though it were a little woolly Lamb. And Men eat both the Fruit and the Beast. And that is a great Marvel. Of that Fruit I have eaten." [3]

Punching the air with an enthusiastic fist he cried, "Behold! The Scythian Lamb!"

A volley of exclamations greeted these words. Simultaneously, the sailor reached beneath his coat, reverently brought out the object of curiosity and held it aloft. About eight inches long, it appeared to be a lamb-like

---

[3]   Mandeville, J. 1964: 174. The Travels of Sir John Mandeville, New York.

organism that shared both plant and animal characteristics.

It had a head, ears and four legs and was covered all over with a reddish, silky down, except on its ears and legs, which were bare and were of a slightly darker, golden-brown colour.

"But if the Fruit be allowed to ripen and the Lamb be brought forth as in birth," the owner orated. "From its Navel groweth a Stem or Root by which this Plant-Animal is attached like a Gourd to the Soil below the Surface of the Ground, and according to the length of its Stem or Root, it devoureth all the Herbage which it is able to reach within the Circle of its Tether."[Lee, H. 1887: 6 The Vegetable Lamb of Tartary. London.]

There was a lot of shoving as people jostled one another to get a better view.

"Is it alive?" they quizzed.

"It is fact unalive," said the lamb's proprietor, "in which Condition it was obtained by Myself. Be it known that these Lambs do perish outside of their native Habitat. Nevertheless it remains a great Wonder, which doth excite the Curiosity of many respected European Scholars, and it is much in demand for Exhibitions."

"Will ye be allowin' us to touch the t'ing?"

The sailor shook his head regretfully. "Alas, such Rarities do quickly fade to Dust if over-handled. Let it be enough that ye have seen, for there are many who would give Purses of Gold merely to set eyes upon this Phenomenon." Carefully he tucked the lamb back under his coat. When it was secured, he patted it tenderly.

"How did you get your hands on the wee beastie?" was the next question. The sailor settled himself comfortably, called for another drink and began relating some of his adventures in far Tartary. Presently some of his ship-mates took up the tales, allowing the storyteller a few moments to swallow his beer.

Lizzie turned to Katherine. "Well, Katie, what do you think of that!" she said. But her sister volunteered no reply. Her gaze was fixed glassily upon the sailor, and she was edging closer to him.

"What on earth is the matter?" Lizzie said blankly. She looked at the sailor, to try to divine the reason why Katherine was watching him as attentively as a hound stalks a deer. She saw a mop of straw-coloured hair, which was straggling in wisps from its horse-tail, a golden hoop earring in the left lobe, a saucy, lop-sided grin, a firm jaw and twinkling eyes. The glow from Rafferty's oil-lamp, which swung from the rafters, reflected like polished bronze from his golden curls. Suddenly, the truth ignited her inner vision. She recalled Katherine telling her about her St. Valentine's dream— "... a gentleman with a kind of yellow shine around his head, and he bearing a young four-legged creature in his arms... "

By now the sailor had caught sight of Katherine. His gaze was locked with hers. He stretched out his hand.

"Plenty o' room over 'ere," he invited, indicating a clear section of the bench beside him and moving along to allow more space. "Come an' sit wiv me, darlin'."

Boldly, Katherine squeezed into the place next to him. She avoided Lizzie's dismayed stare.

"Thank you sir," she said breathlessly. "I was just thinking, you must have seen a fair lot of bizarrities on your travels."

The sailor looked down at her. He placed his arm along the table behind her back, and smiled dazzlingly. One of the village men growled and made to elbow his way towards the couple, but his comrade shook his head warningly, and reluctantly he fell back.

"No dou' about that, darlin'," the sailor said. "Would yer like to 'ear about the time I saw a phoenix?"

Lizzie's hand flew to her mouth. Nervously she started chewing at her fingernails. What should she do? Surely something terrible was happening! Foolish Kitty was falling for a saucy Sasunach...

There seemed no remedy for this latest disaster. Katherine would not heed her pleas to come away, and Mary was on the other side of the room listening to the yarns of the first mate. An hour or two passed, with Lizzie hovering anxiously and wondering whether it was appropriate for her and Katherine to be in Rafferty's at all. They had never before set foot in the place. Presently Rafferty looked up and noticed the couple conversing animatedly beneath his oil-lamp. Instantly he lurched to his feet and came barging through the crowd.

"Miss Kat'erine!" he growled, standing unsteadily over her, "your Da will have the worry on him about you, you and your sister here. You'd better be gettin' on home." He shouted to the other side of the room, "Get them home, Mary. What are you t'inking of, woman! They don't belong here!"

"She's not our nursemaid any more," complained Katherine, but no one heeded her.

Guiltily Mary retrieved her charges and shepherded them out the door, not without many a backward glance from Katherine towards the blond sailor, who saluted her jauntily.

Rafferty was always stewing about the loss of his sons, and he blamed the English as a nation. It must have cost him dearly to rein his bitterness while the sailors patronized his bar. When he noted Katherine looking favourably upon one of them, his self-control exploded like a powder keg. As they departed, they heard Rafferty roar, "The devil take the English! Damn them all to hell!"

A serious brawl might have broken out between the armed sailors and the unarmed cottiers, except for the fact that Rafferty, who had an enormous capacity for liquor, had for once taken too much of his own drop that evening. With one last curse he crashed to the floor, insensible. After an awkward pause the revelry resumed, although its tone was now somewhat subdued.

CHAPTER 26

There We Lost Sight of Your Sailor Boy

Petty officer of the Napoleonic Wars wearing straw hat, reefer jacket and neckerchief.

A sailor's life is a merry life.
They robs young girls of their hearts' delight,
Leaving them behind for to weep and mourn,
They never know when they will return.

"Oh there's four-and-twenty all in a row,
My sweetheart cuts the finest show.
He's proper, tall, genteel withal,
If I don't have him I'll have none at all."

"Oh father, build me a bonny boat,
That on the wide ocean I may float.
And every Queen's ship that we pass by
There I'll enquire for my sailor boy."

Now they had not sailed long upon the deep
Before the Queen's ship they chanced to meet.
"You sailors all, pray tell me true,
Does my sweet William sail among your crew?"

"Oh no, fair maid, he is not here,
For he's been drownded, we greatly fear.
On yon green island as we passed by,
There we lost sight of your sailor boy."

Now she wrung her hands and she tore her hair
Much like a damsel in great despair.
Her little boat 'gainst a rock did run.
"How can I live now my William is gone?"

A Sailor's Life (Traditional)

312

The next day was Sunday. On their way to St. Finbar's, battling against the strong gusts, the villagers beheld most of the crew of the Spice Queen walking up the road towards the Protestant church. The sailors waved cheerily. "Good morning' to yer!" they called. "The wind's against us and we cannot get clear of the 'arbour!"

But instead of the jovial bonhomie of the preceding night, they were met with cold stares. They shrugged and trudged on, some voicing execrations under their breath.

That afternoon the westerly wind was still strong, and honed by the premonition of more snow. It made the sea roar like a wordless, tuneless vociferation from the throats of a distant multitude, now swelling, now fading. All along the water's edge a long, wide cloth of white lacy foam was floating. It rose and fell like a mantle on the swell. Spumy waves tossed sea wrack and driftwood onto the rocks. Where the slopes rose, gulls hovered on the vertical gasps rising off the ocean.

The sailor with the yellow hair was then to be found among the fisher-cots by the harbour. He was seated on the blowing grass, telling stories to amuse the little children. Even the mothers of some of the tots braved the wind and drew near to hear his fascinating yarns and see the 'Scythian Lamb'. They asked him why he wore an earring, and he explained the old mariners' superstition that pierced ears would sharpen their eyes and give them vigour. He told them, too, that he had been pressed into military service when he was only ten years old, taken as cabin boy in a British naval vessel. By the age of thirteen he had talked his way out of the navy and aboard a trader. By then he had discovered in himself a love of seafaring and adventure, and as soon as the opportunity arose he joined the crew of the East Indiaman.

"Been plyin' the trade routes for five years now," he said proudly.

When the women heard he had been the victim of a press-gang they softened towards him. They liked the way he juggled and performed tricks to make their children laugh. Besides, he was the same age as many of Allanwell's sons, whom they missed fiercely. Some were disposed to feel kindly towards him and his good-natured comrades, despite their nationality.

"Me grandmothers was both Irish," he added diplomatically, "by the names of Kearney and Mulcahey. I'm half Irish meself."

"Dem sailor-boys is not too bad, for Englishmen," remarked one or two of the fisher-women tolerantly.

Katherine and Lizzie happened to be out on a jaunt down by the harbour that very afternoon. Seeing the sailor, Katherine greeted him, raising her voice against the roar of the sea— "Good heavens, what a great surprise to meet you here, Mr. Watson!"

Soon all three were walking along the edge of the sea-grass where it met the pebbled shore, with a trail of youngsters milling about their legs. The wind whipped their hair and tangled the skirts of the girls. They were forced to hold down their hats.

"Lizzie, this is Mr. James Watson," said Katherine without preamble.

"How d'ye do, Miss Lizzie." James Watson gave a neat bow. He could not doff his own hat—it was stowed in his pocket in case the wind should scoop it from his head and fling it into the sea.

"Lizzie is very interested in vegetable lambs too, aren't you Lizzie?" Lizzie nodded mutely, miserably. "Mr. Watson has to leave when the wind changes," Katherine said. "He does not have much time."

"Oh," said Lizzie.

"Lizzie is sometimes a little hard of hearing," said Katherine meaningfully, "aren't you Lizzie?"

"What?" said Lizzie.

"Oh, nothing. Mr. Watson and I are just making conversation."

Lizzie nodded. She looked off into the distance, past the sudden jets of spray bursting up from the rocks, and the moored fishing boats that bobbed like ducks about the great pelican-hull of the East Indiaman, out beyond the graduated swathes of silken water, to the wind-scoured sky. As she had pledged when Katherine pleaded the night before, she tried not to listen. The rag-tag mob of children pulled at her skirts. They turned their flower faces up and deluged her with questions.

James Watson was similarly subject to a quizzing.

"And how fares the lamb today Mr. Watson?" Katherine's words were snatched from her lips by a gust.

"Same as always Miss Kate," said the sailor with a grin. "'E just sits abou' lookin' woolly. 'E ain't complainin', though 'e's made no' a penny in this village."

"Sure, a lamb like that would be on wonderful wages anywhere else," said Katherine.

"It's not unusual for 'im to make five shillin's in a night," said James Watson. "See, I'm accustomed to chargin' tuppence a time to look at 'im, fourpence if the audience looks well-'eeled, and up to a shillin' if they're aristocracy."

"Really?" Katherine dropped her sarcastic tone. "Why did you show him around for all to see in Rafferty's, and not a word spoken of payment?"

"I musta' taken too much drink," said the sailor with an air of regret.

"Oh indeed, then how could it be you appeared as sober as a Puritan when I was talking to you?"

He only laughed.

"Where will you be taking the lamb next?" Katherine enquired.

"We're headin' back to Bombay and Calcutta. But first, to the Port o' Dublin to pick up some racing-nags, then to Venice to deliver 'em."

"Venice! My Uncle Francis lives there. At any rate, I think he does. It's been quite some time since we heard from him."

"Wot's 'is line o' work?"

"Well, I'd rather not be saying, Mr. Watson. 'Tis rather a sore point with my family."

"Gambled away the family fortune, eh?"

Katherine was shocked. "How did you know?"

"A lucky guess. 'Appens all the time darlin', 'e's not the first one."

Every time the sailor familiarly called her sister 'darling', Lizzie sighed and rolled her eyes. She wished he would address her as "Miss Katherine," but there would be no use in protesting. Neither of them would be likely to heed her pleas for formality.

"My sisters and I know what our uncle has done, but my father is not aware of it. We think it would break his heart, if he knew. I can hardly bear to think about that gentleman after the shameful way he betrayed us all."

"Kay serah, serah," her companion quoted with his strong Cockney accent. "That's life, innit."

"Oh, so you speak French, Mr. Watson!"

"A smatterin'. A bloke picks up a bit o' lingo in 'is travels."

"Where is your home?"

"I don' 'ave no 'ome. The ship's me 'ome." The sailor leaned down and collected three pebbles from underfoot.

"When will you be coming back this way?"

"I dunno darlin'. Not soon enough, I'll wager."

"You ought to stay here."

"They don' like us 'ere my duck. We're English."

"Sure, I'm English too."

"You 'ad me gulled, I took ye for an Irish colleen." Lazily, Mr. Watson began to juggle the three pebbles.

"I'm Irish-English."

"So you don' 'ate the English then?"

"Really, I only know one Englishman—" Katherine said airily.

He waited for her continue. When she did not, he chuckled and said, "Well go on, Mistress Teasel!"

"—and I do not hate him," she concluded primly.

"I do not 'ate you either, Kate Delacey."

"Then why did you call me 'Mistress Teasel'?" she said, feigning vexation. "The teasel is a prickly plant. Are you saying I have a sharp tongue, or are you referring to my temper?"

"Neither! I call you Teasel because you like to tease and chaff! But do'nt scorn the teasel, for the fuller loves it for raisin' the nap on 'is cloth and will pay good money for the 'arvestin'."

"I remain unconvinced of the name's merit!" she challenged.

"And," he said, "and, mark you Mistress Teasel, I've not yet finished listin' the fine qualities of teasels, by which any one ought to be proud to be called such. Where I come from, they say the rainwater tha' collects in the 'ollow cup at the bases of the leaves o' teasel is a cure for warts if the 'ands are washed in it, and from this, folk call it the Bath o' Venus. It's also a good remedy for sore eyes. Now if anyone is a sight for sore eyes it is the girl who walks beside me. No one ever told me Irish-English colleens was so pretty."

"You and your nonsense," exclaimed Katherine, smiling and blushing despite herself. "I don't believe a word of it. I daresay you tell that to every girl."

"True," the sailor unexpectedly replied, tossing the pebbles high, out into the sea, "but with you, darlin', I mean it."

"You've travelled the world over, you've see queens and princesses no doubt, and the wives of rajahs and such-like. How can a poor country girl compare?"

Katherine was fishing for compliments. He knew it, and deliberately rose to the bait, seizing both her hands in his and whirling her once around.

"All the queens and princesses and rajah-esses in the world cannot 'old a candle to you, Mistress Teasel! 'Pon my word, you're the best-lookin' twist I ever clapped eyes on. This time I'm sure to make me fortune in India and when I do, I'll come back and marry you, tha' I will."

"A fortune, is it? I suppose fortunes are easy to come by in India."

"They're growin' on trees, darlin'. When they're ripe they fall straight into a man's Saint Martins, or on 'is 'ead if 'e's not quick enough."

"I should hope so! D'ye think I am fool enough to marry a poor Jack Tar with no more'n a couple of brass pennies in his pocket?"

"Well, are you not?"

"That's for me myself to know, Monsieur," flirtatiously said Katherine.

"I b'lieve I know your mind better'n you do!" he bantered.

"Si tu veux, faisons un rêve!" she said offhandedly, as if challenging him to make sense of it, to discover if his claims to being multi-lingual were true.

"Orright then!" he returned with ambivalence, confounding her. "And seein' as 'ow I've mastered French, I 'spect I might learn a bit o' Irish next, if someone'll lesson me." He stepped a little closer.

She smiled up at him. "Well sir, I know hardly any Gaeilge. It's not a language anyone is supposed to use, you know. The authorities are trying to stamp it out."

"No' allowed to use your own lingo?" The sailor scratched his golden head.

"It's not really my family's language," Katherine said.

"But you're real Irish, ain't you? Ah, I don't understand Ireland."

"I shall explain it to you! You see Mr. Watson," said Katherine bluntly, "my family is Catholic, an Irish family of Norman-English descent. The Delaceys have always been loyal to the English Crown."

"A bit lonely for you, innit?" quipped the sailor.

"Not at all. The land-owning Irish blue-bloods don't exactly love the English but they revert to being loyalists if their assets are threatened by insurrection. And they may be either Protestant or Catholic, although they're mostly Protestant."

"But Pro'estants and Catholics are at each other's throats!" said the sailor. A glitter from the small cross on its chain around Katherine's neck caught his attention for an instant.

"Not always," its owner said. "Catholic and Protestant land-owners are willing to join forces to protect their estates from the landless Irish if necessary. The Irish parliament is filled with Anglican landowners, but the British rule them—"

"And the Catholics with no land, they're opposed to all 'eretics, aristocrats and Englishmen. Right?"

"Well yes, but with good reason, they are so cruelly oppressed..."

"And the landless Protestants, they can't abide papists, Sas'nachs and upper-crust, right?"

"Well, at this given moment that's true, but there have been times they've been loyalists, and some remain so."

"It's worse 'n a bloomin' game o' chess!"

"Not forgetting another group," said Katherine merrily, "the Presbyterian settlers from Scotland, who hold a great many estates, especially in the north—"

Their interchange was interrupted by a shout. The small children who were grouped around Lizzie lifted their grubby hands and pointed. Along the shore marched a group of three men, headed by Rafferty. One bore a quarter-staff in his hand, another carried a pitch-fork.

The sailor's hand flew to the haft of his knife, but he hesitated to draw the weapon.

"Jesus, Mary and Joseph!" exclaimed Katherine. "What is it they're after?"

"Look," Lizzie gasped. A couple more were approaching from the other direction, striding determinedly along, their expressions fierce and grim. The children ran off. James

Watson stood his ground. Neither did Katherine or Lizzie move—the latter because she was petrified. It was evident by their bearing that the men were bent on violent deeds.

"You!" shouted Rafferty as he came near the trio. "English scum!"

The sailor did not reply, but his face darkened.

"You!" yelled Rafferty again.

Deliberately, the sailor turned to look over first one shoulder, then the other. "I canno' see who you might be addressin', sir," he said.

"'Tis you I'm addressin'," said Rafferty, breathing heavily, "and I'll t'ank ye to show yerself a man and stand away from these two ladies."

"Being engaged in a particular topic, I do not see why we should be interrupted for your sake, sir. Bide your time and you may stave in me noggin when we're finished the conversation, if that's what you're brandishin' them twigs for."

"And why else would we be carryin' shillelaghs?" sneered Rafferty, "but to knock some sense into the skull of a Sasunach dog?"

"I fancied you might be out to dibble some 'oles in the sand and bury your own 'eads," replied James Watson undiplomatically and somewhat suicidally. With a bellow, Rafferty launched himself at the Englishman. His colleagues closed in behind him.

Lizzie gave a faint cry, staggered a few paces and fell to the sand, her eyes tightly shut so that she would not see the splashing of the blood, would not see the young man beaten to death by the five angry villagers. But through the wind-storm inside her ears and the protracted soughing of the sea, instead of yells and the thwack of wood on bone, Katherine's voice sliced like a blade.

Lizzie looked up.

She saw her sister standing between the sailor and the cottiers, her arms flung out as if to form a barrier of fragile bone and flesh. A haze obscured Lizzie's vision—for one appalling moment she thought she had seen her sister being crucified on the sky.

"If you touch this man you will have to knock me down first!" Katherine was screaming, her face suffused with rage. "It's half-Irish he is! He's related to us on me mother's side— that's what we've been chatting about of course, what did ye think? For God's sake, look at yourselves—five grown men against a poor Irish lad who has had the misfortune to be born with a drop of English blood in his veins. What are you going to do—kill the Sasunach half of him? Where has your good sense gone, Mr. Rafferty, Mr. O'Rourke, where are your Christian principles? What d'ye think Father Joseph would have to say about this?"

She bombarded them with questions and rhetoric until they drew back, uncertainty gleaming in their eyes. Their quarter-staffs were still raised, poised to strike.

"And what do you think the rest of the crew would do if he went missing?" Katherine pressed on. "They'd come for vengeance, that's what they'd do, and then where would we be? We'd have the entire East India Company on our backs in addition to the rest."

"He's a heretic," said Rafferty, but Katherine knew it was a half-hearted last stand.

"So's Sir Robert on the hill. Are you going to massacre him now and all?"

Katherine knew she had said enough. If she threatened his dignity too severely, Rafferty would be likely to throw all caution to the currents of the ocean and begin bludgeoning the sailor for the sake of honour.

But Rafferty lowered his staff. The other men followed his example.

"Half Irish or not, ye're not welcome here," the inn-keeper glowered at the sailor. "Get ye gone, and leave our womenfolk alone."

Katherine bit her lip. She longed to make a furious retort, but she walked a knife-edge and dared not utter another sound lest she destroy the delicate balance. She could see the anger in every line of the sailor's stance and guessed he itched to come to blows with Rafferty, despite that he was out-numbered.

"Come, Mr. Watson," she said loudly and quickly. "I'll prevail upon you to walk with me and my sister back to where your rowing-boat is moored." She was about to add, "we are in need of your protection because there are some stupid great thugs in the vicinity", but thought better of it.

She hoped her spoken comment would satisfy Rafferty and his men. It did appear to, for they made no move as James

Watson helped Lizzie to her feet and walked away with the two sisters. When they had marched far along the strand, Lizzie timidly peeked back and saw the men still there as motionless as church gargoyles, watching sullenly.

The sailor remained silent until they reached the jetty and walked out to where the small boat was tied up. There they halted, and he directed his gaze at Katherine.

"What can a man say?" he murmured softly.

"You don't have to say anything," said she, and Lizzie thought she saw some meaning pass between them, which she could not fathom. The wind had whipped bright crystals into their eyes and smacked their cheeks red.

"I won't forget you," said the sailor. Then he seemed to recollect himself and subjoined, "Not in an 'urry, anyway, Mistress Teasel."

"For certain, you will," said Katherine coquettishly, avoiding his glance. "With all those rajah-esses to divert you. Go now, you'd better, before something else happens." She could feel the pressure of his observant eyes on the back of her neck.

The sailor turned to Katherine's sister. "God bless you Miss Lizzie," he said.

"Thank you," Lizzie stammered. "Farewell."

"I will no' say good-bye to you, Mistress Teasel," he said, turning his attention back to Katherine. "I say instead oh-revwah." He unhooked the painter from its bollard and made as if to embark, but hesitated. He seemed to be about to say something, however at the last moment he merely shook his head.

"You'd better go now Mr. Watson," said Lizzie anxiously. "I can see the fisherfolk looking at us, and I think that's Rafferty coming along the shore."

The sailor bent his head close to Katherine's. He said in a low voice, "Katie, I ain't half-Irish and I was not pressed into the navy. Sometimes I talk a lot o' bilge. Forgive me."

"You are not talking to the village idiot," Katherine replied. "Do you think I don't know pig-swill when I hear it? I am aware that you rattle on, but do you think I care? You're the brightest spot of sunlight this old place has seen for many a day."

"What are you going on about Kitty?" Lizzie said nervously, staring at the approaching men. "This is neither the time nor the place for idle chatter."

If Katherine heard her sister's warning she gave no indication of it. "Lord have mercy on me for my foolishness," she said to the sailor. "I ought to be hanged for stupidity, for even thinking of looking at a rover like you, with no fortune. You've muddled my wits with your blarney, that you have."

"Aye, I'm a poor man Katie, but I love you just the same."

"Oh, to be sure. You do indeed talk a lot of bilge. You've known me for almost five minutes!"

"'Tis enough. D'ye love me?"

"Oh Mr. Watson," cried Lizzie woefully, "make speed to depart! They'll be here any minute!"

"I ain't leavin' yet," he said, immovable as a rock. Lizzie began to wring her hands and call upon the saints.

"D'ye love me?" the sailor persisted.

"Jesus!" Katherine cried uncouthly, "What difference does it make, you'll never come back. By the saints I think I do! Bless you Mr. Watson!"

As she laughed, he grasped her hand and kissed it. Lizzie's eyes widened at the brazenness of their behaviour, and hoped no one else had seen. "Rafferty's coming," she squeaked. "Hurry!"

Katherine glanced towards the shore. "Au revoir to you, Mr. Watson," she cried, "and bon voyage, but if we do meet again, I dearly hope it may be under more auspicious circumstances."

The sailor tossed the painter into the wooden shell and stepped expertly aboard after it. Although it was rocking and bobbing agitatedly on a chop whipped up by the wind, he timed his step to coincide with the motion, entering the boat with poise and no jarring. As he sat down he said, "When we meet again, Mistress Teasel." He winked, took up the oars and began pulling strongly away from the jetty.

Now he was laughing, together with Katherine. Their laughters mingled, possibly tinged with a note of hysteria. "This is ridiculous!" gasped Katherine, steadying herself on the bollard. "By George, I believe I must be flying!"

Lizzie could not understand the behaviour of the two of them. They were acting like a pair of fools. The sailor rowed away rapidly and was far from shore by the time

Rafferty's band arrived. Relieved, Lizzie allowed her gaze to wander, scanning the shoreline to find out who else might have observed the scene. To the right, the towering bulk of Madigan's Leap jutted into the sea. A small figure was standing at the summit. At this distance Lizzie could not make out who it was. She did not have to see—she knew.

It was Rose, waiting for Keane.

CHAPTER 27

A Ship There is and She Sails the Sea

"Royal Navy First-Rate Battleship Shortening Sail" by Samuel Scott
(c.1702–1772)

The water is wide, I can't swim o'er
And neither have I wings to fly
Give me a boat that can carry two
And both shall row, my love and I

A ship there is and she sails the sea
She's loaded deep as deep can be
But not so deep as the love I'm in
I know not if I sink or swim

The water is wide. Cecil Sharp published the song in
Folk Songs From Somerset (1906).

Another full year passed with no sign that any who had been torn from the shores of Allanwell would ever return. During that time, news was relayed from London that Edwin Westbourne, now a lieutenant in the Royal Rathskillen Dragoon Guards, had married an Englishwoman before departing with his regiment for a campaign in Austria. Margaret and Katherine felt mildly and unaccountably disappointed to hear of these nuptials, but by then the sisters had practically forgotten what he looked like, and the sentiment soon passed.

Every day, Rose accompanied many of the other bereft villagers to church, where they prayed under the auspices of Father Joseph. Every other day, even in the depths of winter, she would climb to the top of the cliff to look out across the ocean and call Keane's name into the wind. Sometimes, when she was out of earshot, Rose's sisters discussed her haunted aspect and single-mindedness.

"She is not like us," Lizzie said pensively. "She has never really been like us and since Keane was taken she's even further removed. When I was little I used to conjecture that she was the child of an angel, abandoned on earth, and that Mama and Papa found her lying beneath a bush of holy roses."

"What nonsense," Margaret replied automatically.

"I know what you mean, Lizzie," Katherine mused. "Rose has always been the best of us. Mary once said she's too pure, too good for this world."

"Do not say that!" Margaret's reprimand was sharp.

"I mean nothing ill by it," Katherine retorted. "It is just that these days there's a sort of remoteness about her, as if she's half in this world, half away with the fair—I mean, the Good People."

"Half away with Keane O'Connell, rather," said Lizzie. "What about their strange dreams, the pair of them? If that is not magic, I'm a codfish. Keane is another that's too good to be true. I daresay he's really a fairy prince of the Daoine Sidhe." She raised her hand and sketched the sign of the cross above her heart.

"Ryan told Ilvenna something about Keane," said Lizzie. "Something their mother said to both the boys."

"Well, what is it?" asked Katherine.

"That before Keane came into the world, when their mother was carrying him, she was worried the baby might be born sickly, like so many others in the village. So she went to consult a wise-woman who was known to have dealings with

331

the Good People. And she got a spell from the woman, so that her child would be well-favoured, strong, kind and wise. And Keane was born strong and healthy, and as he grew to manhood everyone said that the boy was so handsome he could only have got his looks from the fair—from the Good People. And by the time their mother was carrying her second child the old woman had died, but everyone said that some of the magic must have lingered in the mother's womb, because her second son was so comely too."

"Fairies and angels!" scoffed Margaret. "Leave off your fanciful whimsies. Keane is a mortal man and Rose is just a girl. She's your flesh-and-blood sister, for heaven's sake."

Despite her protestations, Margaret took to thoughtfully observing Rose, and trying—unsuccessfully—to coax her from her miasma of abstraction.

December of 1796 brought, once again, foul weather for mariners, but stirring news came into Allanwell. The hopes of the United Irishmen and their supporters rose high, for Napoleon had granted his support to the cause of the Irish rebels. A French fleet of forty-three ships arrived in Ireland's Bantry Bay, with Wolfe Tone aboard, and fifteen thousand French soldiers intending to invade Ireland and help the insurgents put an end to British rule. Perhaps the rebels came close to victory then—but the French expeditionary force never landed.

A strong gale had seized Bantry Bay in its teeth. It was said by some that the rough seas and inexperienced sailors prevented the French from coming ashore, but others contended that they would have done so except that they were leaderless. The French naval commander refused to allow his troops to disembark until General Hoche, his Commander in Chief, arrived. After waiting a few days in vain for him, the French fleet was scattered by what some called the 'Protestant Wind'.

The villagers were bitterly disappointed at this turn of events.

"Are we disappointed, Father?" Lizzie asked John Delacey. "Where do we stand? Are we loyalists still, even though we have lost our land?"

Her father regarded her wearily. "Lizzie, once I called myself a loyalist. In hindsight I fear I took that stance purely by force of family tradition. I had never thought to examine my beliefs to any great depth. As master of Charter Hall I knew my cottiers, of course, but it was not until we lived amongst them that I was rudely awoken to the true pitifulness of their circumstances.

"After your mother went to heaven I could not care about anything much at all, let alone politics, and if anyone had asked me I would have said I was neither loyalist nor republican, but a man struggling to find some meaning in existence. Now, though, we are all forced to choose one side or the other. I would rather see food on the tables of my neighbours and some reason for them to hold their heads high, and if that is somehow to be brought about by opposing the British, then yes, I am a republican."

"We are republicans," Lizzie told her sisters solemnly.

"I'm not," said Katherine.

Margaret said, "Do you harbour a death wish, Kitty? Publish that idea in the streets of Allanwell and there are some fanatics who would as soon beat you to pieces as look at you; even your family name would be no protection. Everyone's a republican here, except the Westbournes, didn't you know? Three more boys from the lower cots went off to join the United Irishmen this very morning."

"I'm not a fool," snapped Katherine. "I'm keeping my mouth shut."

That night as they lay abed in their small chamber, Margaret said to Katherine, "And why are you calling yourself a loyalist? Pandering to the British, that's a Protestant behaviour."

Moonlight pierced slantwise between the curtains in spindleshafts of clear silver. Softly it poured essence of pearls on the bleached frills of the girls' mob-caps and the downy snowscapes of their pillows.

"No it is not," argued Katherine, levering herself up on one elbow. "I've heard that there are Irish Catholics aplenty joining the ranks of the British army. The United Irishmen come from every religion, that's a fact—Presbyterian, Protestant and Catholic, they're all in it together. Republican or loyalist, it's not to do with religion."

Margaret folded her arms behind her head. "You're only declaring you're loyalist because of your English sailor, are you not? He is a rake, I daresay, with a girl at every port, and hardly worthy of your political support."

Katherine thumped the pillows. "He's no rake and I'll thank you not to miscall a man behind his back. It reflects ill on you. As for being a loyalist, what about family tradition?"

"Is that a good enough reason? Papa does not think so!"

"An obedient daughter I may be," hissed Katherine, trying to subdue her vehemence so as not to disturb the household, "but I do not have to think like my father."

"He is head of the household!" Margaret said disapprovingly.

"But I have my own head for thinking!"

"I believe you call yourself a loyalist just to be contrary, and if we all agreed with you, you would turn republican in the blink of an eye."

"Believe what you like, since it seems nothing I can say will alter your opinion!"

Katherine lay down, turned her back on her sister and tugged the bedclothes over her shoulders.

A few days later Rose asked the same question of Katherine; "Are you really a supporter of the Crown?"

"No I am not, of course! But don't tell Margaret I said that. She'd triumph over me. However if I must hate the British, I cannot include Mr. Watson."

"Dear Kitty!" exclaimed Rose, giving her sister's hand an affectionate squeeze. Tears began to flow swiftly down Katherine's face, dewdrops on glassy ribbons.

"I am confused," she said wretchedly. "Everything has become so hateful."

But worse was to come.

It was the same in Allanwell as elsewhere. After expectations were foiled at Bantry Bay, Irish society became divided into two opposite extremes. Loyalists thronged to join the British army in Ireland, while the United Irishmen's numbers substantially increased.

Throughout that year grim tidings filtered through from Ulster to the little seaport of Allanwell on the west coast. In that northern county the United Irishmen, comprising middle-class landowners of Catholic, Protestant and Presbyterian faith, were not only violently opposed by the ultra-Protestant Orange Lodges, they were also constantly under attack from the local Catholic peasants, who were motivated partly by extreme rancour at Protestant privileges and partly by the revolutionary ideals of French-trained priests. For the first time, the British army had stepped in and applied military coercion against Catholic rebels in Ulster.

It was only the beginning.

Sir Robert Westbourne proudly informed John Delacey that a baby boy had been born to Edwin's wife in London. They had named him Charles Robert Edwin George Osmington Westbourne. Unfortunately the infant's mother failed to thrive after the birth, and in February 1797 she had passed away, leaving Edwin a widower.

In the apple orchards of Allanwell, the leaves turned palest gold and sombre brown. Rose continued to wait, still with hope, for Keane's imminent return. Months passed, then another year. There came no word of the O'Connell brothers. Yet she did not give up, because from time to time the dreams played into her sleep, as they always had. She dreamed many dreams, all of tall ships and the sea. Though the visions were harrowing she welcomed them, believing that as long as she dreamed of him, he lived.

On a fair night in Autumn[October 15th] when the swallows had nearly all flown south and the last bronze-in-wine leaves were falling from the apple trees, the final dream came to Rose Delacey.

As she slept, she saw a shingled beach at night, lit by the moon and stars. The shadowy shapes of men were climbing out of a rowboat in the shallows. All were dressed in rather grimy white trousers and blue coats, their draggled locks scraped back into horse-tails. Four of the men carried muskets, and seemed to be overseeing the rest, who lugged wooden kegs on their shoulders. Keane O'Connell was amongst the cask-bearers. This enterprise had a familiar look to Rose—it was a landing party from a ship, in search of fresh water. In her sleep she tried to identify the shadowy shore, but it was impossible by the dim radiance from the night sky. Wavelets washed up among the pebbles, their hems rimmed with silver. She could hear no sound, but could not help imagining the clatter and sigh of the water, and the soft splash of the men's boots.

The dream faded, then returned.

Keane was alone in the gloom. Bushes and trees rose up all around him. He was glancing from side to side, crouching low, tearing off his blue coat and throwing it on the ground. Abruptly he sprang forward and began to run. Vegetation loomed out of the dark and rushed past him, sometimes whipping him, or tearing at his shirt. He leaped over rocks and small watercourses, and then his feet were pounding on the rutted surface of a country lane, bordered by hedges.

Rose's heart began to race. Keane was escaping from his captors.

And the punishment for desertion, if they caught him, was surely death.

She moaned and writhed, longing to aid him but caught fast in her trance. Unexpectedly Keane whirled about, facing the direction from which he had fled. Three British marines were dashing up the lane after him, at full pelt. One paused briefly, braced his musket on his shoulder, took aim, and fired. Yellow light flared, and smoke puffed, but Rose could not hear the weapon's roar. She shuddered, but to her relief, she perceived that Keane had turned back and was again running. Something whizzed past him—a second bullet? Now he was dodging and swerving to avoid the third. He was gasping for breath. A second time he turned to face his hunters, like a fox at bay, and prepared himself to make a last stand.

With their guns now fully discharged, the three men came at him with blades. The Irishman had undoubtedly retained his physical condition and prowess. Keane took the first man by the arm and, with a rapid flick of the wrist, bowled him over, disarming him at the same time. The attacker landed flat on his back. Keane took the man's musket in both hands and began to wield it as he would have wielded a shillelagh. There in the middle of that moonlit country lane he fought for his freedom and his life, batting aside their thrusting bayonets and cutlasses, whirling his makeshift cudgel so fast it appeared no more than a blur against the stars. The butt of his musket connected with a skull, and a second man toppled. The first was struggling to rise but Keane spun on his heel and dealt him another blow to quieten him, before ramming the gun's muzzle into the third man's ribs. When the sailor doubled over, Keane brought his weapon hard across the back of his head, and he crumpled. Three men sprawled senseless in the dust of the lane. Dropping the firearm, Keane fled. The roadway darkened as clouds sailed across the moon's face, but not before Keane—and Rose— had glimpsed movement among the hedges ahead.

An ambush.

Perspiring and flailing about in helpless panic, Rose saw Keane glance over his shoulder. Down the lane, the dim outlines of his enemies could be seen, hastening after him. In front, more enemies waited. He was trapped. There could be no way out. Suddenly the world tilted, and he fell. Blackness closed in. Keane was gone; gone completely, to a place she could not follow.

The dreamer woke and sat bolt upright, giving Lizzie another heart-pounding fright. "He's killed, Lizzie," Rose said, blank-eyed and too overcome with anguish to weep.

"He has been shot. He's dead. He and I shall never meet again on this earth."

That was the final time she dreamed of Keane.

Even when the dreams ceased she did not give up hope straight away but, over time, her confident expectations gradually faded. She grieved and would not be comforted. She shunned Madigan's Leap, and instead of going to church nearly every morning she only went on Sundays.

To her sisters, choking on her sobs, she asserted she would never marry.

Once, Rose went to Ilvenna and asked her if she could see Keane in the future.

"D'ye t'ink I've not tried?" said her friend, unable to control a revealing tremble in her voice. "We all want to know if—" she checked herself "—when our boys will come home."

"Have you seen anything at all, Venna?" Rose pleaded.

"I can see that there is a future," was the reply, "which is somet'ing to be t'ankful for. And it seems to me, 'tis like the waves of the ocean, with grand, sparkling crests, and deep, gloomy valleys. I see that much, but I cannot see more."

"Thank you," murmured Rose.

"All I know is," said Ilvenna, "'tis certain to be fierce excitin'".

THE END

This story continues in -
Madigan's Leap Book 2: The Cloven Ring
and
Madigan's Leap Book 3: Words of Power

THE END

If you enjoyed this book, please write a short (or long)
review on Amazon.
Reviews signal to potential readers that others are
interested in the book, and like it.
Writing and posting book reviews on Amazon is a small, but
powerful thing you can do to support authors from whose
work you have derived some value.

~ Cyberchicks in Love ~

"Science Fiction with a Good Dose of Humor"

"Cyberchicks in Love" is an eccentric combination of humor and sci-fi-fantasy. The story, revolving around a group of young women infatuated with a movie star, offers a delightful spoof of various genres - from fanfiction to chick lit and science fiction.
~ The Reader's Gazette

www.professorsbookshelf.com

- THE PROFESSOR'S BOOKSHELF -

The books that inspired Tolkien's "The Hobbit" and "The Lord of the Rings."

Introduced by Cecilia Dart-Thornton

Some titles in the series:

1. The Song of the Nibelungs (illustrated)

Translated by Margaret Armour, previously published as 'The Fall of the Nibelungs', illust. W. B. MacDougall, pub. 1897

2. The Poetic Edda (illustrated)

Translated by Olive Bray, previously published as 'The Elder or Poetic Edda', illust. W. G. Collingwood, pub. 1908

3. The Story of the Glittering Plain (illustrated)

By William Morris, illust. Walter Crane, pub.1894

4. The Red Fairy Book (illustrated)

By Andrew Lang, illust. H. J. Ford and Lancelot Speed, pub. 1907

5. The Princess and the Goblin (illustrated)

By George MacDonald, illust. Jessie Willcox Smith, pub. 1920

6. The Saga of Eric Brighteyes (illustrated)

By H. Rider Haggard, illust. Lancelot Speed, pub. 1891.

For more about the Professor's Bookshelf series, visit
www.professorsbookshelf.com/